DEATH

A LIE

By

PETER HARPER

Copyright © Peter Harper 2019

This book is sold subject to the condition that it shall not, by way of trade or otherwise, be lent, resold, hired out, or otherwise circulated without the publisher's prior consent in any form of binding or cover other than that in which it is published and without a similar condition including this condition being imposed on the subsequent publisher.

The moral right of Peter Harper has been asserted.

AUTHOR'S NOTE

Although this is a stand-alone novel, the reading of *Cascade* beforehand might further enhance the enjoyment of the storyline and characters.

The sequel to *Death of a Lie*
(*The Indiscriminate Agenda*)
will be released shortly.

For
Brock and Nige

Vikings and Pirates,
and the River Blythe.

*"'We are determined
that nothing shall stop us from sharing with you
all that we have...'"*
Harry Hopkins (advisor to Franklin D. Roosevelt)
speaking at the Russian Aid Rally,
Madison Square Garden, June 1942.

*"By the end of June 1944 the United States had
sent to the Soviets under Lend-Lease more than
11,000 planes;
over 6,000 tanks and tank destroyers; and 300,000
trucks and other military vehicles..."*
American Historical Association

CONTENTS

PROLOGUE.. 9 1
PART 1 IN THE SHADOW OF AN ILL WIND... 20 12
CHAPTER 1. 20 12
CHAPTER 2. 33 26
CHAPTER 3. 43 37
CHAPTER 4. 61 55
CHAPTER 5. 82 77
CHAPTER 6. 92 87
CHAPTER 7. 99 95
PART 2 DOUBLE-EDGED FOE.. 118 115
CHAPTER 8. 118 115
CHAPTER 9. 134 131
CHAPTER 10. 148 145
CHAPTER 11. 167 164
CHAPTER 12. 175 172
CHAPTER 13. 196 193
CHAPTER 14. 212 209
CHAPTER 15. 225 222
CHAPTER 16. 241 238
CHAPTER 17. 259 256
CHAPTER 18. 280 278
CHAPTER 19. 293 291
CHAPTER 20. 314 313
CHAPTER 21. 325 325
PART 3 A SNAKE IN THE GRASS. 344 345
CHAPTER 22. 344 345
CHAPTER 23. 357 358
CHAPTER 24. 368 369

CHAPTER 25. 380 381
CHAPTER 26. 402 404

This is a work of fiction. Names, characters, businesses, organizations, places, events and incidents either are the product of the author's imagination or are used fictitiously. Any resemblance to actual persons, living or dead, events, or locales is entirely coincidental.

PROLOGUE

September, 1944

Gore Field Airbase, Great Falls, Montana, USA

First Lieutenant Augustus Steinbeck threw off his coat and tossed it across the annex alongside the Base Operations Room. He stared ahead at the floodlit apron, squinting his eyes while closely following the B-25 Mitchell with the Soviet Red Star on its wings and fuselage.

'You see that?' he growled finally. 'You *see* it, for Christ's sake?'

'I see it,' acknowledged Jack Irvine, Steinbeck's assistant for the evening. The B-25 had started to leave the apron, building up thrust and making the windows rattle in their steel frames. Irvine looked around, and noticing they were still alone: 'They givin' you front, Gus?' he asked. 'Like they give the poor ol' Major front the other night? Yeah?'

Steinbeck was used to Irvine addressing him informally – after all, they'd played together for the baseball first team at their high school – but if people were around, then Jack always gave him his rank. He shook his head in a gesture of utter bewilderment. 'The co-pilot even threw himself across the trunk I wanted to inspect. "Diplomatic immunity!" he shrieked. "You call Mr Hopkins. You call him!"'

'You know the latest name for Lend-Lease round here?' Irvine was still watching the B-25 trundle towards the north-facing runway. 'Push-button service.' He laughed briefly, sarcastically. 'You gonna let it go, Gus?'

'What can I do about it?' Steinbeck took out a bottle of bourbon from a drawer on his desk, poured a shot and downed it. He wiped his lips with the back of his hand. 'The Major can't do anything. Classified information haemorrhaging into Stalin's hands and nobody's listening, even in Washington.' He felt the knot of patriotic outrage in his chest tightening his lungs, limiting his breathing. 'Sometimes I think I'm dreaming all this. We're building the Soviet's infrastructure for them. You know that, Jack? That's what San Francisco and Seattle's been all about, the ships leaving stacked to the gunnels with our gear and know-how.'

Irvine lit a cigarette and sat back in the bucket seat, glancing every so often at the B-25 before it faded into the night and the foul weather that had plagued

Montana for the past couple of days. 'You know, Gus, there's talk of Harry Hopkins being a commie spy.'

Steinbeck poured himself another shot. 'No smoke without fire.'

'How can that be, Gus? He's right next to the President.'

'The world's upside down, that's why,' reacted Steinbeck, realising if he didn't calm himself he would be in for an asthmatic attack – but he simply couldn't help himself! 'I'm telling you, Jack. I'm telling you straight. Upside friggin' down. As if handing over these planes to Russian pilots up in Fairbanks isn't enough. Now this one's being allowed to take off in front of our eyes. Moscow's laughing at us.'

* * *

Thirty-two hours later

Steinbeck had just unbuttoned his fly in front of the urinal when the door burst open.

Irvine gave an excited glance around himself. Empty. 'Gus, you heard?'

'Jesus, Jack, can't a guy take a leak in peace?'

'Remember that B-25 you had trouble with?'

Steinbeck was in mid-flow. 'Yeah. What about it?'

'The pilot might have to make an emergency landing. They were taking a southern route—'

'I was told they were taking the usual ALSIB route.'

'You know you can never believe what they say. I've just heard it's being diverted over Romania. An engine's out, and the other one keeps feathering – then kickin' back in.'

Steinbeck spun his head, looking over his shoulder. 'You sure, Jack?'

'Come through from RAF Ballyhalbert, County Down, where the plane was refuelled. What do you reckon, Gus?'

Steinbeck turned back to the business in hand. 'If that B-25 comes down, questions are gonna be asked.' He finished off, buttoned his fly and went over to the washbasins. 'It's gonna be a ball, Jack. Shame for the crew, I don't wish them that amount of grief, but if that plane comes down then someone over in Washington has some explaining to do. I can only guess what's in those "diplomatic immunity" trunks. Uranium – pure as the saints above us.'

* * *

Timişoara, Romania

Andrei Bălcescu started to tether the flap at the entrance to the tent. This was the first occasion he'd used it and he hadn't expected to be sharing it with a girl. Rodica was nice but annoying at the same time – like most girls, he'd decided. Her parents had been friendly with his parents for years. In fact, Rodica's father was his godfather, and the nice thing about Uncle Mihai was that he always gave him exciting presents – like tents and things.

'Did you check to see if there are any bulls in the field?' came the small voice over his shoulder.

''Course I did. Anyway, Papa moved them all out last week.'

'You're sure? He might have left one behind. Perhaps you should check the field again.'

Andrei pursed his lips. Girls! 'For someone who's eight years old, you're bossy. You're not this bossy at school.' He finished the last tie. Then spun around with his fingers pointing upwards like horns on his head and gave a roar.

Rodica screamed and started hitting him before they fell about laughing. 'I'm going to get into my sleeping bag,' she said finally.

Andrei started to do the same.

'What are you doing?' asked Rodica.

'Getting into my sleeping bag. What does it look like?'

'You have to kiss me goodnight first.'

'Kiss you?'

'The man always has to do that. It's manners.'

'Where've you heard that?'

'It's manners,' insisted Rodica.

'To kiss you?'

'Is there a parrot in this tent?'

'A parrot…? Funny!' Andrei felt at that moment his life had taken on a worrying turn. 'If I did kiss you, you'd keep it a secret? Not tell anyone at school?'

'We're in different forms.'

Rodica's reply hardly put Andrei at ease. If his classmates found out he'd kissed a girl – let alone an *eight*-year-old girl – then his life wouldn't be worth living. 'And you'll keep it a secret?'

'If you want me to.'

'Cross your heart?'

'I'll keep it a secret—' Rodica glanced at the tent's flap. 'What's that?'

Before Andrei had time to react to the unearthly shriek overhead, the air detonated around them, culminating in a secondary explosion that shook the ground and caused the tent to partially collapse. An orangey light glowed immediately beyond the tent's canvas flap amidst another reverberation and what sounded like scraping metal.

Andrei caught his breath, the explosion having expelled the air straight out of his lungs. He struggled feverishly to untether the flap, Rodica's ear-splitting screams compounding his confused state and sense of panic. His fumbling fingers untied the last tether and he threw back the flap – to see a river of fire across the field that ran down into a shallow valley and a neighbouring smallholding. He looked at Rodica who'd started to whimper, her hands tight as fists pushing against her face.

'Get your shoes on,' he told her, while doing so himself.

'It's a big rock,' Rodica blurted. 'It's come from space. We've done them at school.'

Andrei didn't comment because he wasn't at all sure himself what had happened. They were stuck in the middle of a warzone, that's all he knew, and it had been that way ever since he could remember. Something from space seemed too fantastic for words.

They left the tent, the heat and swirling acrid smoke that shrouded the piles of twisted metal driving them away. Andrei coughed and felt his eyes water. He wiped them with his sleeve, making out in the diffused glow a ghostly-looking object with a red star on it. 'It's Russian. Let's go into the valley.'

'No!' objected Rodica. 'Let's go home. I'm scared. I want to go home!'

'Maybe we can help the crew. It's our duty.'

'They won't be alive. Not in that.'

'Give me your hand.' Andrei looked at Rodica. 'Give me your hand, will you!'

Hesitantly, Rodica did as she was told. 'I don't want to see a dead person.'

'It's our duty to help them,' repeated Andrei. 'They're our friends now. Fighting with us against the Germans.' Another detonation thundered across the fields, visibly extending the river of fire just as a huge object rolled, as if in slow motion, down into the valley. 'I bet that's the cockpit.'

Rodica started to whimper again. 'Let's go—' She tripped and fell straight to the ground. 'Andrei, help me!'

Andrei hauled her roughly onto her feet. Something glinted briefly on the ground nearby amongst the sheets of paper that were blowing about. He reached down and picked up what looked to be a black folder – a shiny strip of metal fastened to the cover, no more than a centimetre wide and as long as the cover itself.

'Let's go,' repeated Rodica. 'It's too dangerous.'

'I'm taking this.' Andrei ran his fingers along the strip of metal.

'It doesn't belong to us.'

'It's on Papa's land. 'Course it belongs to us.'

'Leave it here.'

'See this strip? I reckon it's silver.'

'It's stealing.'

'I could get someone to make a ring out of it for you.'

Rodica looked up at him, a different kind of intensity in her brown eyes. 'A ring?' she echoed. 'Like…like a wedding ring?'

'That sort of thing.' Andrei attempted to get his fingernails under the strip.

'What are you doing?' asked Rodica.

'Trying to get the silver off the folder. That's all we need.'

'Don't do that. You might damage the silver. Let's take the whole thing. We can do it properly at home.'

They set off and made their way back across the fields, a near full moon guiding them safely between wire fences and over dilapidated wooden gates. They constantly looked behind themselves, the flames around the wreckage beginning to diminish. As they neared the farm's outbuildings, they could hear their parents calling them.

Rodica pointed at a small barn. 'Hide it under the straw in there!'

'Why?' asked Andrei.

'Because they might take it off us when they see the silver.'

Andrei realised this was a sensible idea and wished he'd thought of it first. As he stuffed the folder under some straw in the far corner of the barn, he was even moved to say, albeit cautiously, 'Sometimes, I think you could get nearly as smart as me.'

'It's horrible to think there are dead bodies near to where we were standing,' said Rodica.

'They'd be ashes now.'

'Ashes?'

'Their bodies will have melted with the heat.'

'Do you think? Do bodies do that?'

They left the barn. ''Course they do. I've seen pictures.'

'Who can we get to make the ring?'

'I'll find someone.' Andrei hadn't the heart to tell Rodica that for the past month he'd had his eye on a set of fishing rods at her father's store. He'd just had his birthday, and it was ages until Christmas, so

Uncle Mihai wasn't going to give him any presents until then. Funny, he thought, a piece of silver falling from the sky just when he needed it to.

All the lanterns seemed to be lit at the farmhouse, and their respective mothers rushed forward.

'Children! Children!' they cried.

Andrei and Rodica were smothered in kisses and hugs, their ears filled with sighs of relief and a torrent of ardent though virtually incoherent blessings to God, the Father Almighty.

'Where's Papa?' asked Andrei. The surrounding lanes were now teeming with headlights converging on the crash site.

'He's gone with Uncle Mihai to see if they could find you,' said Ileana Bălcescu. 'We've been so worried. I can't begin to tell you how worried we've been.'

'Was it a plane?' asked Rodica's mother, Constanta.

'Yes,' answered Rodica. 'A huge plane with a red star.'

They all looked back towards the crash site with renewed relief and awe, and at the trucks arriving from all directions.

PART 1
IN THE SHADOW OF AN ILL WIND

Timişoara, Romania
October, 1993

CHAPTER 1

Lucian Bălcescu looked back at his wife as he reached for his socks and sat on the bed.

'Next weekend I've been given more overtime,' he said.

'You're doing too much.' Zinsa struggled to raise herself up the bed. 'I mean it, Lucian.'

Lucian stood and put on his corduroy trousers, hopping on one foot when he nearly lost his balance. 'In a short while, there's going to be four of us. We can't live here forever. As much as we love them and they love us, we have to strike out and be independent.' He reached for his shoes and sat back down on the bed. 'Believe it not, they've actually made a start on building those apartments on Strada Lorena, not far from the water tower. Lots of trees there for you. I know how you like your trees.'

'How far from the water tower?' asked Zinsa.

'A few hundred metres. The other end of the street.'

'There's something that unnerves me about that tower. It's so big, and looks derelict. Some of its windows are broken.'

'All the same, a fascinating building – architecturally speaking.' Tying his laces, Lucian looked back at his wife. 'Are you coming down for breakfast?'

Zinsa nodded. 'In a moment.' She rubbed her swollen belly. 'They were kicking most of the night. But I didn't mind. I think it's the girl bossing her brother about, keeping him in order. Probably his own fault for trying to take up too much room. What do you think?'

Lucian smiled and knelt beside the bed, stroking Zinsa's hair; her ebony skin had never before looked so radiant. 'We're both orphans, Zinsa – your journey more hazardous than mine. But we're here now, at this point, and I don't care if my daughter is going to be bossy. I rather like that. She'll have her own mind. And my son…I know he'll protect her.'

'Like you always protected me at school against those bigots?'

'No question.'

'You always say the right thing, Lucian. I love you.'

'Love you, too.' Lucian kissed his wife and stood to leave. 'See you at the table.'

* * *

On Saturdays, without fail, a feast awaited the household. Though Rodica Bălcescu complained that she was forever chained to the cooking range, in truth she wouldn't have it any other way. The range was the focal point of the kitchen and her pride and joy. It had come from Germany years before the Revolution, but before Rodica could exhibit it to her neighbours the badge with its manufacturer's name and country of origin needed to be removed. Now, of course, German goods were considered prestigious, though to Rodica's frustration she couldn't recall what she had done with the badge and suspected she'd probably thrown it away all those years ago.

Lucian liked Rodica's quirky ways, and her diplomacy when it came to Zinsa's pregnancy: she kept her distance, but was always on hand to advise should she be asked. Lucian often wondered, with sadness, what Rodica and her husband, Andrei, must truly be thinking at times, since they had no children of their own. To help fill that gap in their lives, they'd adopted him a few months after his eighth birthday. Two years earlier, Andrei, during an anthropological expedition in the West African state of Séroulé, found himself caught up in a coup. At a nearby village, he'd come into contact with a terrified, dumbstruck child. Her name proved to be Zinsa Dangbo, and she was the only surviving member of the former ruling family. By some miracle, Zinsa had managed to escape before her father, President Tuma Dangbo, her mother and her older siblings were massacred by the current president, General Odion Kuetey – the epitome of a cruel and contemptuous despot who, over the past two decades, had allowed the West to systematically rob Séroulé of its mineral wealth.

'There's been an earthquake in India,' mentioned Andrei. 'A place called Latur.' He lowered the newspaper. 'Six-point-two magnitude.' He took a sip of orange juice. 'Could be up to ten thousand people lost their lives, it says here.'

'How awful,' commented Rodica, serving *balmoş* straight from the range.

Lucian gazed down at his bowl, and knew from the yeasty aroma that apart from having boiled the cornmeal in sheep's milk, Rodica had added all the necessaries: cheese, sour cream and butter.

'Is Zinsa coming down?' asked Rodica.

'In a moment,' said Lucian. 'She said they were kicking through much of the night. She thinks it's the girl doing most of it – bossing her brother about.'

'How sweet! I just can't wait to see what they look like. Adorable, of course, but…' Rodica sighed and served her husband his *balmoș*. 'I just can't wait, that's all. Andrei, don't let your *balmoș* grow cold.'

Obediently, Andrei lowered the newspaper. 'Ah, the finest *balmoș* in all of Romania, I tell you.'

'I'm probably the only one in Timișoara who still makes it this way,' quipped Rodica. 'A dying tradition, I have to say. Not many shepherds these days with all this modern technology. We're no better off, in my opinion.'

'It's progress,' Lucian said. 'There's instant photography now – more instant than Polaroid. And mobile phones are going to get smaller. There won't be a single person without one in ten years' time.'

'Well, I don't like it,' said Rodica. 'I was at the shops the other day and a man nearly walked straight into me, too busy with his phone to look where he was going. Serve him right if he'd walked into a lamppost.'

'Given the choice, my dear,' remarked Andrei, 'I think I'd prefer the lamppost to being assaulted by your handbag.'

Zinsa appeared and Lucian left the table to pull out a chair for her.

'Morning, Andrei,' said Zinsa. 'Morning, Rodica. Everyone sleep well?'

Andrei put down his spoon. 'Not bad at all, thank you, my dear.'

'Lucian told us they've been kicking again.' Rodica placed a bowl of *balmoș* in front of Zinsa. 'And that you think it's mainly the girl.'

'Just a feeling really, Rodica. I'm sure she's going to be quite headstrong.'

'Goes without saying,' interjected Andrei.

Rodica's head snapped round. 'Meaning?'

'Andrei…' Lucian tried to keep the grin from his face. 'Do you like living dangerously?'

'Just a casual observation from my sixty years of existence on this planet.'

'And look what that existence has done to me.' Rodica put a tray of thinly sliced *slănină* onto the table – the pork belly fat having been smoked by their neighbour in return for jars of currant and berry jam. 'My hair's almost completely white.'

'Why don't you tint it?' said Zinsa.

'Too much of a fiddle, I think, darling. A woman up the road tried to do it herself and some of her hair fell out. It's all round the neighbourhood. If that happened to me, I wouldn't leave the house.' Rodica took a tray of fried eggs from the range. 'No, my grandchildren can see me just as I am, that's what I say.'

'Rodica, come and sit with us,' said Andrei. 'I'll do the coffee.'

Rodica took off her apron and forked a slice of *slănină* onto a plate. 'What are you two doing today?'

'I'm tidying up the shed,' said Lucian. 'I promised I'd do it back in the spring, if you remember.'

'I think I'll go for a little walk,' mentioned Zinsa. 'I'll post that letter for you, Rodica.'

'If you would. Has to be there a week Monday, otherwise the car will be uninsured, and then where will we be? How's your back, dear?'

'It was all right yesterday,' said Zinsa, 'but I might lie on the settee later. Do some sewing for you, perhaps.'

'Lucian, if you find time, could you run over the lawn?' said Andrei. 'Front and back. There's a rumour we could be in for more power cuts.'

'And the electricity bill will still go up,' said Rodica. 'They really have a nerve, those people. Andrei, did you say you were going to make a start on the coffee?'

'After my *slănină*,' said Andrei. 'It's perfectly delicious, let me tell you.'

* * *

Lucian had everything out of the shed at the end of the garden, and now found it hard to believe everything had fitted inside it in the first place. He'd completely forgotten about there being a set of fishing rods. It came to him that perhaps he and Andrei should go for a day's outing on the Beja. He wiped the dust off them, seeing a Horrocks-Ibbotson transfer on the thicker cane. The rods still looked in mint condition and, although the name meant nothing to him, Lucian had the impression they might be worth a small fortune to a collector. He exchanged the rods for a broom and swept out the shed, before wiping the cobwebs away from around the windows – something, he realised, he ought probably to have done before sweeping the floor.

'Lucian?'

Lucian left the shed, seeing Zinsa coming down the garden. 'Have you been for your walk?'

'Yes.' Zinsa perched herself on a stool that belonged to the shed. 'It was something of an excuse. Sorina had a letter for me, so I popped round to collect it and had coffee.'

Lucian began to roll a slender cigarette. 'This penfriend you have in Séroulé concerns me, Zinsa.'

'She's not going to mention me to the authorities.'

'Not for a thousand dollars, or whatever? Kuetey's a monster. If he discovers you're living here in Timişoara, he could send people to track you down. And then what? You're a danger to him – last of the Dangbo family. There's no telling what Kuetey's capable of doing.'

'Lucian, you're making too much out of it.'

Lucian shrugged his shoulders and lit the cigarette. 'Maybe.' Sometimes Zinsa's complacency infuriated him, particularly when it came to her background. 'Just remember Andrei, Zinsa. He's paid out a small fortune to keep your anonymity and get all the necessary paperwork, often circumnavigating the authorities – no easy task when Ceauşescu was driving the country over a precipice. He took risks.'

'Lucian, I know I owe my life to him. But this is why Afia sends her letters to Sorina. Afia doesn't know this address – and neither will she.'

'What does the letter say?' Lucian took a draw on his cigarette.

Zinsa shrugged and adjusted her posture on the stool. 'Just the same, really. Although she mentioned somewhat cryptically that there are rumours the rebels might try for another coup.'

Lucian was quick to shake his head. 'I'm sorry, Zinsa – they won't succeed. The West won't allow it. They'll back Kuetey, despite his atrocious record when it comes to human rights. The problem you have is oil and minerals. Your father wanted the Séroulèse to benefit entirely from that. Kuetey doesn't give a damn about the people, as long as he knows that at any sign of an uprising the West will defend him and his hideous regime.'

'It's horrible. Where's the justice?'

'Greed comes before justice. Talk justice to the multinationals and they'll laugh at you behind your back – if not in your face.' Lucian put out the cigarette. 'Changing the subject for a moment, look what I've come across.' He took a black folder with a torn cover from a wheelbarrow. 'It was propped up down in the corner of the shed behind an old fireguard.' He opened the folder. 'It's full of letters in squares—'

'Like a code,' interrupted Zinsa.

'Exactly.'

'Not many pages.'

'About ten, that's all.'

'Perhaps it has something to do with Andrei's work. Or maybe part of his thesis after he graduated.' Zinsa gave a brief grimace and put a hand on her bump. 'I'm going to have to go inside and lie down. My back's starting up again. I'll make you a cup of tea first.'

'I'll come in with you.' Lucian tucked the folder under his arm and walked with Zinsa towards the house, passing Rodica's cherished rose beds as they did so. 'I forgot to mention, I said I'd meet Serghei this evening for a quiet drink. You don't mind?'

'Of course not. I like Serghei. He's a good friend to you, Lucian.'

* * *

'Don't talk to me about those fishing rods,' said Rodica, putting down the kitchen cloth. 'I'm surprised he's still got them, let alone that folder.'

Zinsa brought the cups of tea to the table.

'Zinsa, you should let me do that,' said Rodica. 'Or Lucian.'

'I want to make myself as useful as possible. And Lucian works all week. This should be his day of rest. I'm going to go and lie down on the settee.'

'Call us if you need us,' added Rodica.

'I will.'

'So what's the story with the fishing rods?' asked Lucian.

'Well...' Rodica came and sat at the table. 'Towards the end of the Second World War, when the plane came down – you know about that, don't you?'

'Andrei mentioned something about it years ago. Can't remember all the details.'

'We were around ten years old... Let me think... 1944. Andrei was ten, so I must have been eight. My father – Andrei's godfather – gave him a tent for his tenth birthday. Our parents let us try it out – mine were staying at Andrei's parents' farm that particular night. That's when the plane came down, a hundred metres or so from the tent. I still have nightmares. While we were looking at it, we found that folder. On it was a strip of silver. Andrei said he was going to get someone to make a ring for me. Of course, even then I was taken in by his charm and what I took to be his worldly knowledge. The next thing I heard he'd sold the silver and bought a set of fishing rods from my father's store.'

Lucian smiled.

'I was livid, I don't mind telling you.' Rodica put forward her left hand. 'Not until he bought me this did I finally forgive him.' She eyed the 18-carat gold ring encrusted with a central band of minutely detailed sapphires.

'It does look beautiful,' said Lucian.

'I can't deny that...'

'And what of this folder?' asked Lucian. 'It's like the contents have been written in some sort of code.'

Rodica looked up from the ring. 'We could never work out what it was. A lot of nonsense, more than likely.'

'Is Andrei in his study?'

'Probably. Do you think Zinsa's all right?'

'It's just her back. Only natural, I suppose, at this stage of her pregnancy. What with twins, as well.' Lucian stood up from the table. 'It's strange when you think about it. But you and Andrei were childhood sweethearts, and likewise Zinsa and myself.'

'I think it's nice,' said Rodica, finishing her tea. She left the table, put her cup in the sink and gazed out of the window. 'You know, I need to make a start on pruning the roses. Providing I do it now, there's a chance of three blooms next year if we have a mild winter, should there be any truth in what the weather people are saying.'

CHAPTER 2

Lucian left the kitchen for the hallway and knocked on a door at the top of the stairs, next to what used to be his bedroom. Their adoptive parents' bedroom lay beyond Zinsa's and the bathroom. By the age of fifteen, both he and Zinsa knew exactly which floorboards creaked and which didn't – a near zigzag from one bedroom to the other. Years earlier, at school, he'd wanted to touch her skin more than anything, but what dreadful damage might he cause if some of the blackness rubbed off? Zinsa's skin captivated him far more than the lessons he was supposed to be engaging himself in. Then, when that moment finally came, when she allowed him to kiss and explore her body, he could only think of ebony as being the most gorgeous – and certainly the most sensual – colour in the world.

'Come in, come in!' called Andrei.

Lucian entered the study, seeing the usual clutter – which Rodica had given up on years ago, declaring the area a 'hazard to all living creatures'. Precarious piles of paper sat on shelves, punctuated by alien-looking figurines, sculpted mainly in West Africa where Andrei had conducted much of his anthropological research. It was the Goma tribal mask on the windowsill, though, that had always unnerved him as a child. Slit-eyed, with pursed lips, it appeared ready to bring all manner of curses down on the onlooker. Typically, Zinsa loved it – along with the rest of the weird figurines.

'What are you working on?' asked Lucien.

Andrei swung around from his desk. 'Galleys have come back from the publisher. Just running my eye over them. A rather depressing tale, in fact, as I come to look at it after several months of not seeing the script.'

Lucian closed the door. 'What makes it a depressing tale?'

'The various demands on pastoral societies in Uganda and neighbouring countries, with regards to population growth and loss of herding lands to farmers.'

'Causing migration?'

'The evidence of dislocation can be described as dramatic – drought, famine and civil war.' Andrei's eyes widened as he seemed to recognise what Lucian was holding. 'Where did you find that?' he asked. 'In the shed?'

'At the back, behind an old fireguard.'

'I'd forgotten all about it.'

'Rodica said you discovered it when the plane came down in the Second World War.'

'Indeed…'

Lucian noticed Andrei's face had grown solemn. 'I sense the memory's making you uncomfortable. It must have been frightening-—'

'It's not that,' said Andrei sharply.

'What then?'

Andrei looked up, his eyes grey with apparent sorrow. 'I've only ever made the suggestion to Rodica, and Dr Cheban. But it's my belief that whatever cargo was on that plane made me sterile. And rumour has it, it was uranium—'

'Uranium?'

'Amongst other toxic materials.'

'Why would America send uranium to Russia, of all places?' Lucian asked, thinking he really needed to wash his hands.

'It was done under the Lend-Lease Act, from what I can make out.'

* * *

As Andrei seemed keen to return to his galley proofs, Lucian closed the study door behind himself, deep in thought. What he'd heard made little sense to him: that, under this 'Lend-Lease Act', which he'd never heard of before, America was transporting atomic materials directly into the hands of Stalin. How could that possibly be?

At the foot of the stairs, Lucian thought he heard a muted whimper from the living room. He found Zinsa lying on her back on the settee, tears on her cheeks. He rushed towards her.

'God's sake, Zinsa – what is it?'

Zinsa wiped her tears with a tissue. 'I'm just being silly.'

Lucian knelt beside her and stroked her hair, both upset and mystified. 'I've never known you to be silly. Let me be the judge.'

She turned her head to face him. 'Why can't my parents be here to see the birth? It's my fault.'

Lucian reached for her hand. She hadn't mentioned the coup for over two years, and he'd hoped he had finally convinced her to dismiss her guilt. 'Zinsa, I've said it before, they would have shot down that helicopter. You *know* that. You're not to blame.'

'My mother kept calling me, but I was more interested in climbing the tree. I can still see my father on the terrace, gathering my siblings and ushering them towards the helicopter, my mother all the while calling me. Only then did I climb down from the tree, not knowing we were in danger but believing we were going to have "a party in the sky". Papa would organise crazy things like that when we were on vacation. I saw the dust on the horizon, but I never made the connection that it was the start of the coup.'

'How could you? You were six years old.'

'I should have climbed down the tree the moment my mother called me.'

'You were a child, having fun. And, as I've told you over and over again, the fact that you saw the trail of dust on the horizon is a clear indication it was already too late. Kuetey would have shot the helicopter out of the sky with a surface-to-air missile.'

Zinsa laid a hand on his cheek while dabbing her eyes with the tissue. 'Where would I be without you, Lucian?'

Lucian kissed the palm of her hand and then her brow, his eyes aching with emotion. Life was just too cruel at times. 'They live on. You know that, don't you, Zinsa? They live on inside you, and within our children. No one can take that fact away from you. And you have to believe me, from the way you have always described it to me, it's a blessing that you didn't climb down from that tree straight away... You wouldn't be here now had you done so.'

* * *

'Not this one, Serghei,' said Lucian, shaking his head. 'It's a dump. And I swear they water down the *țuică* to the point of gnat's pee.'

'I'll only be a moment,' insisted Serghei. 'Wait here.'

From the pavement, Lucian watched Serghei disappear into the crowded bar. A bunch of roughnecks, in his opinion. There were times, this moment being one of them, when he wondered why he was still friends with Serghei Sapdaru, although he supposed it was a case of blood being thicker than water. Serghei's father had run the orphanage at whose entrance he had been abandoned by God knows who – his mother, presumably. Six years later, with Serghei sitting on his left in Class 2B, a black girl arrived out of the blue, the teacher instructing her to sit on his right. Skin colour aside, he was intrigued from the start when he saw the shiny metal tin in which she methodically kept her pencils and crayons and a plastic crocodile sharpener. The fact that she refused to communicate with anyone became both a mystery and a challenge to him. The breakthrough came when it dawned on him that he needed to take an interest in a country called Séroulé in a place called Africa. A short while later, something remarkable happened to him: at the suggestion of Zinsa herself, her adoptive parents decided to adopt him from the orphanage.

Serghei emerged from the bar. 'We can go.'

'What were you doing in there?' asked Lucian. 'Wheeling and dealing, eh?'

Serghei put a hand on his shoulder. 'I'm happy. Are you happy, Lucian? Lighten up, man. Be cool!'

Lucian winced. He detested such phraseology and felt it was contributing towards a decline in morality in the cities across Romania – which he knew sooner or later would infect the towns. *And then where will we be?* he all but heard Rodica say.

'Why are you so down?' persisted Serghei as they walked along the street, headlights a silvery gleam in the light drizzle.

Lucian was surprised Serghei had picked up on his mood. Although, on reflection, he supposed he hadn't been particularly talkative since leaving the house. 'I'm worried about Zinsa,' he said. 'I think her hormones are running riot.'

'How long, now?'

'Four weeks. But they say twins often come early.'

'She'll be happy then. Not long to wait.'

'She's started talking about the coup again, and how she's to blame for her family being wiped out.'

'I'm sorry... Give her my love and a massive hug, won't you?' Serghei glanced at him. 'Where do you want to go? The Subterranean?'

'It's only in the next street.'

'I'll get him to make us up a bottle of *țuică*.'

Lucian took out his wallet.

'No need,' interrupted Serghei. 'I'm flush.'

Lucian didn't comment. The fact that Serghei was 'flush', coupled with his overly buoyant mood, concerned him. He still hadn't a job, so where had the money come from? What deal or scam had he pulled to get it? Leaving Serghei to order the *țuică*, Lucian sat at a table opposite the bar. The building itself was supposed to resemble a London Underground tube station, with posters even stuck to the concave walls. He cast his eyes back to Serghei, chatting vivaciously to the owner of the bar, who seemed keen to edge away from him. Lucian wondered…and wondered again, praying with all his heart that Serghei hadn't been stupid enough to make the same mistake twice. Like Zinsa, he wanted to see Serghei settle down with a sensible partner. He had the looks and charm, but sadly not the domestic stability to satisfy such a woman.

Seeing Serghei leave the bar, Lucian took the folder he'd found earlier in the day from a carrier bag.

'What have you there?' Serghei put a couple of double-shot glasses and a bottle without a label of any kind on the table. 'Looks old. Does it hold something valuable?'

'I doubt it.' Lucian looked up and, in the diffused light, noticed a sore under Serghei's jaw. 'I discovered it today while emptying the shed. Andrei said he found it in the wreckage of that B-25 plane that came down at the end of the war. You remember the story?'

'The one supposedly en route to Moscow from America?' Serghei's nose had started to run. Instead of using a tissue or handkerchief, he wiped the mucus onto his jacket sleeve. 'What's in it?'

'I can't make it out. It's in some sort of code. What do you think?'

Serghei turned the folder around and flicked through several pages. 'Like algebra to me. And I was crap at algebra, if you remember.'

Lucian watched Serghei ponder a moment longer, scratching at the sore as he did so – his worst fears now virtually realised.

'Mario!' Serghei reached for his glass. 'Remember Mario from the orphanage? He was nuts on crosswords and fathoming out riddles and things like that. I'm still in touch with him. I know where he lives.' Serghei wavered his left hand ominously. 'Shade dodgy, but heart's in the right place.'

'Didn't he end up as a caretaker for some private college?'

'He's still there.' Serghei downed a shot of *țuică*.

'What do you mean, "dodgy"?'

'Does a bit of dealing.'

'Drugs?'

'Er...no, don't think so.' Serghei shrugged. 'Whatever stuff comes his way, I guess.'

'Tomorrow's Sunday,' said Lucian. 'I'm not at work. Can we go then?'

'Sure. Cool.' Serghei filled their glasses, his hand with a noticeable tremor. 'Now let's finish this bottle – and for Christ's sake, Lucian, lighten up! Zinsa's going to be fine.'

CHAPTER 3

The following day, they travelled by bus across the city. It didn't take long for Lucian to notice Serghei's mood had taken a nosedive, and that the sore under his jaw appeared flakier and angry-looking. For much of the journey they didn't speak a word to each other and Lucian found himself downhearted about what was happening to his friend. The evening before he hadn't dared tell Zinsa what he suspected was going on with him. Upsetting her at this stage in her pregnancy would be cruelty itself, particularly now that she had started to blame herself again for the massacre of her family in West Africa a decade and a half ago. His hope was that when the twins were born she would refocus and that would be the end of the matter – preferably, forever.

Serghei stood. 'This is the stop.'

Lucian reached for the folder and left his seat. The only time he could recall being on this side of the city was on a school outing. 'Do you remember coming here to the zoo when we were kids?' he asked Serghei.

'Vaguely,' said Serghei.

'Next stop along or so, as I recall. We did the Banat Village Museum at the same time.'

Serghei didn't comment, as if he were in some other world. Lucian shrugged inwardly and directed his attention at the imposing houses that had started to appear, some of them flamboyantly Baroque in style, like in the old quarter of the city. It looked to be a classy area. Lucian wished he and Zinsa could live in such style, but he doubted they could ever afford to. An architect's draughtsman often earned below average pay – unless a progressive company that sought to go places happened by chance to open its door. Since joining Crăciun & Fieraru, he'd realised neither partner had any such fire in their bellies, and he had watched with dismay as other architectural firms took profitable projects from under their noses. He vowed that once Zinsa had settled down with the twins he would make 'enquiries' with a view to moving on.

'His room's over on the right,' said Serghei abruptly.

The building they'd arrived at was in the unusual style – for its geographical location – of Art Deco as opposed to Baroque, its façade typical of the period with bold cubist geometrical forms. As they waded through crisp leaves fallen from a line of now virtually naked sycamores and headed towards a side gate at the top of the driveway, Lucian suspected it had originally been designed for a large family rather than for a foreign language school – and that the architect might even have been slightly eccentric.

The door at the foot of a short row of steps squealed open on rusted hinges, pulled back by a skinny youth with unkempt dark hair and pock-marked cheeks. Lucian was surprised by how little Mario Nemescu had changed since the day he'd been expelled from school. Like himself, Mario had also been caught up in what became a nationwide social catastrophe – a consequence of Nicolae Ceaușescu's belief that population growth by outlawing abortion and contraception and taxing childless couples would boost the economy. However, by a stroke of luck their orphanage happened to be 'humane' in comparison to the majority, to the point whereby they even received an education.

'Come in, you guys!' ushered Mario vigorously. 'Serghei, I have the gear you wanted–'

From his peripheral vision, Lucian noticed Serghei raise a finger to his lips. He followed them both into the windowless living space, which clearly doubled as the bedroom, with a mattress on the floor over in the corner.

Mario spread his grubby hands theatrically. 'My paradise! And all I have to do is to open up, do a bit of cleaning and then, when the day is over, do a lock-up. How are you, Lucian? Must be a few years…'

'I'm doing okay, Mario.' Lucian's eyes took in the three handguns on the pedestal table next to the mattress, the largest one in several pieces. 'Zinsa's pregnant with twins. It wasn't planned, but obviously we're overjoyed.' Curiosity moved him towards the table to take a closer look at the guns. 'A side-line?' he asked.

'Yeah, yeah,' brushed off Mario, as if realising he should have removed them from plain sight. 'Just a hobby. They've been deactivated, but a little filing and drilling here and there and they're as good as new.'

Serghei picked one up, its barrel a couple of centimetres shorter than the one that lay in pieces. 'How much you knocking them out for?'

'Well, like I said, it's just a hob—'

'How much?' repeated Serghei. 'This one. How much for this one, say?'

'That one? Er, well, that's a Beretta. Nice model. That one, er…eight-hundred thou'.'

With inflation having gone berserk, it might have sounded like Mario was asking the earth for it – but in fact Lucian thought it a reasonable price, not that he knew much about such things. Serghei was still examining the gun, turning it over repeatedly in his hands. Fearing what was rattling around in his mind, Lucian altered the proceedings by handing the folder to Mario.

'I'd like you to take a look at it,' he said, 'with a view to deciphering the code.'

'Code?' asked Mario. 'Code for what?'

'That's what I'm hoping you can tell me.'

Mario opened the damaged cover. 'Where did it come from?'

'The wreckage of a B-25.'

Mario turned his head towards Lucian, seeking clarification.

'My adoptive father found it. He was camping out when the plane came down in 'forty-four. It was on its way to Moscow, having started its journey in North America – so the rumour goes.'

'Bullshit,' said Mario.

'Pardon?'

'It's a bullshit rumour, in my opinion.'

'Why do you say that?'

'Europe was at war. Why fly across a war-zone, dropping south and then veering north? I've never reckoned that plane was heading for Moscow.' Mario looked at Serghei and Lucian in turn. 'The area where the plane came down is still sealed off, you know that? I went past it a couple of months ago.'

'Andrei, my father, reckons it had uranium onboard, as well as other stuff. Toxic stuff, that is.'

'Doesn't surprise me. Probably part of some crooked policy going on in the background.' Mario turned a couple of the pages, nodding to himself as he gave each page a moment's thought. 'They've based it on the Polybius Square,' he announced. 'No question.'

'"Polybius"?' queried Lucian.

'Greek historian. Centuries ago. Before Christ, I think.' Mario looked up from the folder. 'Go lose yourselves for a couple of hours,' he said. 'This is interesting. I want to be alone with it. Might just get the gist of the first set of letters for you.'

* * *

Lucian walked back up the side road with Serghei and told him he wanted to take a look at the zoo, keen to see if it had changed much since the school visit. A bus came soon enough and took them to the next stop, and to the end of the line as it happened. They walked along the zoo's perimeter towards the entrance, their silence punctuated by some exotic bird chirping vociferously behind the high-rise fence. There was no one to take their money at the kiosk behind the wooden barrier.

'Let's just go in,' said Serghei, his monosyllables as leaden as the November sky above them.

Lucian bought him a sandwich from a stall alongside the meerkats' enclosure after Serghei claimed he'd left his money at home. A man came over and asked if they'd paid. Lucian paid the man for their tickets while thinking how costly the afternoon was becoming, what with the bus fares as well. Still, on the upside Mario had clearly taken an interest in the folder.

They sat on a bench overlooking the ostrich enclosure, although there didn't appear to be any birds venturing out from the shed adjoining it.

'What deal are you doing with Mario?' asked Lucian at length.

Serghei turned to him. 'What?'

'It's drugs, isn't it?'

'Drugs?'

'Show me your arms.'

'What?'

'Show me your arms.'

Serghei had a look of annoyance on his face. 'What do you want to see my arms for?'

'Because you're mainlining again, aren't you.' It was not a question but a statement. Lucian was that confident. He lowered his voice while noticing the flicker of alarm on Serghei's face. 'Jacking up junk. Heroin.'

'Go to hell.'

'Ah! I knew it. You idiot!'

'You don't know nothing! You don't know the shit I have to go through to put food in my mouth, to pay the rent, to have one bulb for heat and light. Mario...he understands—'

'At least he's got himself a job.'

'Leave me alone.' Serghei dipped his eyes. 'Just leave me alone.'

'I can't. I've known you all my life.' Lucian rolled two cigarettes, lit them both and handed one to Serghei. 'So, what's the deal with Mario?'

Serghei drew hesitantly on the cigarette. 'It's not drugs.'

'What is it, then? I'm hardly likely to mention anything to anyone, am I?'

Serghei held the hand-rolled cigarette in front of Lucian. 'These. French. Real posh ones. I'm selling them on in the hotels and restaurants.'

Lucian nodded, feeling somewhat reassured. 'Hope you do well out of it. But if you are mainlining, for Christ's sake cut it out. Don't go back to it. I couldn't bear it – and neither could Zinsa.'

Serghei's head jerked upwards. 'Zinsa? You haven't mentioned anything to her?'

'No. It would break her heart.' Lucian changed the subject, with Mario now at the forefront of his mind. Sharp as a razor, that was his impression. Probably entirely untrustworthy, too. 'A while ago, I heard Mario was living in Bucharest—'

'In the sewers, with other kids,' confirmed Serghei, seemingly relieved that the conversation had shifted from narcotics. 'He should never have been taken out of school. The whole thing was a set-up to get rid of him. That teacher was a queer son-of-a-bitch. He got what he deserved from Mario...a solid pasting.'

'I remember,' said Lucian. He could still vividly recall the ambulance arriving at the school entrance. 'How long did he live in the sewers for?'

Serghei shrugged and drew on his cigarette. 'Couple of years.'

'Clever, isn't he? I mean, if he put his mind to it, he could go places – like university. It's not too late for him.'

Serghei snorted, as if amused. 'All those airs and graces? That's not Mario's style. Anyway, where's he going to get that sort of cash from?'

Lucian nodded soberly, as if to himself. 'I guess you're right.' He had visions of Mario punching a professor's lights out for 'unjust' marking. 'We'd better head back.'

* * *

When they arrived at Mario's, they found him lying across the mattress in the corner, completely engrossed in the folder's contents.

'There're bottles of beer in the cupboard under the sink,' he muttered without turning his head towards them.

Lucian opened the cupboard, and while taking the tops off the beers watched as Serghei went and picked up the Beretta handgun. He knew that somewhere down the line Serghei was going to try for a deal with Mario to get his hands on it permanently. He debated again whether to distance himself from him. In a month or so he'd be the father of two beautiful children. Why would he want to hang out with a man who no longer listened to common sense?

'This is major,' insisted Mario. 'And I'm only on the second set of letters.'

Lucian went over to the mattress. 'What do you mean by "major"?'

'I'm going to have to keep hold of this.' Mario finally turned his head. 'How long can you let me have it for?'

'Not that long,' said Lucian cautiously. He'd noticed that Serghei was now taking an interest, having put down the gun and drifted over.

'What have you deciphered so far?' Serghei asked.

Mario left the mattress and got himself a beer. 'It mentions a unit, simply called 17 – in numerals. Hitmen, I think.'

'*What?*' Lucian stared at Mario. 'No, that can't be right. You've got to be doing it wrong – deciphering it wrong. Surely?'

In the blink of an eye, Mario deftly struck the cap from the bottle on the edge of the filthy stove – evidently a frequent habit since much of the enamel had chipped off on that particular corner. 'I don't think so, Lucian.' He swigged back some beer. 'Could be a global thing. Seventeen hitmen to sort stuff out. Political stuff, you know? One for each zone.'

'Zone?' probed Lucian.

'That's what it'll be in the end, "zones". Not countries.'

'Why don't you leave it here?' proposed Serghei. 'Let Mario spend time on it. Like he says, this really could be big.'

Those last five words from Serghei, coupled with Mario's decisive interest, sent Lucian's head spinning, because he knew what Serghei was likely to be thinking. For that reason, he needed to keep hold of the original. A small white lie was required. 'I told my father I'd get it back to him by this evening.'

'Pity,' said Mario.

'But I know what I can do. Tomorrow, my firm is expecting delivery of a replacement photocopier.' Lucian opened the folder. What if he *could* convert it into cash? It might just pay the deposit to set himself and Zinsa up in a modest house of their own. A collector of war memorabilia would surely pay handsomely for such a mysterious document. 'I'll photocopy every page and bring them round after work,' he said.

'You never know,' said Mario, 'if I'm right, maybe it was someone from this unit who hit JFK.'

'Kennedy?' queried Serghei.

'Why not?' Mario took another swig of beer. 'Kennedy had started to piss people off – the right kind of people, if you get my drift. This folder was on a plane carrying uranium, heading from America to what would become the Eastern Bloc. It's easy to make the connection, isn't it?'

Lucian looked at Serghei and saw the bewilderment in his eyes, too. They both turned back to Mario. 'Go on,' said Lucian.

'The Soviet Union was handed the atomic bomb by the Yanks, or more precisely by a powerful underground faction operating inside America. Maybe Kennedy was about to expose the fact that the Cold War was a hoax. A complete set-up.'

'That doesn't make any sense at all,' said Lucian, annoyed now that his time was being wasted because the man was talking garbage. 'I mean the Cold War being a hoax.'

'Listen to me...' Mario took a long cigarette from its elegant, gold-striped packet – utterly incongruous with its surroundings – and lit up. 'When I was in Hotel Sewer in Bucharest, I met a guy who told me a lot about this stuff. It makes sense if there's a body of people – like really wealthy people – who are set on organising massive upheavals, and out of them they build a world government while the ordinary governments show themselves to be useless against what's being thrown at them. That's what this guy told me, and since that day every question I've put to myself always points to exactly that. He told me that before long this faction will hijack the United Nations.'

'That's a rubbish organisation,' said Lucian. 'Has no bite to it at all. What's it doing about ending the Rwandan Civil War? It might have quietened off for now, but I guarantee you all hell will break loose again next year.'

'So, it's ripe enough to be hijacked then, isn't it? It's a ready-made world government. Look at all the organisations that trail off it. It's like a giant cobweb spreading itself across the planet. This faction has only to worm its way inside, if it hasn't already done so, adopting a smoke and mirrors strategy. Believe me, Lucian.'

Lucian looked down at the folder he was holding, feeling the blood drain quite suddenly from his face. He spoke barely above a whisper. 'And you think this could be instructions, or whatever, to members of the faction operating in the East? If what you say is at all true, there would have to be co-conspirators in the East to synchronise with those in the West. Right?'

Mario shrugged. 'Why not? So far as the faction is concerned, East and West have never been *dis*united. It's all bullshit this communism and capitalism. I repeat, smoke and mirrors to keep everyone distracted from what's really going on.'

'So was Stalin a member of this faction?'

'A *puppet* of the faction. All the leaders we see up-front are puppets.'

'I'm not so sure about that—'

'It's obvious, Lucian. They keep themselves in the background, pulling the strings.'

'All right, all right,' said Lucian, confused and wondering whether the exchange between himself and Mario had reached a point of make-believe. 'Going back to the plane…you don't think it was heading for Moscow, itself?'

'I don't know, Lucian. It just seems odd that the plane went south. By my reckoning, if it were heading for Moscow it would have come down from the north – less chance of it being blown to pieces by the Germans. No one knows for sure why that plane came down, do they?'

'No,' admitted Lucian, before his mind veered towards Zinsa. He didn't like leaving her for too long, unless he was at work and had no choice in the matter. 'Lots of rumours, of course.'

'I heard it ran out of gas,' said Serghei. 'Maybe some flak punctured a tank.'

'Could be just that,' said Mario. 'Couldn't it, Lucian?'

'Possibility, for sure.' Lucian glanced at Serghei. 'I need to get back to Zinsa,' he said, closing the folder. 'Mario, I'll catch you tomorrow after work.'

* * *

Lucian felt himself to be buoyed-up on so many fronts as he turned back the starched cotton sheet to join Zinsa. The imminent birth of the twins. The fact that relatively affordable apartments were at last being built over on Strada Lorena, barely three kilometres away – meaning Andrei and Rodica could visit them with ease, and vice versa. And now the discovery of the folder. As he gazed up at the ceiling's shadowy contours, Lucian wondered again whether he could make money from it. He'd yet to mention to Andrei what Mario had told him about there being a possible unit of assassins capable of creating mayhem by taking out world leaders and other prominent figures. If that was the case, what other extraordinary information did the folder contain? The United Nations aspect didn't make much sense to him. If the faction had that much power, instead of 'hijacking' the organisation why not start it from the beginning in the first place with a view to making it a world government?

He felt Zinsa stir. 'How have they been today?' he asked.

'Not so much kicking and wriggling.'

'Good. It's high time they gave you a moment's thought.'

'Did you go and see what's-his-name?'

'Mario? Yes, Serghei took me. He lives over by the zoo and has a job as a caretaker for some school. Has his own flat. Well, more like a windowless, semi-basement of a room.'

'Isn't he the one who hit that teacher?'

'The teacher interfered with him apparently, if you remember.'

'He wasn't a very nice teacher. I found him a bit creepy. So did some of the other girls. What happened to Mario when he left? Do you know? Did he say?'

'He lived in the sewers in Bucharest. By the sound of things, he met some interesting characters. Knowledgeable. I found him to be just that. I wouldn't trust him, though.'

'You wouldn't?'

'No. From what I can make out he's wheeling-an'-dealing on the side. He's selling French cigarettes to Serghei, who then hawks them around hotels and restaurants.'

'Serghei told you this?'

'Yes,' replied Lucian cautiously, not wanting to mention the drug issue. 'I'm trying to straighten Serghei out, but it's hard work.'

'He just needs to meet the right girl.'

'I suppose…' *But what decent girl would want to know Serghei in his present state?* deliberated Lucian. He leant on an elbow to kiss Zinsa. 'I'll go to sleep now. Work tomorrow, unfortunately.' He kissed her again, just lightly on her brow. 'Love you.'

'Love you, too, Lucian – always.' A moment later she said, 'Are you seeing Mario again?'

'Yes. Tomorrow. I'm going to photocopy the contents of the folder and drop them off after work.'

CHAPTER 4

Four days later, Lucian caught the bus from work at 4:30, as usual. It was a blustery day, and as he sat at the back of the bus he watched a paper bag twirl skittishly in the air. The driver was waiting for the lights to change, but Lucian found himself captivated by the dancing paper bag. It felt like a private performance, just for him – until suddenly it swirled violently and swept under a lorry. The bus moved forward, and Lucian straightened himself in the seat. An unexpected thought entered his head: that, in those few seconds, the paper bag had emulated life itself. Discovery, liberty, passion and death – though not necessarily in that order.

When he left the bus fifteen minutes later, he noticed that a car had coincidentally followed the bus route – a Dacia Liberta, a car he particularly fancied since they had enough room for a family and a quality second-hand model was now virtually within his grasp when it came to affordability. Another reason for noticing it was that the nearside door happened to be a lighter shade of blue. The car, with its single occupant, continued to follow the bus down the street.

One day, he vowed, he'd get to own one of those.

* * *

Zinsa put a slice of apple tart on a plate for him.

'I can do that,' said Lucian, taking off his anorak. 'Take the weight off your feet.'

'I'm okay. No need to fuss.'

'Where are they?'

'Rodica's gone up the road to have coffee with Mrs Bãlan.' Zinsa took a seat opposite him and wriggled to get herself comfortable. 'I think Andrei's in his study.'

Lucian tucked into the tart that either Rodica or Zinsa had made. Or perhaps they'd done so together, which was often the case. 'How's it been for you today?' he asked. 'I get the impression you're quite exhausted. Not surprising, of course.'

'I'm okay...'

'Sure?' Lucian met her eyes, as brown and as mesmerising in their beauty as the day they'd first caught his breath in Class 2B. 'I'm not fussing.'

'I know...'

'But something's on your mind. I can tell.'

'It's a silly thing.'

'Then share it and let me be the judge.'

Zinsa stood and went over to the drainer to pour mint tea from the pot. 'I think there might be someone watching me.' She turned to look at him. 'There, that's how silly it is.'

'Watching you?' Lucian took his cup from her, frowning. 'What's given you that idea?'

'For the past two days, a man has been sitting in a car nearly opposite – like he's watching the comings and goings of a certain house. Maybe this house.'

Lucian found himself recalling the blue Dacia, but said nothing. After all, that was pure coincidence.

'You're not saying anything.' Zinsa sat down at the table.

'What colour was the car?'

'The colour? Oh, sort of pale green... Why do you ask?'

'I just wondered if it had caught my attention.'

'It seems to arrive after you go to work, and leaves before you return.' Zinsa sipped some tea and put the cup back on its saucer. 'You don't think it could be...do you?'

Lucian's head jerked upwards. 'That General Kuetey has tracked you down?'

'Yes.'

Lucian felt as if he wanted to laugh, to suppress the perpetual fear he lived with – that they *all* privately lived with. 'I can't imagine he would have a person sitting in a car watching you.' He met her eyes to drive home his point.

'You know he's obsessed with wiping out my father's bloodline?'

'So why is this person simply watching you?' Lucian shook his head. 'I can hardly bring myself to say it.'

'Say what?'

'The President of Séroulé wants you bumped off. I don't dispute that. We know it to be true. So why hasn't this person merely knocked on the door and committed his heinous deed?'

'I don't know...' Zinsa gave a lengthy sigh and shook her head. 'Like I said, it's just a silly thought.'

'Let's see what happens tomorrow.' Lucian forced a smile. 'Perhaps your condition is making you a shade paranoid.' He pointed at her belly. 'Over those two treasures.'

Zinsa laughed. 'Do you think?'

'I'm no psychiatrist.'

'Are you going to see Mario, like you said?'

Lucian glanced at the kitchen clock. 'Yes. I should get going. If I'm not back in time for dinner, put some aside and I'll reheat it.'

* * *

The bus drew up to its stop before the zoo and Lucian disembarked. He could hardly contain his excitement, eager to know what Mario had discovered from the photocopied pages he'd handed him earlier in the week. He veered off into the side-road, just as he had done when being directed by Serghei. The streetlights seemed brighter in this particular neighbourhood – one of well-to-do families, living comfortable lives. *One day…*

Lucian pulled up sharply and blinked, unable to believe his eyes. Surely not? He couldn't see the nearside door, but the rest of the Dacia was the same colour. He took to a tree-lined alley, his heart beating wildly in his throat. Standing in a daze, he recalled Zinsa's words to him less than an hour before.

I think there might be someone watching me…

He backed away and walked the length of the alley, arriving at what resembled a skewed T-junction. The uneven path to his left happened to run adjacent to the gardens of the houses in the road. He followed the path until he came to the rear of the Art Deco building, with Mario's basement studio somewhere to the left of it. Dusk had now fallen, but there were no lights on. Did that indicate Mario had locked up for the day? There was a chain-link fence, perhaps a couple of metres tall, surrounding an overgrown garden.

Something wasn't right; he could feel it at the core of his being, the ominous feeling of an ill wind. Nothing at all to do with Zinsa, he was certain about that, but possibly to do with him – or more precisely, the folder. Or was he, himself, now becoming as paranoid as Zinsa?

Lucian scaled a metal pole that supported the fence and swung himself over into the garden. Keeping to a line of shrubs and checking constantly for faces appearing in the windows of neighbouring houses, he made his way up the garden. He located Mario's studio with ease, surprised to find it on the latch. It was pitch black inside. He stood there, detecting a musty smell that he hadn't noticed on his previous two visits. His senses were on high alert, particularly his hearing. Would it matter if he put the light on? He couldn't recall the room having any windows. Out of necessity he was going to have to – briefly so, hopefully. He just needed to locate those eight photocopied pages!

Lucian lightly ran his hand over the wall on both sides of the entrance. His right shin knocked into something whilst doing so, causing him to curse under his breath, before he finally found the switch. The low-wattage bulb shed enough light to reveal that the pages were absent from the mattress. He resumed his search while debating what might have happened. Mario, in his infinite wisdom, had likely started to hawk the pages around town, contacting acquaintances, hoping for a decent price… Lucian's anger started to rise as he pulled open drawers. He'd been a fool for trusting Mario. He wondered whether it had all been nonsense about there being a unit of seventeen assassins. There again, if it were true, Mario knew he could get decent money for it. World War Two memorabilia found in the wreckage of the B-25 that had 'mysteriously' come down – and now with an even more remarkable story to tell.

He yanked open the bottom drawer of a chest of ill-fitting drawers and came across a complete gun. He hesitated. What if Mario had got out of his depth, and now there was a gang after him…and himself, because he had the original – and the original of anything was invariably worth far more. He took the Beretta and a handful of bullets, then went back to searching for the pages: under the porcelain sink, running a hand over the top of the wardrobe... Nothing. *Damn it!*

Lucian left the basement and checked that both handgun and bullets were safely tucked away in his anorak. He wanted to see if the Dacia was still there, parked up in the street. He kept himself inside the thick shadows from the line of sycamores and edged his way down the drive... *Still* there. He could see the nearside door. It was hard to make out because the car was parked between two streetlights. Nevertheless, it did look a lighter shade of blue. The only occupant was the driver, sitting motionlessly – until he started to get out of the car!

Lucian withdrew, and realised that in his haste he'd left the door wide open and the light on in Mario's studio. *Idiot*, he told himself. Too late, now. Just then, as if he were trapped inside the most isolated of nightmares, he realised he could predict what would happen next. The figure hesitated, turned to the right, and then sure enough headed up the drive towards him. The individual was tall, and perhaps had a slight limp... Curious, but that limp and the height of the figure gave him the impression he'd seen the man before.

Lucian made an abrupt about-turn. Dismissing any noise his footsteps made on the dead sycamore leaves, he bolted to the rear garden and over the chain-link fence. The moment he rejoined the path, he debated whether he should have taken the Beretta handgun. But if Mario had got himself caught up in something, he might while under duress blurt out his name. The very thought began to unnerve him. A good enough reason to take and keep the gun, then. He had a family to protect. And if somehow he'd managed to get hold of the wrong end of the stick, then fine – he'd return the weapon to Mario and all would be as if nothing had happened.

Walking back along the road towards the zoo, fighting off a temptation to look over his shoulder, Lucian kept his hearing primed for vehicles approaching and then rapidly decreasing in speed behind him. But *who* was the driver of that Dacia Liberta?

Lucian caught a crowded bus with seconds to spare and discovered a vacant seat at the back. Settling himself, he found he wanted to feel the gun in his hand, as if he couldn't quite believe he had actually taken the thing. He casually put his hand over the pocket of his anorak. The trigger housing, the barrel itself and the outline of a bullet. God Almighty, he thought. A complete gun, *and* ammunition. Naturally, he hadn't a permit. Apparently, they were notoriously difficult to get hold of from the police, an inheritance perhaps of the dictator, Nicolas Ceauşescu, and his diabolical paranoia.

Lucian gazed out of the window at the headlights of cars shimmering towards him. If caught, then he could always bring General Kuetey into play. The fact that the President of Séroulé wanted – as Zinsa succinctly put it – to eradicate her father's bloodline gave him a reason to possess a gun. If discovered, the authorities would certainly rap his knuckles and at best the crime might result in a non-custodial prison sentence. A small price to pay to protect his family, although Rodica would be horrified. *What will the neighbours say?* He glanced over his shoulder. The traffic was heavy; the tail end of the rush-hour. With no Dacia Liberta following from what he could see, he made a snap decision to leave the bus three stops before he intended to get off.

Lucian waited at the stop. Camouflaged by graffiti strewn across the Perspex shelter, he watched the cars follow the bus. Definitely no blue Dacia in the traffic. He nodded to himself and left the shelter, walked a couple of streets and knocked on a door that was in desperate need of a coat of paint. *Not the only thing that feels 'desperate'*, thought Lucian.

A girl with braided blonde hair eventually answered. Lucian knew her as one of five housemates.

'Hi, Denisa. Okay if I go up and see if Serghei is in?'

'Yeah, he's in.'

Lucian followed the girl into the murky hallway, hit by a waft of cannabis. In the kitchen at the end of the corridor a knot of people sat around the table, drinking and smoking, Reggae music playing in the background. The girl went and joined them. Lucian climbed the stairs. Whenever he came here, he left feeling both relieved and grateful. A bunch of wasters. He'd smoked spliffs in the past, and enjoyed them. They heightened his creative edge in some inexplicable way. But since the day Zinsa announced she was pregnant he'd kept to straight cigarettes, and intended to give those up once he'd set himself up in the right frame of mind.

Lucian knocked on a door on the landing at a point where some of the floorboards had been removed, most likely for firewood, he suspected – recalling Serghei's remark about having just a lightbulb for heat.

'Yeah, come in!'

Lucian attempted to turn the knob. 'It's locked!'

'Shit... One minute, Lucian.'

Lucian waited, and took a rough guess at what Serghei might be doing. When the door opened, he stepped over a bare joist and just came straight out with it. 'Jacking up, were you? Hence the "Oh shit, it's Lucian!"'

Serghei gestured for him to enter the room. 'Take a look. You won't find a gram of junk anywhere.'

Lucian stepped inside, his mind refocussing. 'I might have a problem.'

'Like what?'

'Shut the door.'

Serghei did so, his face a sheet of concern. 'What's happened? Is it Zinsa?'

'She's fine.' Lucian sat cautiously on a threadbare armchair, one of its front cabriole legs missing and replaced by several paperbacks. He looked around the room, the Bob Marley poster switched for some other reggae artist. 'Who's that?' he asked.

'Gregory Isaacs.' Serghei sat at the end of the bed. 'Want a drink? I can scrounge some *țuică* off the others.'

Lucian waved the offer aside. 'I need to get back.'

'So what's the problem?'

'I'm only guessing, but I think Mario's stirred some shit up.'

'How do y—?'

'I reckon I'm being followed. A blue Dacia, with a paler shade of blue on the nearside door, seems to be featuring somewhat prominently in my life.'

'Oh... A blue Dacia? For how long?'

'Since leaving work.'

'Today?' Serghei chuckled. 'Spare a smoke? I've got some papers.'

'I'm being serious, for Christ's sake.' Lucian took a half-filled pouch of tobacco from an inside pocket of his anorak. Should he tell Serghei about the gun? He handed over the pouch. No. He would face Mario if he ever caught up with him again. 'According to Zinsa, there's been a car parked outside the house these past two days. The odd thing is that it's only there when I'm not there.'

'But it's not the blue Dacia?' clarified Serghei before locating a packet of papers amongst the items of clothing strewn across the bed.

'No. Pale green, she said. Of course, she thinks agents from Séroulé have finally caught up with her.'

Serghei glanced up while rolling his cigarette. 'Probably a street census thing.'

'For what, exactly?'

'We had a car parked up by the lights for a whole month. We thought they were monitoring this house, but it turned out they were monitoring the flow of traffic to see if the street needed widening.'

Lucian nodded as it slowly dawned on him, because he remembered now. 'There's been talk they might widen our street.'

'Well, there you go. Just monitoring the traffic.' Serghei sat back down on the bed, clutching a grubby seashell for an ashtray. 'So, what happened today – with you?'

'I left work as normal, caught the bus as normal. As I was waiting to board it, I noticed this blue Dacia Liberta. You know I've always wanted one. The prominent feature on this one being the paler shade of blue on the nearside door. It followed the bus route until I got off.' Lucian shrugged. 'Coincidental, I thought. Why wouldn't I? Then once I'd had tea, I went over to Mario's. What should be parked outside? None other than the blue Dacia.'

Serghei drew reflectively on the cigarette. 'Did you see Mario?'

'No.'

'He was expecting you?'

Another shrug. 'Sort of,' said Lucian. 'It was a loose arrangement.' He decided to roll a cigarette for himself. 'Anyway, there's no sign of the pages I photocopied for him.'

'How do you know?'

'I climbed over the fence. The door to his studio was on the latch.'

Serghei nodded. 'He often leaves it like that. Reckons he's living in an area where people trust one another.'

'With one lousy, untrustworthy bastard living in the centre of it!'

'That's a bit hasty, isn't it?'

'Not really,' said Lucian with conviction. 'I can figure out what he's done. He's approached someone – someone out of his league. Now they want the original and are sizing me up. I could get done over. I'm not going to spell out the worst-case scenario.'

'Aren't you being a shade dramatic?' said Serghei. 'I mean, why don't you just wait for Mario to turn up?'

Lucian sighed. 'You know, Serghei, when Zinsa told me about the car, I mentioned partly in jest that she was getting paranoid because of the two treasures she's carrying. But is it me who's now getting paranoid?'

'You're concerned, I get that. But look, why don't I go over to Mario's tomorrow while you're at work and check out the scene?'

'You'll do that?'

'For sure. Christ, Lucian, I've got a backlog of favours I owe you.'

* * *

Lucian wrapped the Beretta and accompanying bullets in a carrier bag and placed it carefully inside the somewhat larger bag that contained the original folder. Turning off the light in the kitchen and hallway, he climbed the stairs and joined Zinsa, already in bed.

'Is that the folder?' she asked, turning her head towards him.

'The original, yes.'

'It's a bit cramped up here, Lucian. Why not put it back in the shed, where you found it?'

Lucian made space for it in the bottom drawer of the chest, where he kept his pants and socks amongst the burgeoning pile of pink and blue baby clothes, the majority of which had been knitted by Rodica. 'I think it could be quite valuable,' he said, pulling off his sweater and unbuttoning his shirt.

'Does Mario believe it to be?'

'He wasn't there.'

'A wasted journey?'

'I suppose.'

'What makes the folder valuable?'

'World War Two memorabilia, for starters. Then there's the code itself—'

'I'm worried by it, Lucian.' Zinsa turned onto her side, her brown eyes a pointed gaze. 'Why has a code been used? It's a secret, only to be deciphered by certain people. Not the likes of us.'

'It'll be related to a war fought fifty years ago.' Lucian was satisfied he was telling her the truth – up to a point. 'We could sell it at an auction—'

'With Andrei's permission.'

'Naturally, with Andrei's permission. We could then put the money towards an apartment, or even a house, of our own.'

'I imagine in a couple of years' time we're going to need a house, Lucian.'

Lucian tied the cord on his striped pyjamas. 'I know. But I've been told that half the apartments they're building on Strada Lorena will be two-bedroomed, with an adjoining box room. I'm going to make enquiries this coming week.' He started to leave the bedroom. 'Just brush my teeth.' As he walked across the landing, he heard soft classical music from the radio in Andrei's and Rodica's bedroom. At 10:40 on the dot it would stop and all would fall silent, save for the occasional creak here and there as the house cooled down.

Lucian squeezed toothpaste onto his brush. The Beretta handgun… He now seriously regretted introducing it into this innocent household. He'd never been in trouble with the police and didn't intend to be at any time in the future. What should he do with it? Throw it away? Or bury it, just in case it was required to threaten someone to get them off his back – like the driver of the blue Dacia? Keeping the gun in the house would likely make him restless, his mind overreacting by conjuring scenarios such as what would happen if there was a police raid due to a mix-up with an address? Only a couple of months ago such an incident had occurred at a house further down the street, giving the elderly owner a heart attack by all accounts.

Lucian brushed his teeth. *More* to the point, what if the police became suspicious that Serghei and his housemates were taking drugs, or happened to discover Mario's illegal dealings? The police would likely pay him a visit and insist on conducting a search of this house.

Turning away from the concern on his face in the mirror above the basin, Lucian dried his lips on Zinsa's towel and pulled the cord for the light. He did have an idea of sorts. The question being how much would it cost? He retraced his steps along the landing to the bedroom.

'Zinsa?' he said, keeping his voice low.

'What is it?'

Lucian turned back the sheet to join her. She was now lying on her left side, facing him as he drew the sheet back up. He put a hand on her warm belly. 'I can't get over this miracle,' he whispered. He kissed her brow. 'Two miracles, I should say. It's just unbelievable.'

Zinsa giggled. 'You're like a little boy, Lucian, at times. Brimming with wonder.'

'Don't you feel the same?'

'I feel like an elephant. What were you going to say?'

'I was just thinking what to do with the folder, to keep it out of the way and perfectly safe. That girl you used to be quite friendly with at school, the one who went to work for Banca Comercială Bănăţeana. Do you know if she still works there? Only I haven't seen her behind the desk lately. Not that I've been in that many times—'

'Oh, Elena?'

'Yes. Elena. Is she still at the bank?'

'Yes. I bumped into her last month. We had coffee. She's been promoted. That's why you won't see her at the front. Why do you ask?'

'I want to put the folder somewhere safe, and thought about using a safe deposit box at the bank.' Lucian felt Zinsa's look of surprise in the darkness, and ploughed on before she could interrupt him. 'I mean, say we went down the road of putting it in an auction...well, it wouldn't be for a while. It has to be deciphered first, so we know what we're dealing with.'

'It all sounds very intense, Lucian.'

...Then he could put the gun in the safe deposit box, too – along with the half dozen or so bullets. Everything in one place under lock and key. 'I certainly don't think we should put it back in the shed,' he said. 'The damp won't do it any good, especially now we're coming into winter.'

'Will it be expensive putting it in the bank? We need to be careful. Our budget is tight enough as it is.'

'I know. That's why I'm going to speak to Elena. See if she can cut us a deal. By the way, on the way back from Mario's I called in on Serghei. He thinks the car you've seen in the street is likely to be monitoring the traffic to see if the road needs widening. There's been a rumour about the possibility, hasn't there?'

'Yes, of course,' sighed Zinsa. 'Hopefully just that. Did I tell you earlier, the Tourist Information Centre called today?'

'I don't think so. I'd have remembered.'

'They've finally got around to making a decision. They're allowing me two months' maternity leave.'

'I wish it was four. Bonding with them is going to be important.'

'It'll be okay. We'll make it okay.'

'Try for three months.'

'I will. Being winter, there's not going to be that many tourists. So, it might just work.'

Lucian's thoughts swung back to the blue Dacia. It was too sinister for words. Two completely separate locations in the same afternoon. A definite concern.

'I'm tired, Lucian... Love you.'

Lucian kissed her brow again and then her lips while drawing the sheet protectively around them both. 'I know I keep saying it,' he whispered, 'but I'm just so lucky. I can't wait to take them down to the coast to play on the sand.'

'The little boy in you again,' teased Zinsa.

'I know... Love you, too.'

Bloody Mario! Lucian rolled onto his back. He should *definitely* never have trusted him!

CHAPTER 5

The irony was that he was taking a gun and several bullets into a bank: Banca Comercială Bănățeana, to be exact, on Strada Teiului. Lucian didn't see it as an act of folly, despite the bank being a stone's throw from a police station. The gun wasn't primed and, from films he'd seen, no one needed to be given a description of the items one intended to place inside the safe deposit box. If that wasn't the case, then he'd withhold the Beretta and bury it. Or perhaps chuck it in the river. To hell with bothering to give it back to Mario.

Lucian walked up to the front desk and realised that the bank had been partially refurbished since his last visit, the desk itself rather stylish – a sweeping curve of polished maple. The 'natural effect' was the new look, although trying to explain that to Crăciun & Fieraru, the staid architectural outfit he seemed stuck with, was nigh on impossible.

The attentive girl at the desk wore a jersey blazer with a pink badge on the breast pocket sporting her name, Silvia. Lucian kept a firm grip on the carrier bag, his mood starting to change about the gun he was carrying – so much so that he felt he was on the verge of perspiring.

'I'm looking for Elena,' he said. 'Wondered if she had a minute to spare.'

'Elena?' queried the girl, looking up at him as she tucked a wisp of flaxen hair behind her ear. 'We have three Elena's. Which one did you want to speak to?'

Lucian thought back to the school register and ended up with two choices. He should have asked Zinsa before he left home. 'I think her surname's Văduva – or possibly Șerban.'

'We have an Elena Văduva.' Silvia picked up the phone beside her. 'She should be in by now. What name shall I give?'

'Lucian Bălcescu. She knows my wife better – Zinsa.' While Silvia made the call, Lucian looked around. The bank was filling up, queues forming at three of the four cash desks. What would it take, he considered idly, to pull the gun from the carrier bag and demand millions of lei? Chronic psychosis, or desperation, he supposed. The bespoke clock above the cash desks, sporting the bank's motif of a silver bird against a turquoise skyline, showed the time to be 9:20. He would be late for Crăciun & Fieraru – again. He really needed to find some excuse other than the traffic. Although the delay on this occasion had been caused by a visit to the bank, and the switching of trams three times as a precaution against anyone following him.

Silvia put down the phone. 'She's on her way.'

'Thanks for your help.' Lucian stepped aside, allowing the customer behind him to approach the desk. A mere blink of an eye later, Elena Văduva appeared, dressed formally in a black knee-length skirt and white blouse, garnished with a blue and green neckerchief. Her cleavage, so universally admired by his classmates at school, now seemed even more profound.

'Lucian.' Elena extended a manicured hand.

'Elena.' Lucian took her hand, undecided about whether he liked her perfume. Harsh, rather than mellow. Still, it seemed to complement her cleavage in terms of subtlety. 'Thanks for your time.'

'How's Zinsa?'

'The due date's in three weeks. But as we're having twins, we've been told it could be sooner.'

'Excited?' Elena smiled pleasantly.

'Nervous – or at least getting that way.'

'It'll be fine. You're still working as a draughtsman?'

'Yes, although the company I'm with feels like it's on its last legs, so I'm looking around.'

'How can I help you?'

Lucian drew Elena's attention to the carrier bag. 'I've a couple of items I need to put in a safe deposit box...' He felt her pale blue eyes all but pierce him. Was his request odd in some way? Or was he being overly sensitive? And now a hesitation – on her part. 'The bank does have deposit boxes?'

'Oh, indeed. But they are rather expensive, Lucian. You feel these items wouldn't be safe enough at home?'

'Not really.' *Dear God*, thought Lucian, *I haven't come here to be given the third degree!* 'Zinsa and I are moving shortly, and until that happens we just want to keep these family heirlooms we treasure perfectly safe.'

'Well, come to my office and I'll give you the prices,' said Elena. 'We have three sizes. By the looks of things, you're going to need the largest.'

'You've done well for yourself, Elena,' commented Lucian for something to say while following her down a glacier-white corridor.

'I've really found my niche, Lucian. Some people that grew up with us haven't been so lucky. Do you still see anything of Serghei?'

'Only yesterday evening, actually.' They ended up in a square white box, with no pictures on the walls – completely sterile. *Eight hours in this space and I'd be screaming my bloody head off,* decided Lucian.

Elena closed the door. 'How true it is, I don't know…but someone told me he was taking drugs.'

'I think he's over that now,' said Lucian, annoyed with Serghei for making him lie. 'Fortunately.'

'Good.' Elena opened a drawer under her desk and took out a folder. 'So,' she murmured, turning the pages, 'thirty-five centimetres by twenty-five with a depth of ten centimetres. That comes to…' She looked across her desk. 'Lucian, we're looking at thousands upon thousands of lei per annum.'

'Really?'

'The board is obviously having to consider current inflation issues. It's literally rocketing. Two-hundred and fifty percent.'

Lucian stared in amazement. 'I thought it was around a hundred and fifty. I'm sure it was that in September.'

'Two hundred and fifty-six point one percent, to be precise. I've heard there's going to be a massive demonstration on Thursday, starting at the University. They're going to march over the river, towards the Cathedral, and from there to the Opera House. It'll feel like '89 all over again. I'm quite nervous... Lucian, do you have your bank book with you?'

'Yes.'

'Do you mind if I take a look at it?'

Lucian handed it over, hoping for a ray of hope – but Elena's face twisted abruptly into disappointment.

'You haven't enough in your account for a reduction.'

There and then, Lucian gave up on the idea. He should be putting all his wages towards their new home – wherever that was going to be. That aside, the twins were going to be a costly business, too. Betting on the encrypted material inside the folder being worth anything was too much of a gamble.

'There is another way,' Elena said. 'I could be your agent, or so called "joint renter". I'm allowed two guests who don't have to pay anything to the bank. A perk of the job, you might say.'

Lucian straightened himself in the chair. This was more like it. 'And you're prepared to give a deposit box to me – and Zinsa?'

'I don't see why not. But it will mean that I will hold the spare key.'

Lucian hurriedly debated whether he should conceal the gun in the garden shed, the only issue with doing so being Rodica ferreting around inside for something. He'd never hear the end of it. Throw the Beretta away, or sell it? The latter had more risks than putting it in a safe deposit box. He was reluctant to throw it away, because of the blue Dacia and the man with a limp…

He became conscious that Elena was waiting for a response from him.

'Of course, I've no interest in opening it,' she said. 'Your heirlooms will be kept completely private. That I can assure you.'

'I have no doubt about that, Elena,' said Lucian, before making an excuse for the hesitation. 'I was just contemplating whether they would be safe at home. I really don't want to put you to any trouble. It's just that there's been a spate of robberies in our neighbourhood—'

'Same with us,' interjected Elena, closing the folder. 'It's perfectly dreadful. I thought things were going to get much better after Ceauşescu. A cousin of mine went to England and apparently they have these neighbourhood-watch schemes. We're thinking of starting one…'

If he buried the Beretta, would the damp affect it? And what if an animal dug it up? And where would he bury it, anyway? In the local park? Or the garden itself?

'…a sort of trial run. We're going to get stickers made up. The idea is that you stick them on a window in full view of the front door to warn—'

'Elena,' interrupted Lucian without realising, 'I would like to take you up on your kind offer.'

* * *

The paperwork seemed to take an age, and it was now past ten o'clock. He was going to have to bring Zinsa into play, use her as an excuse for arriving late at Crăciun & Fieraru, something he had managed so far to avoid doing. Elena then showed him to a cubicle with a privacy curtain. He put the black deposit box on the shelf in front of him. *Just like in the movies*, he thought. After placing the Beretta and the bullets – a total of eight – into the box, he started to remove the folder from the carrier bag. As he did so, his index finger detected a very slight swelling, ten or so centimetres square, under the cloth material bonded to the board on the back of the folder. Straightaway he assumed it to be a flaw in the manufacturing process and, aware Elena was just a couple of feet away waiting for him, he hurriedly slid the box back into its outer sleeve. The identity of the box on the end-plate corresponded with the paperwork: BCB1634. He made a note of it on the brown A4-sized envelope that Elena had given him along with photocopies of the transaction.

Sweeping aside the curtain: 'I'm so grateful, Elena,' he said, and meant it. 'Thank you.'

'Happy it's worked out for you. Do give my love to Zinsa, won't you?'

'Of course. When we're more settled,' said Lucian, 'we'll bring the twins in to show you. I know Zinsa wants to keep in touch.'

Outside the bank, under an iron-grey sky, Lucian felt as if a weight had lifted from his shoulders. The right decision had been made. If Elena did open the box, then he would simply have to invent an excuse about why the Beretta was inside it. While waiting for the bus, he thought it might be quite a good line in a novel or a film, that the robber would plant a gun inside the bank a couple of months beforehand. On collection, he would hold Elena's equivalent at gunpoint, gag and tie him or her up and then proceed to drill out the locks on the deposit boxes.

Lucian caught the bus and took a seat at the back. Now to deal with Crăciun & Fieraru and the two-hour absence from his desk.

As the bus waited at the first of a string of lights and inevitable roadworks, he realised safe-cracking via such a strategy probably wouldn't make for a plausible storyline. There were bound to be security cameras all over the place, a couple of which would undoubtedly be directed at the wall of safe deposit boxes.

In fact, a totally crap idea, he told himself.

CHAPTER 6

It happened three days after he had visited the bank. Lucian arrived at the offices of Crăciun & Fieraru after measuring up a possible extension for a former client to find Miss Dobre, company secretary and elder cousin of Mr Fieraru, in a state of high excitement.

'Lucian, thank goodness! Have you enough money for a taxi?'

Oh, brilliant! thought Lucian. 'Another job?' he asked. Had to be important. Usually he was told to take the bus.

'No, no, no!' Miss Dobre came around her desk towards him, tweed skirt swirling. 'It's Zinsa. She's called. Her waters have broken—'

'Broken?... *Broken?*' Lucian's pulse soared. 'Are you sure?... I mean—'

'Zinsa's been on the phone. She wants you to call her.'

Without asking, Lucian seized the phone on her desk. It seemed to take an age for it to be answered. 'Zinsa, where's Rodica? Andrei?'

'They're having coffee with Mrs Bālan. She doesn't have a phone… Lucian, it's happening! I've tried to get an ambulance. The service seems permanently engaged.'

'Zinsa, I'm getting a taxi. Ten, fifteen minutes. Did they take the car?'

'No. Hurry, Lucian… I think there's a contraction coming.'

'I'm on my way.' Lucian threw down the handset.

'Lucian, do you need money—?'

'No. I've enough. I'm okay.' Lucian bolted down the stairs rather than opt for the antiquated gated lift. He was in luck. Out on the street a cab caught in traffic, the lights changing up ahead. He dived into the front passenger seat.

'My wife,' he panted to the bemused driver. 'She's in labour. Hurry. I'm telling you, just *hurry*.'

* * *

The driver recognised the urgency, frequently blasting his horn while slicing through the traffic. At journey's end – a mere seven but tortuous minutes –

the driver was presented with a fistful of notes in his lap.

'Whatever's there, take it,' said Lucian, leaping from the car.

Zinsa was in the kitchen, propping herself up on the worktop.

'Thank God, Lucian. I can't get in a comfortable position...don't slip on the floor! It just happened.'

'Straight to the hospital. Now.'

'My overnight case...it's still upstairs.'

'I'll bring it later. I just want you in that hospital.' Lucian snatched a set of car keys from the ornamental bowl in the hallway and guided Zinsa out onto the driveway.

'I'll sit in the front,' said Zinsa before they'd reached the Volkswagen. 'Get me the cushion from the back seat.'

Lucian did so, fumbling with the keys. He set the front passenger seat to its farthest position, then helped Zinsa into the car. 'I can't believe it, Zinsa!' He stuffed the cushion into the small of her back. 'It's actually happening! Comfortable?'

'As I'll ever be. Let's get going.'

Lucian sat in the driver's seat.

'They told us the contractions would start before my waters broke. I've only had a couple of small contractions since. I'm worried about infection, Lucian.'

Lucian rammed the key into the ignition. 'They also said things might happen differently with twins. They're two weeks early as it is.'

'They can't wait to see the world.'

Lucian reversed out of the drive.

Zinsa puffed out her cheeks. 'I'm perspiring like crazy – on a day like this, middle of November.'

'Blood pressure, probably,' said Lucian, turning left at the lights at the end of the street. 'Must be rocketing. Mine is, for sure.'

'Hope everything's okay.'

''Course it is. We'll be at the hospital in a matter of minutes.'

Two police cars shot past them, sirens blaring.

'They're in a hurry,' said Zinsa.

'Won't sell ice cream at that speed.'

Zinsa giggled, but then winced. 'Ooooh, I think there's a contraction on the way. Don't make me laugh.'

'Keep your legs— Christ! What's going on ahead?' Lucian noticed two columns of smoke rising rapidly in the distance. Or was it three? He couldn't quite tell in the grey sky. Another police car loomed in the rear-view mirror, siren blaring as it shot past, followed by a police van. 'Something big's going down,' he said. Just at that moment, he recalled Elena mentioning a demonstration at the polytechnic on Thursday. 'Zinsa, what's today?' he asked.

'Lucian, just get me to the hospital!'

'Thursday. Elena said there was going to be a demonstration.' Lucian turned left at the Metropolitan Cathedral to cross the Beja River, only to find the road choked-up with demonstrators. To reverse would add possibly twenty minutes to the journey because, judging by the size of the crowd, it was likely that the police had sealed off nearby streets. He glanced at his wife, and noticed her wince. 'Another contraction?'

'Yes, I think so. Oh, God…'

Lucian kept his hand on the horn, forcing the Volkswagen through the crowd, the car rocking as people were pushed up against it – the scene, if anything, tribal. 'This is insane.'

'Lucian, I'm frightened!'

'We're making progress. We're over the river. Once we're through this then just a couple of minutes to the hospital.' Between the mob's frenetic faces, anti-government placards and a sea of red, yellow and blue flags, Lucian saw more plumes of smoke and realised the protestors were setting fire to cars in the side streets. 'Hell, this is a bad one…' Something hit the back of the Volkswagen, a stone or similar projectile, but suddenly Lucian could see an end to it. 'Look, Zinsa, a barricade. I'll get them to move it—'

'I'm going to give birth to them in the car! They'll come to harm, Lucian. We'll lose them!' Zinsa clamped her eyes shut. 'God, God, oh God – help me. Please *help me*!'

Lucian forced the door open against the crowd and fought his way the few yards to the barricade. 'Make way for me!' he screamed at the cordon of police, their faces masked by riot gear and shields. 'My wife's giving birth!'

An officer started to move along the line towards him. While he was doing so, a glass bottle ricocheted off his helmet, causing him to stagger briefly. Lucian wondered if he was in overall charge. 'My wife!' he yelled. 'You have to let me through. She's giving birth to twins!'

The officer shook his head and started to speak when Lucian leant over the steel barrier and grabbed his shield so he could eyeball him. 'You let us through, you idiot!'

'We'll get an ambulance for you—'

'I'm coming through – now!' Lucian turned on his heel, pushed a demonstrator out of his way, and got back in the car.

'Are they letting us through?' demanded Zinsa. 'For God's sake, *are* they?'

'I'm driving through.'

'I can't hold on much longer.'

'I know that.' Lucian looked across at her. Pain, perspiration, tears. 'Sweetheart, I'll get you to the hospital—' A stone shattered the rear window. 'That does it!'

Above the barricade a paper bag suddenly swirled high in the air. Amid the panic fuelled by outrage churning up his presence of mind, Lucian had a disturbing sense of déjà vu. A collection of images collided with the barricade, the most prominent being the blue Dacia and the man with the limp. Because Lucian remembered now. The man actually gave a lecture at their school on how to be responsible citizens. He was with the police. And not only that… He couldn't believe it. They must have been in it *together*!

A protestor became entangled with the offside wing-mirror, tearing it from its mounting. Lucian revved the engine and inched up to the metal barrier. A policeman unexpectedly raised a semi-automatic rifle. Zinsa screamed. The Volkswagen touched steel, pushing the barrier. The policeman took aim. He wouldn't dare, it would be insane, thought Lucian, and took his foot off the brake pedal.

CHAPTER 7

'Don't you think she's lost weight?' said Andrei to his wife as they walked back down the street.

'I'm worried it could be cancer,' said Rodica, adjusting her scarf against the icy breeze. 'Remember, she had that scare a couple of years ago.'

'We really missed her,' recalled Andrei. Until last autumn, Mrs Bãlan had been their home help for seventeen years, often extending her domestic duties to caring for Lucian and Zinsa when they were children whenever academia took him, and on occasion Rodica, to Bucharest, or further afield. 'But she's eighty-two now, so I suppose we must expect…' Andrei tailed off, seeing a figure leaving the driveway of their house and head in the opposite direction. 'Isn't that Serghei?'

'I think it is.'

'Serghei!' called Andrei. The figure spun around, and started trotting towards them. 'It is him. What's he doing here?'

'Nightmare…' spluttered Serghei, closing down the gap. 'I've heard something dreadful has happened, Mr Bălcescu.'

Andrei noted his breathlessness and anaemic complexion. He knew, or at least suspected, that Serghei took drugs whenever he could get his hands on them. At times, he disliked Lucian's friendship with him, although by the same token he admired his son's loyalty to stand by his friend. 'What's up with you?' he asked.

'It's not good.'

'What's not good?'

'The rumours.'

'Rumours?' interrupted Rodica. 'What rumours?'

'Zinsa…it's awful.'

'For God's sake, man!' shouted Andrei. 'What's happened?'

'Shot. Police have shot her—'

'*What…?*' Andrei could barely control himself. 'What have you been injecting this time?'

'Nothing. I swear, Mr Bălcescu. I'm clean. There's a demonstration going on by the University. A big one—'

'I've heard about that,' said Andrei. 'But what's this about Zinsa? What do you mean she's been shot by the police?'

'A green car. A black woman, pregnant. It *has* to be Zinsa. And a man shot, too. That has to be Lucian.'

The car was missing from the drive. Andrei started running towards the house. Then he had the front door open. In the hall he grabbed the phone's receiver, vaguely aware that Rodica and Serghei had caught up with him. He dialled the number for Crăciun & Fieraru. The call was answered by Miss Dobre, her voice familiar to him since they occasionally crossed paths at the local greengrocer's store.

'Miss Dobre, I take it Lucian isn't with you?'

'Oh, Mr Bălcescu, isn't it wonderful news. He left about an hour ago. Zinsa called, you see, because her waters had broken—'

Andrei cut the call. 'We need a taxi.' He started dialling.

'What did the office say?' pleaded Rodica.

'That Lucian left there an hour ago. Zinsa called, saying her waters had broken.'

'You need a police car,' suggested Serghei. 'The demonstration's still going on, blocking the route to the hospital. I've heard there are barricades around that part of the city.'

'You're right,' said Andrei, mildly surprised by Serghei's presence of mind.

'Shot...' Rodica sat on the wicker chair they kept beside the phone. 'What could have happened? And the twins...'

Andrei made the connection with the local police station. 'Who am I speaking to?'

'Sub-inspector Cazacu. And who am *I* speaking to?'

'Bălcescu. Andrei Bălcescu. Listen, Sub-inspector, I understand my son and daughter have been caught up in a demonstration. My son was trying to get his wife to the hospital, driving a green Volkswagen.' There was a pause and, amidst the panic steadily demolishing his composure, Andrei wondered if the call had caused confusion. 'I should add that we adopted—'

'Their names?'

'Lucian and Zinsa Bălcescu.'

Another pause.

'Sub-inspector—'

'I suggest, Mr Bălcescu, you drive over to the County Hospital. I believe you will find them there.'

'That's all very well, but we do not have a car,' argued Andrei. 'Secondly, I've reason to believe the demonstration is still in progress, therefore a taxi will be of little use to us – the streets apparently barricaded.'

'If you would just hold the line, Mr Bălcescu.'

Andrei turned to his wife. 'I've got to hold the bloody line.'

'Shot, Andrei!' exclaimed Rodica. 'Serghei says Zinsa has been shot.'

'We don't know for sure.' Andrei turned to Serghei. 'Do we?'

'It's a rumour…' Serghei wrung his hands. 'It can't be true, can it, Mr Bălcescu?'

'Your address?' cut in the Sub-inspector. 'We're going to get a car over to you.'

Andrei gave the address. 'They're at the main hospital, then? It's definite?'

'Apparently. Because of the demonstration, I wouldn't take anything literally at the moment.'

'Fine. Thank you, Sub-inspector.' Andrei cradled the receiver and turned to Rodica and Serghei. 'They're sending a car.'

'What should I do, Mr Bălcescu?' asked Serghei. 'Should I come with you?'

'I think this is likely to be a very private matter, Serghei. What, with the twins, you understand.'

'Of course.' Serghei edged towards the open door. 'I'll be on my way, then.'

'We'll get news to you somehow, as soon as we hear anything.' Andrei closed the door.

'We need to call the hospital!' Rodica stood up from the chair.

Andrei found the number in the address book. 'My head's spinning,' he said. Rewarded with an engaged tone, he cradled the receiver.

'Is that a car I can hear coming up the drive?' said Rodica.

Andrei stepped out into the porch to find a blue Dacia on the driveway. Turning his head back to Rodica: 'That was quick, if it is a police car. Doesn't appear to have any markings.'

A besuited man climbed out: no uniform or badge to say he was a policeman. 'Mr Bălcescu?'

'Indeed.' The man took a couple of steps towards them. Andrei absently noticed that his right leg hardly bent at the knee, giving him a distinct limp.

'I'll be the one taking you to the hospital—'

'But we need a siren,' objected Andrei, 'to get us through the demonstrators. Has that car got one?'

'No need. I'm in radio contact with my colleagues. We'll detour the main arteries to the hospital. Rest assured, any barricades we happen to come across I'll be allowed through without a moment's delay.'

* * *

They came to two barricades with just a smattering of protestors at each. True to his word, the driver was let through the moment he flashed a card.

Andrei considered what his position might be in the force, before leaning forward from the back seat. 'Can you try again and get some information on Lucian and Zinsa?'

'We're nearly there, Mr Bălcescu,' said the driver, who had yet to volunteer his name. 'My colleagues are overwhelmed with this demonstration.'

'Might I ask your position in the force?'

'I'm a detective, Detective Breban. I was nearby when your call came through. My job description doesn't usually involve ferrying people from A to B.'

'Well, we're grateful,' said Andrei as the hospital's enormous green façade came into view, a cluster of sirens now distinctly audible. 'Drop us both at the entrance and we'll take it from there.'

'It has to be a mistake,' said Rodica. 'They don't use real bullets at demonstrations these days, do they?' She leaned forward, her face taut with dread. 'I mean, that sort of thing went out when we got rid of Ceauşescu, didn't it?' She turned to her husband when there was no response from Detective Breban. 'A mistake, that's all it can be. Serghei was given the wrong information, wasn't he?'

Andrei squeezed her hand. 'Best not to speculate, darling,' he said, trying to keep himself, let alone his wife, in check. 'Hopefully we'll find them in the maternity unit and all is well with the both of them.'

'And the babies.'

'Of course.'

Detective Breban could only drop them off in the street; the entrance to the hospital choked up with ambulances, while sirens blared from those departing to ferry more of the injured.

'This is outrageous,' muttered Andrei.

'I'd better leave you here,' said Detective Breban. 'I might be needed.'

'Yes, yes, fine.' Andrei leapt from the car, took Rodica's hand and pulled her towards the entrance, passing a sign in red lettering:

SPITALUL CLINIC JUDETEAN DE URGENTA

'What state are we going to find them in, Andrei?' said a tearful Rodica.

'God only knows.' They climbed a row of steps, bloodied faces and crooked limbs on stretchers passing them by. 'An absolute outrage,' persisted Andrei. 'I really thought such a scene would never be repeated after the Revolution!'

The entrance's main set of glazed doors had been locked open. Once inside the reception area, they were confronted by chaos: people crying, in search of loved ones, while somewhere in the throng a women's ululating shrieks suggested full-blown hysteria.

'Perhaps we should head for the maternity ward,' said Rodica. 'Zinsa's in labour. Miss Dobre said so.'

'Yes, you're right,' agreed Andrei. 'Where the hell is it? This building, or some other building?'

'This building, I'm sure. But I don't know which floor.'

'Rodica, keep hold of my hand.' Andrei shouldered his way through the distraught crowd, aiming for an exit that he hoped would emerge into something with a map, or signage of some description. When they reached it, he looked anxiously around. No clues as to where the corridor might take them. 'We'll just carry on,' he said. 'We're sure to bump into a nurse, or someone who can help us.'

The chaotic din at reception began to fade as the corridor widened into what Andrei determined was an arterial route through the hospital. They passed a cross-section of staff, many of them hurrying to and fro, dismissing their questions as if they didn't exist, such was their resolve to deal with the catastrophe.

In desperation, Andrei buttonholed a middle-aged woman carrying a mop and bucket.

'Look, we need help,' he said. 'Can you tell us where we might find the maternity ward. Is it in this building?'

The woman nodded in the direction of the corridor. 'Down to the theatres and get the lift.'

'Thank you.' Andrei turned to Rodica. 'Now we're getting somewhere.'

A couple of nurses from the opposite direction wheeled a stretcher past them; the figure on it looked to be unconscious, its bandaged head masking its gender.

'Poor soul,' said Rodica. 'Just out of the theatre, by the looks of it.'

'The police have a lot to answer for.' Andrei pointed suddenly. 'I can see the lift.'

As they approached it, a member of staff wearing a blue cow gown emerged from a corridor on their right.

'Excuse me!' called Andrei.

The man hesitated. 'Yes, can I help you? I'm in such a hurry.'

'I understand that,' pacified Andrei. As he drew closer, he could read the name embroidered on the gown: RADU. 'Radu, we're looking for two people. We're desperate to find them. We've heard they've been shot, but we don't know if it's true – and if it is, then obviously we have no idea how badly injured they are.'

'Two people?' clarified Radu.

'Indeed. Lucian and Zinsa Bălcescu are their names.'

Radu's jaw dropped.

'Have you come across them?'

'W-what relation…?'

'Yes?' prompted Andrei, then took a guess at the question being asked. 'I'm their father, and Rodica here is their mother.'

The blank expression on Radu's face deepened.

'We adopted them when they were very small. Zinsa is black, born in West Africa. I repeat, have you come across them?'

Radu stood stock still, staring blankly at Andrei.

'Can you help us?' demanded Rodica. 'Please. We need to find them.'

'The lift,' said Radu. 'I'll take you.'

'To the maternity ward?' asked Andrei.

Radu didn't reply, and simply waited for them to enter the lift. Seven floors later, he ushered them into a carpeted corridor with numerous doors on both sides. It didn't make sense to Andrei; it looked as if the floor was for administrative purposes only. Seconds later they stopped at a door bearing the name: *Di Panait*.

'Please wait,' said Radu. He knocked on the door, and a man mumbled 'Enter'. Radu entered.

Andrei turned to Rodica. 'For heaven's sake, what's going on?'

'Something's not right, Andrei,' Rodica said. 'That man who brought us here…he knows what's happened to them. Why isn't he telling—'

Radu came back out of the room. 'Please, Mr Panait is asking to see you.' With that, Radu scurried away from them, down the corridor towards the lift.

A tall, good-looking man in his mid-forties greeted them without a smile of any kind. Just a handshake each. Andrei couldn't help but notice that the man's eyes looked red and tearful. He also appeared half-dressed: no tie, and a pink shirt loosely tucked into his trousers.

'I'm Darius Panait. Please, call me Darius.'

'Andrei Bălcescu, and this is my wife, Rodica.'

'Yes... Let me find another chair.'

Andrei halted the half-dressed man. 'My wife can take the chair. I will stand – while you explain to us both precisely what has happened to Zinsa and Lucian.'

Panait seemed to shrink into himself as he sat down behind the desk, on which sat a revolving chrome calendar, a couple of sheets of paper and a white telephone. 'I'm presuming you adopted Zinsa?'

'Indeed.' Andrei steered Rodica towards the vacant chair. 'Lucian, too. Due to a condition I have, we were unable to have children.'

Panait leaned forward and put his face in his hands.

'For God's sake, man, what's happened to—'

'I have awful news for you.' Slowly, Panait lifted his head, his eyes even redder than before. 'Lucian died at the scene. I believe a police officer panicked—'

'Died?' Rodica left the chair and came to the desk. 'What are you saying?'

'And Zinsa?' asked Andrei with surprising calm, as if what he had intuitively feared had now become fact. 'What of Zinsa?'

'I finished operating on her half an hour ago. Of the three of them, only the baby girl has survived—'

'"Survived"?' shrieked Rodica. 'Only the baby girl has *survived*?' She thumped the desk with her fist. 'You're lying. I know you are! Why are you lying? Who has told you to do this?' Rodica spun on her heel to Andrei. 'Ask him why he is lying to us. Ask him!'

Andrei tried to take her in his arms. 'He's not going to lie—'

'Why are you lying?' shouted Rodica at the surgeon. 'Has the government told you to do this?' She started hitting the desk again. 'Tell me. Tell me. *Tell me...*' Her fist started to slide away from the desk.

Andrei managed to reach her, softening her fall.

Panait snatched the receiver on the telephone, dialled a number, demanded a stretcher and replaced the receiver. 'Someone will be here shortly,' he said, before swiftly checking Rodica's pulse at her neck. 'I believe she's fainted, nothing more. Better to leave her as she is, rather than put her in the chair – unless she becomes fully conscious. Just loosen her clothing.'

Numbly, Andrei did as he was told, before turning her head to one side to assist her breathing.

'Mr Bălcescu?'

Andrei looked up. 'Yes?'

'I can't continue with the facts as I know them to be with your wife present. Do you understand?'

'Yes.'

'Does your wife have any medical issues that you are aware of?'

'No.'

A knock on the door. Two nurses entered with a stretcher. Panait turned to Andrei. 'They will take her to a side room on a ward to recover. If necessary, Mr Bălcescu, do we have your permission to administer a mild sedative?'

'Whatever you suggest,' said Andrei.

The nurses lifted Rodica onto the stretcher. Without opening her eyes, she gave a muted moan.

'I can't think clearly myself,' Andrei said. He turned to the nurses. 'Please, take good care of her. I'll be along to sit with her shortly.'

As the nurses were leaving, Panait said, 'Monitor her blood pressure, and be sure someone stays with her until Mr Bălcescu arrives.' The surgeon re-seated himself. 'I will be brief. You need to be with your wife, Mr Bălcescu.'

Andrei sat in the chair and faced Panait. 'Then be brief.' Half of him expected to wake up at any moment. How he wished it could be like that!

Panait returned to his chair and leaned forward. 'I mentioned that Lucian died at the scene. This is a fact. What is conjecture is that a policeman panicked as Lucian tried to break through the barricade. I can only imagine the policeman was equipped with a semi-automatic. Perhaps he was ordered to give a warning shot but his finger froze on the trigger. Or the gun developed a fault. Whatever the reason, Zinsa received a total of five wounds. All of them, I believe, to have been ricochets.'

'God Almighty…' Andrei lowered his head, feeling queasy. He snatched a couple of deep breaths and told himself he had to keep going for Rodica's sake, if not his own. He couldn't permit Rodica to receive the details in such a forthright manner as this. In fact, there and then he decided she would receive a substantially edited version, delivered by himself once they'd got out of the place and back home. 'And the babies? You said only the girl—'

'It's my belief one of the ricochets killed the boy outright.'

'And the baby girl? She's not in danger?'

Panait interlocked his fingers and rubbed his palms together, keeping his hands close to his chest. 'There's…there's an issue with her left foot.'

'Why? What's wrong with it?'

'I can't tell if it was damaged by the ricochet that killed her brother, or if the damage was done by a fragment of bone from Zinsa. But the damage is extensive, so much so that I have asked a colleague to operate. A highly respected paediatrician. As we speak, he should be on a flight from Bucharest.'

'And worst-case scenario?' asked Andrei. 'I mean, you're saying there's a risk the foot will have to be amputated?'

'Yes. I'm sorry. Because the trauma appears to be so extensive, involving what I suspect to be severe nerve damage, any attempt to repair the appendage will leave her in a position of discomfort and hindrance, whereas a prosthesis would enhance her life considerably.' Panait parted his hands. 'But I could, of course, be wide of the mark.'

'Is Shani nearby?'

'Shani, the—?'

'It's what they were going to call her.'

Panait reached for the telephone. 'Let me just find out where your wife is.'

While the surgeon made the call, Andrei lowered his head again and clasped his hands together between his knees. Someone was to blame for this, but already he could see an issue that might prevent him from taking it to court: Zinsa's background in Séroulé, and all that had occurred before he'd taken her out of the country and into safety – *supposed* safety.

Panait lowered the handset. 'Your wife is on Level Three, your granddaughter on Level Five, two below us.'

Andrei rose. 'Then can we see Shani on the way down.'

* * *

The baby girl appeared remarkably peaceful inside the incubator, considering the trauma she had endured inside her mother's womb. A loom of wires spread around her like a web, her left foot heavily bandaged. Shani had her eyes closed, head to one side. So angelic, and so very precious. Sacred. A wisp of black hair curled onto her brow. Andrei thought he could detect Zinsa's high cheekbones.

But how could this be? Already the child was parentless. Another orphan, for God's sake, to add to the country's appalling statistics! Andrei felt close to breaking as tears started to well up in his eyes.

Then, conscious of Panait standing alongside, Andrei turned to him. 'This morning…this morning we woke up and had breakfast as a family. Lucian was typically late for work, so bolted his cereals and toast. Zinsa had her hand on her stomach, saying they'd kept her awake until the early hours. I glanced through the paper. A strike at some industrial plant on the outskirts of Bucharest, I seem to recall. Rodica pouring freshly ground coffee for everyone. And now…*this*.' Andrei wiped his eyes with a handkerchief. 'I just don't understand,' he said, turning back to the baby girl. 'When can we see her mother and father – and baby brother?'

Panait took the chair next to Andrei. 'If you can hold off until tomorrow. Your wife is not in a stable enough condition to see them. Besides, we need to… Perhaps you could bring fresh clothes for them.'

Andrei nodded. 'Yes, of course.' He shook his head, but this did nothing to quell his bewilderment. 'Questions need to be asked,' he muttered, knowing perfectly well he could not ask them himself. Any media coverage could prove fatal to Shani; General Odion Kuetey would have little trouble locating the new-born infant, who was now the sole survivor of the Dangbo dynasty. He wiped his eyes again.

In fact, there was no alternative. No other option whatsoever left open to them. He and Rodica – and this divine miracle before him – were going to have to leave Romania. Never to return.

PART 2
DOUBLE-EDGED FOE

Oxford

...Present day...

CHAPTER 8

It was her first Stated General Meeting at St Thomas Aquinas College, and so far it had done little to enthral her. She looked down the table in the Grand Hall, past scores of Fellows and an avenue of portraits of various notables spanning six hundred years, and on towards the President, seated at the far end. Bearded and serene-looking, he waited for the latest round of voting slips to be gathered by a youthful male Fellow who was almost as junior as herself. No one could be morejunior, since no one had been elected since February, three months ago – the craziest months of her life. And none of them spent at St Aquinas, apart from a brief visit before the onset of a horrendous nightmare.

The junior Fellow had reached her, and she put her voting slip into the silver bowl. She had ticked *YES*: that a Risk Register should indeed be implemented for both staff and Fellows.

The nightmare. Now that it was over, that's where she wanted to be, in Séroulé with Nicolas. An unforeseen and radical shift had occurred in her disposition. Three months ago, she might well have found a Stated General Meeting such as this absorbing, part and parcel of academia and college life. Since then, her boredom threshold had eroded dramatically and she wasn't looking forward to revealing her 'deviation' with her supervisor. She could see him way down the table, a couple of chairs away from the President. He was fiddling with a piece of paper, possibly a redundant voting slip. Harry Rothwell had become an unexpected father figure to her.

The President stood abruptly and the murmurs in the Hall gave way to silence.

'We welcome three newly elected Fellows...'

God, no! She stiffened by reflex. This was the moment. If only she could crawl under the damn table!

'Two Senior Research Fellows: Professor Julien Berger, European Medieval History, and Professor Joanna Cartwright, International Relations. This year, we elected just the one Junior Research Graduate, Shani Bălcescu, formerly at Corpus Christi – continuing with her subject, History of Economics.'

The President sat down, and immediately smacked the table with his right hand. The Fellows duly followed. The applause – smacking the table – continued for what seemed a stomach-churning thirty or more seconds. So, some of her old traits remained. Anxiety. Hating to be noticed. Call it whatever. Basis for depression, really – although the fundamental issue from where it had all originated had now, she was convinced, been dealt with. Just its ghost remained, nothing more.

Everyone stood up. Harry came over to her. The epitome of the eccentric professor, with his wiry physique and tousled mop of perfectly white hair.

'Well done for making it.'

'I had a choice, Harry?'

'Rumour has it that a Fellow actually turned up at an SGM with a drip on a stand and a nurse in tow, who obviously had to wait outside while the vote over whatever took place.'

'Can we talk?'

Harry glanced at his watch. 'I'm meeting Sabine at two at a gallery that's just opened in Jericho.' He slipped off his gown. 'So, yes, we have an hour.'

'I'm going to dump mine in my study.' Shani roughly folded her gown as they wandered through a Tudor archway to the West Quadrangle. 'I'll be over in a couple of minutes. Need to check my phone. I left it on my desk.'

She entered her staircase and climbed the column of quarried-stone steps that led to her rooms. There was a wave of mixed feelings as she unlocked the door to her study. Of course, she was fortunate – that was an understatement. Four years to complete her thesis, although she was expected to do it in three and make up the rest of the time teaching. Lodgings, food, et cetera, all paid for, with a generous monthly allowance on top. But to continue with academia? That was the question – the headache – that was disrupting her otherwise blissful state of mind.

She hung her gown on the hook on the door and turned to her desk and the four mullioned windows overlooking the Priory Quadrangle. In the distance, beyond the lawn, perfectly striped from the morning's mowing, was the Cecil Brampton Library with its intricate gold and azure sundial. A smile touched her lips as she recalled soulmate Christina's apt description while lending a hand to move her possessions from the house they'd shared in East Oxford. *Can you imagine a clear sky at night, stars twinkling and a crescent moon, little goblins running along the parapet, peeping over the crenulations – or whatever the gaps are called. It would be like something out of a Disney film.*

Shani picked up her mobile phone next to the turquoise mug on her desk, and reread the text that confirmed her flight to Timişoara mid-afternoon the following day. She had the feeling she was going to find out considerably more about her birth parents than she had first time around – which included a visit to the hospital where she'd been born, and where her mother had died. The mention of a twin brother had shocked her to the core. In fact, she still cried at night on occasion for Tuma – the name she'd given him, having discovered that was the name of her murdered grandfather: Tuma Dangbo, President of Séroulé.

* * *

Professor Harry Rothwell's study on Staircase VI was unchanged since her last visit, the day he had welcomed her to St Aquinas after her scholarship bid had unexpectedly proven successful. Stacks of books sought to touch the ceiling and there was still the faint aroma of tobacco – a pipe or cigar, she imagined, although she'd never seen him smoke anything.

'I have to make the point,' said Harry, 'that all that's been going on in your life has made your eyes shine and your skin glow. So, tell me.'

'That I will, Harry,' said Shani. 'But your hand... I've just noticed.'

Harry lifted his right hand: three strips of Elastoplast over three knuckles. 'Magdalen Bridge, this morning. Chain came off the bike. Proceeded to fix it and successfully jammed my fingers in the wretched cogs.'

'Ouch. Painful, clearly.'

'Don't mind telling you, the air turned blue. Came close to chucking the lousy contraption into the Cherwell. Fixed now, Ian the lodge porter did it on my arrival.'

Shani smiled, recalling Harry's attempt at installing a letterbox as described by himself at their first meeting. The attempt had cost him a new front door. Sabine, his wife, apparently now dealt with all household DIY issues.

'A glass?' Harry reached for the bottle of Merlot on his desk.

'Thank you. It's good to see you, Harry.' And she meant it.

Harry unscrewed the cap. 'Given to me by an undergraduate for getting him into the Brampton Library for the next three years. Naturally, we're not supposed to accept gifts…' He poured the wine. 'But hey, what the hell's the point of rules if you can't kick them into touch – annoying the self-righteous in the process.'

'Quite.' Shani reached for her glass and sat back in the uncomfortable armchair with its peculiar arrangement of springs beneath the threadbare fabric. 'Perfectly agree, Harry,' she added. And she did agree, more than Harry perhaps realised. She detested pointless bureaucratic rules that choked up effort, industry and progress.

'Of course, I'm not supposed to be leading you astray, my dear.'

'Naturally. Though I rather like it when you do, Harry.'

Harry chuckled and positioned his chair to face her squarely. 'Where do we start? Nicolas, Romania, or the coup in Séroulé?'

'Actually, Andrei's deathbed, Czech Republic.'

'Ah, yes – Andrei, your adoptive father. Or grandfather, perhaps I should say. His wife died some years ago. Yes?'

'Rodica. A kind and generous woman, that's my lasting memory of her.' Shani sipped some wine: a shade metallic for her liking but it had a kick to it that gave her a measure of courage, which she sensed she was going to need shortly. 'Via Andrei and the safe in his apartment, I discovered that my father wasn't Czech but Romanian, and that my mother came from Séroulé, West Africa, not East Africa.'

'So when the tragedy happened with your birth parents, Andrei upped sticks in Romania to prevent General Kuetey tracking you down, since you were the only living member of the Dangbo dynasty he had tried to wipe out all those years ago. Correct?'

'Absolutely.' Shani put her glass on a side table and crossed her legs. 'And now the situation against the Kuetey regime has been reversed. Of course, despite media reports claiming otherwise, I have no qualifications or ambition to be president. A ridiculous notion, in fact. For now, the leaders of the coup will take charge, with democratic elections to follow in approximately a year's time.'

'Do you trust that the leaders will adhere to that?' asked Harry.

'Actually, I do. I had my doubts at first. I was privileged enough to sit next to Khamadi Soglo when he addressed the nation. Obviously, that by itself isn't proof. It's a combination of conversations I had with them, and of course Nicolas knows his stuff when it comes to Séroulé and the likes of Khamadi.'

'Ah, yes… Nicolas. He's French, is he not? A journalist, I think you mentioned in an email.'

'Yes.' Shani shrugged. 'Sounds dramatic, but he changed my perspective as regards to myself, and my outlook.'

'He's here, in Oxford?'

'Khamadi wanted him to stay on for more reporting.' Shani leaned forward when Harry offered to replenish her glass, her heartbeat stepping up in pace as 'the moment' drew ever closer. 'You've read some of the media reports that have arisen these past few weeks?'

'Specifically, about you?'

'Yes.'

'Of course.'

Shani felt herself blush. Not only did Harry now know her intimate history – but plainly so did all the staff and Fellows.

'Fascinating, shall we say? Don't want to patronise, but respect is due.'

'In particular my prosthesis?'

'I had no idea.'

'The point is, Harry, it caused me to retreat into myself, to bury myself in academia.' Shani sipped wine and leaned back. It had to be said. It was only fair that Harry knew. 'When I met Nicolas, he basically dragged it all out of me, more than any counsellor has managed to do. He unleashed the dam – my insecurity. I've learnt a huge amount about myself these past three months, about my capabilities outside academia. I made mistakes – stupid mistakes. But the point I want to make, Harry, is that another world has opened up for me. A practical world, if you will.'

'I see...'

'Fact is, I know I'm going to find it problematic to sit behind a desk and hammer out a thesis.'

'You're saying academia became a convenient analgesic for your insecurities brought about by your prosthesis?'

'Yes, I believe that to have been the case. And, of course, not knowing my birth parents, Lucian and Zinsa.'

Harry topped up his own glass. 'What's the immediate plan?'

'If possible, I'd like you to extend my leave by another fortnight.'

'We're coming into the summer break, so not an issue. To do what?'

Shani found it difficult to gauge Harry's mood: his lined face was ominously impassive. If anything, the slight crags along his jawline looked craggier. Was he getting pissed off with her? That was her fear above all others when it came to St Aquinas. 'With my identity now known in Romania,' she explained, 'I've received a text, and now a call, from someone called Serghei Sapdaru, who was apparently a close friend of my parents. I want to meet him – talk to him. Learn more about my parents, their personalities. How they were regarded by their peers. Perhaps visit the house where they lived, and the architectural firm where my father worked as a draughtsman. It's important to me, Harry.'

'Of course.' Harry nodded and put down his glass. His expression began to lighten as a cloud coincidentally cleared from the sun to send a shaft of leaded light to the left of his desk. 'Nothing's going to stop you from learning as much detail as possible about your background – certainly not me. Actually, one of the articles stated that you wanted to help the many Séroulèse orphans in some way. Correct?'

'Yes. It's an idea I have. A loose idea.'

'An admirable one, obviously. Has Nicolas commented on it?'

'Not really. There was a lot going on, what with the coup. I think he would like to base himself in Séroulé – or at least West Africa – rather than Paris.'

'May I make a proposal?'

'Absolutely,' said Shani, doubting whether the 'proposal' would sit comfortably with what she had in mind. 'Please do.'

'These winds of change, or *discoveries*, shall we say, have been dramatic to say the least. So, you can't – or shouldn't – make concrete decisions until all has settled, enabling a coherent framework to be formulated. What I propose is that you don't jettison academia out of hand – because that's exactly what your gut is wanting you to do.' Harry's eyes sparkled. 'Isn't it?'

It would be pointless to dress up the decision she had arrived at. He was on to her. She should have expected it! 'Yes, it is, Harry. Academia feels like boredom to me, after Séroulé—'

'An intense adventure, you could say. Laced, I'm sure, with fear on occasion. By one means or another, the adrenaline must have flowed. But that intensity is over now. You can't relive it. The fact is you've already squeezed in a Master's. For the D.Phil, you only have to inflate those twenty-five thousand or whatever words. Then, put academia on the backburner, if you so wish. In ten years' time, you might want to return to it in some form or another.' Harry smiled and cocked his head. 'Not quite the answer you hoped for, is it?'

'It's…practical, Harry.' Shani did some hasty calculations, taking into account the progress she had made on her thesis thus far – which amounted to little more than a few diagrams, and quotes from the likes of E.F. Schumacher. 'If I knuckled down to it, I think I could get it done in two years, Harry.'

'I disagree.'

Shani stared at her supervisor, a sinking feeling in her stomach. 'Three years?'

'No. Eighteen months.'

Her supervisor's estimation jolted Shani. 'You think? Really?'

'Put your mind to it. No problem. Besides, I'll be retiring in a year and a half's time. We need it all wrapped up by then.'

'Eighteen months…' deliberated Shani. 'Wow. I'm going to have to go some. Like high gears, you know.' She noted Harry's flicker of curiosity. 'I'm taking my Kawasaki out later. Misplaced analogy, perhaps, but there'll be some tough terrain to scramble over – thesis-wise. Full range of gears, then.'

'I'd forgotten you were a biker.'

'It's the freedom it offers, Harry. The wind, the speed, the required skill – balance, flow. The sound of the engine. A complete symphony.'

'In my late teens, in Canada, I bought a BSA Gold Star for a song. Aimed to go all the way down to Lima – but the thing seized solid in Panama.' Harry looked at his watch. 'I'd better set off to meet Sabine.'

Shani stood. 'Harry, invaluable. You've brought me down to earth in a good way.'

'Practical way?' smiled Harry.

'Yes.' Shani handed him her glass. 'Definitely. I love that word *practical*. It's so physical. My new buzzword, in fact.'

'Then stick with it, and let's see where it takes us.'

* * *

Shani fixed herself a mug of rooibos tea, sat at her desk and took stock of what Harry had said. He was probably right, but she found she was still fighting it – fighting to find a better answer to prevent herself from sitting at this bloody desk. The irony was that many an academic would give their eyeteeth to be here at St Thomas Aquinas, let alone Oxford. She shook her head, knowing it was hopeless to keep contesting the point. She was simply aching to return to Séroulé, to be with Nicolas and those brave rebels who had so successfully trounced the Kuetey regime. Besides, she'd fallen for the country itself: the occasionally annoying dust; the street vendors and the savoury smells of *chin-chin*, or *akara* served with spicy tomato sauce or the hottest chilli powder imaginable – and, everywhere, the awesome ingenuity borne out of necessity, flip-flops from old tyres, intricate and dazzling jewellery from recycled trash. This was the stuff, the kind of *people*, she wanted to learn about, to immerse herself in, not the history of sodding economics. She just couldn't engage herself in it anymore.

Shani reached for her phone and flicked through the recent texts until arriving at Serghei Sapdaru. *Yes, Shani, I knew parents well. At same school. Good people. We talk. Call when arrive.* She put down the phone and gazed across the manicured lawn at the sundial on the library's vast edifice. Serghei Sapdaru hadn't shown up on any internet searches. She wondered what he did for a living, whether he had a family. She supposed he would be around forty-five years old.

She finished her tea, realising that she had a lot to do if she wanted to fit in a ride on the Kawasaki. In the adjoining bedroom, she found herself assessing her hair for the umpteenth time that day. Should she, shouldn't she? There were a few split ends – the endless flow of incidents in recent months had hardly allowed her the time to preen herself. The long tresses looked lacklustre, too. And to appear different to the photographs currently floating around Romania would be an asset. Less chance of being followed by journalists. Although there was little she could do about her mixed race 'dusky' skin. Picking up the magazine she had bought while waiting for the connecting flight to the UK in Senegal, she held the picture of the white girl with the pixie hairstyle alongside herself in the mirror. Would Nicolas approve? Could make her appear alarmingly waifish, she supposed. 'Alarmingly', because she'd unintentionally lost five kilos over the past three months.

Shani put down the magazine and reached for her leathers in the holdall at the bottom of the wardrobe. She would make the final decision while riding her bike.

CHAPTER 9

Shani left the concourse at Traian Vuia Airport and took a cab into the city centre. This being her second visit to Timişoara, she knew precisely where she wanted to go: to the guest house on Strada Răsăritului, a quiet, tree-lined street – and a virtual stone's throw from the Cemetery of Heroes where her family were buried. When it came to their grave, she had it in mind not to make the same mistake twice: a mistake that, on her first visit, had resulted in a photograph of her gazing at the grave below the headline *MISTERUL LUI ZINSA* in a local newspaper. She suspected that the person who'd taken the photograph was the man in the records office where she'd initially sought assistance. Just before she'd boarded her flight out of Séroulé, Nicolas had made the suggestion that if she found herself hounded by journalists then her best tactic would be to give a comprehensive interview to one of them – and in effect deflate the 'mystery of Zinsa' by acknowledging she was her daughter. But she hoped it wouldn't come to that: the pixie hairstyle, grey baseball cap, backpack and unfashionable sunglasses a robust attempt to conceal her identity.

Dusk had begun to fall by the time she reached Strada Răsăritului, where she was welcomed in broken English by the owner of the Sunrise Guest House. His reserved composure reassured her that he regarded discretion as a virtue and that questions would not be asked – nor journalists contacted. He showed her to the same room she'd occupied three months earlier.

After the owner retreated with a brief but courteous smile, Shani relieved herself of her backpack and crossed the room to the window. As before, several treetops blocked her view of the cemetery. No matter, she might dare herself into making a sneaky visit in the morning, while keeping a watchful eye for anyone drifting with intent behind her with camera or mobile phone at the ready. She sat on the bed and replied to the call from her adoptive father's housekeeper, having received it mid-flight from London.

'Dusana, hi! Sorry I missed your call. I've just arrived in Timişoara. How's your arm?'

'They took the plaster cast off last Tuesday,' said Dusana. 'The doctor's very pleased, I have almost full movement in my wrist—'

'Be careful next winter, Dusana. Any sign of ice, take a stick with you for support.'

'But Shani, dear, my arm's the least of our worries.'

'Pardon?' Shani leaned forward on the bed, concerned by Dusana's tone. 'What…what's happened, Dusana?'

'I thought I'd do some light dusting at the apartment. So I went round, opened the door and – oh, Shani, what a mess!'

'What do you mean—?'

'It's been burgled.'

'*Burgled* – oh, my God.' Shani briefly stood up from the bed in shock at what she was hearing.

'Believe it or not, there appears to be at least some good news,' mentioned Dusana.

'Good news? Like what, for heaven's sake?'

'Nothing appears to be missing.'

'Do the police know?' asked Shani, trying to picture what the apartment might look like. Andrei's precious books strewn everywhere, presumably.

'Yes. They've already been, but they didn't seem to show a great deal of interest. Just made a few notes. On reflection, perhaps I shouldn't have told them that I didn't think anything was missing.'

'Not even the Goma tribal mask? Because apparently it's worth quite a bit.'

'No, that's still there, Shani.'

A part of Shani wished it wasn't. She couldn't stand the slit-eyed 'thing' with its pursed lips. It had unnerved her so much in childhood that Andrei eventually shifted it from the living room to his bedroom. 'Do you have any idea when it could have happened, Dusana?'

'Not really. At some point over the past four weeks, because it was last month when I went to turn off the heating. My last visit.'

'What about Mrs Havranek below? She might have heard something.'

'I did go and speak to her. She's quite deaf these days, so no clues there as to when it might have happened. But, Shani, the police seem to think that whoever entered the apartment did so to search for something specific.'

'That's what they've concluded?'

'The safe behind the books has been prised open,' mentioned Dusana, 'but the contents, as I remember them from when you opened it after Andrei died, appear to be intact. My feeling is they must have been quite professional, Shani. They could only have entered the block through the lobby.'

'By tailgating someone, perhaps,' considered Shani. 'Or bribed someone from the maintenance firm, possibly, to cut them a key.'

'I suppose... Not very nice, though, is it?'

'Horrible. On my way back to London, I'll call in. Besides, I want to see you – catch up with you.'

'When might that be?'

'Couple of weeks at the most. How long did the police stay at the apartment?'

'About half an hour. I tried you first of all, but when you didn't answer that's when I called them. Thought that would be the right policy.'

'Of course. I'm sorry you had to witness such a thing. I'll call you tomorrow, Dusana.'

Shani leaned back on the bed and considered the phone call in detail. She was less troubled by how the intruders – plural, or otherwise – had managed to gain access to the block than by their apparent motive as implied by the police, that they were searching for something 'specific'. The day her adoptive father died was the day she realised he had kept information from her about her birth parents – the lie, she now believed, fabricated to protect her from the maniac who had taken control of Séroulé and who, by all accounts, was obsessed with systematically eradicating her grandfather's bloodline. Andrei had always maintained that Zinsa came from Rwanda and that her father was Czech, born in the Bohemian city of Hradec Králové, her parents having been killed in a car accident when she was two years old – a car accident that had left her with a prosthetic foot. It was only when she found a video tape in the safe that she began to discover the truth of what had occurred on that bleak November day in 1993 in Timişoara, a cultural city five hundred kilometres north-west of Bucharest.

So why the break-in? Nothing appeared to have been stolen. The video tape? She would ask Dusana. Even if it had been filched, it would be of little value to anyone; she'd since discovered footage of the demonstration and its appalling aftermath were readily available on the 'Web.

Shani glanced at the time. Not too late to call Nicolas. Besides, he would want to know she'd arrived safely. She readjusted the comfy pillows and made the call to West Africa.

'Hi, Nicolas,' she said, after typically – when it came to Séroulé – having to wait for the connection. 'I'm here, in Romania. How's it going with you?'

'I'm okay. Khamadi's keeping me busy... Hey, got the photo. Hairdo suits you. I didn't think it would, but it does.'

'You think? I'm not so sure.'

'Why? What's wrong with it?'

'I look severe, and a bit boyish!' She heard him laugh. How she missed that Gallic, festive laugh, and how she missed *him*, for God's sake. 'It's true, Nicolas. Boyish. I was something of a tomboy in my teens, and constantly battled with Dusana.' She picked at a loose thread on her jeans. 'Actually, I'm going to have to visit Prague on my way back to London.'

'Your supervisor was okay about you extending your vacation?' asked Nicolas.

'Harry? Yes, he was fine about it. Not a problem since we're heading into the summer break. Thing is, Nicolas, I've just spoken to Dusana. Andrei's apartment has been broken into at some point over the past month.'

'You're kidding?'

'Not at all. Nothing has been taken, apparently. To be honest, it sounds quite mysterious. The police told

Dusana that it appears whoever did the break-in was probably looking for something in particular. I can't think what, though. There's no jewellery to speak of, nothing at all.'

'You know what, Shani, it doesn't come as a surprise to me.'

'How come?'

'Think about it. Up until three months ago, no one knew your true identity, including yourself. And now there's a story to be told, isn't there? So, I'm guessing some cretin from my profession did it.'

'A journalist?'

'At a guess. The individual might have paid someone. It's done all too often, I'm afraid – their prey usually celebs, of course.'

'It's not nice.'

'For sure.'

'I'm missing you like hell.'

'I've got good news, Shani – a break for us both.'

'Go on...'

'In Cornwall. A couple of weeks' time. By then I should have finished my reporting out here – for now, at least. A friend of mine owns a tiny apartment in a little enclave called Trebarwith Strand. The apartment overlooks the sea. Ever surfed?'

'No, never.'

'You're about to learn. When are you meeting this Serghei character?'

'Tomorrow.'

'Be wary, Shani – just in case. Yeah?'

'I will. I'll call you in the evening.'

'Love you – massively.'

'Likewise.' She giggled. 'For eternity, Nicolas. I just wish you were here, for heaven's sake.'

'Two weeks. You should be wrapped up by then, wouldn't you say?'

'Certain to be. Bye for now, Nicolas.'

She gazed at the ceiling with a yearnful sigh. *Nicolas, Nicolas. Dearest Nicolas.* The love of her life. No question. If she sold the apartment in Prague, then for sure they could keep his *pied-à-terre* in Paris in addition to finding somewhere to live in Séroulé. But she would miss Prague and its theatrical Baroque architecture.

Shani returned to the window. She wondered whether the cemetery had closed for the day. Perhaps now would be a good time to visit, with the night sky as her camouflage. She took her keys, phone and cotton jacket off the bed and left the guest house with its tidy front garden. She rather liked the street itself, the terraced houses and the many trees sporting their recent foliage after the bitter winter months. If she ever came into enough money, then perhaps she might consider a modest apartment in this neighbourhood, allowing her to visit whenever and to stay as long as she wished. She was, after all, half Romanian.

She crossed a busy highway and made her way along the cemetery's boundary wall. When she arrived at the gates, a notice stated she had an hour before they closed for the night. The entrance itself was as she remembered it to be, an 'eternal flame' against a marble edifice, attached to which a life-sized steel cross and a date: *DECEMBRIE 1989*. The month and year when President Nicolae Ceaușescu was ousted from power in Bucharest and summarily executed with his wife, ending years of repression. What with General Odion Kuetey in Séroulé and Ceaușescu here in Romania, she felt she'd had more than her fill of dictators.

With nightfall now complete, it took her a moment to recall which path to take. She came to an open space and recognised the partially floodlit domed chapel opposite. Despite possibly being the only person in the cemetery, she realised she wasn't unnerved in the least. Why should she be? Her parents were just a moment away. Veering off to the left, she joined an avenue of graves, some garnished with bouquets of flowers, faintly illuminated by streetlights from the surrounding highway. Before her next visit, she would buy a wreath or a couple of posies from the street-sellers outside the cemetery when they returned in the morning – vividly recalling their presence from her first visit. She wondered what flowers might have appealed to her father and mother. Tulips, roses – hopefully not lilies. She couldn't stand them: always reminded her of funerals, for some reason.

In the next moment, Shani realised she must have passed by the grave and she promptly doubled back. A wooden cross, that's what she was aiming to find in the diffused light. More accurately, a crooked and weather-beaten wooden cross that she had in mind to replace. She knew she had to be within feet of the grave, her emotions bordering a mixture of wellbeing and excitement. Her family lay here, the family that Andrei stated had been cremated in the Czech Republic after the 'car accident'. No mention that she'd had a brother. Never any clue as to her direct relationship with Romania, just that his own grandfather had apparently emigrated to what was then Czechoslovakia. Of course, she'd forgiven him. He and Rodica had given up their friends and Andrei his academic post to protect her from the regime in Séroulé.

She caught sight of the grave further along. Her heart began to race. Intense joy, for just the briefest of moments, before sadness choked off the wellbeing, descending on her like a grey cloud as it always seemed to do, leaving her emotionally drained. She was here now, though, with them. With Lucian and Zinsa, and her little brother, Tuma. The cross appeared straighter than she remembered it and she wondered whether some benevolent soul had tended to it in some way.

But if only, she told herself, if only... Silly, she knew, but if *only* this grave never existed and she had that *physical* contact with her parents and brother! At times, her head ached with the many delightful scenarios that might have taken place in reality rather than in her daydreams.

Shani knelt on the pebbles and bowed her head, whispering:

'I'm here, with you. Love you, lots. Much has happened since my last visit. You'll be happy to hear General Odion Kuetey is no longer. There are battles ahead – political battles. The rebels, headed by Khamadi Soglo, have already stated they will dismiss those international creditors who have – largely through trickery – inflated Séroulé's external debt. We are going to print that so-called debt because as far as we are concerned such an astronomical figure shouldn't exist, that it basically amounts to pure extortion. When the correction has been made, we are going to clean up the country's environment and much more besides. There will be repercussions. That said, other West African countries are genuinely interested in adopting a similar strategy, and so we will support each other against those creditors and their devious methods of entrapment into the New World Order.'

She wiped away a tear that had trickled onto her jaw. 'I've met a man. He's absolutely gorgeous. I met him in Paris. He's a journalist. He wanted to make certain that I am the granddaughter of Tuma Dangbo, and not an imposter. I didn't trust his line of questioning at first, but I shouldn't have worried. I can be a poor judge of character at times. I love him dearly. With straightforward logic, he took away my anxiety over my prosthesis. It's no longer an issue. Can you believe that?

'The question mark that hangs over me is whether to continue with academia. To be honest, it bores me rigid these days. I really want to go back to Séroulé and in some way help the many orphans that the former regime created. But for now, I'm here in Timişoara, hopefully finding out more about you. Tomorrow, I'm meeting Serghei Sapdaru. He claims he was close to you. I'm just hoping it's not a journalistic stitch up of some description.'

She stood and brushed aside the remainder of her tears, kissed her fingers and touched the cross. 'Wish me luck. Massive love, as always.'

Shani turned away, constantly dabbing a tissue onto fresh tears until she emerged from the cemetery. She reminded herself that at least she had found her family. There were many in Séroulé who hadn't a hope of finding their families – their relatives or loved ones thrown into mass unmarked graves, many of which were now overgrown as if nature herself wanted to erase the mindless cruelty that had befallen the nation over the previous forty years.

CHAPTER 10

The address Shani had been giventook her on a journey several kilometres across the city. Waking up both excited and with her nerves on edge over how the meeting might pan out, she'd merely taken a croissant and a cup of strong coffee for breakfast. And now here she was, the cab driver turning into a street cluttered somewhat with mopeds and bicycles, the latter leant against rustic buildings with flaking paint. Shani judged it to be a neighbourhood that, if she were honest, she wouldn't feel comfortable walking through after dusk.

More to the point, what might Serghei Sapdaru reveal to her about her parents? Direct her, perhaps, to the school where they graduated? The actual building where her father had worked? Of course, she could see the trap of becoming obsessed, of wanting to bring them back to life – and in so doing recreating the 1990s in the form of a nostalgic womb around herself. Music, films, documentaries, books – not to mention a motorbike from that period.

The driver pulled up and pointed to a building with a weathered set of grey double doors, a lopsided83 in white paint alongside the vintage octagonal knocker. Above the doors, an unlit neon *HOSTEL* sign. Could this be, Shani asked herself while leaving the cab, Serghei Sapdaru's line of business?

Nervously, she watched the cab drive off up the street, abandoning her to the prospect of what lay beyond those inscrutable doors. Would she find disappointment or relief – or perhaps joy of some description. At least, given the shabby look the neighbourhood projected, it now seemed unlikely that she was being set up by a journalist. A meeting in a café instead, perhaps, rather than here. As the cab disappeared from view a bunch of children spilled out of an alleyway further up the street, kicking around what appeared to be an inflated carrier bag.

There was no bell that she could see. Shani used the brass knocker, and as she did so the door opened slightly of its own accord. She supposed that made sense – the time of day and with it being a hostel. Once inside, she was confronted by a set of metal gates that reached the ceiling, the chain used to lock them together dangling towards a scuffed wooden floor. Shani shivered; the dreary interior several degrees cooler than outside in the street. The reception desk amounted to a foldaway table, featuring a portable television set watched by a man far too old to be Serghei.

The man stood up. He was tall and wore clothes that seemed to blend in with the floorboards. When he stepped away from the table, he had a noticeable limp and Shani suspected that, given his age, he had an arthritic knee or hip.

She announced herself and the man raised both hands as if in recognition. A smile of sorts touched his worn face, before he shook a small brass bell, its muted tinkle leaving her to wonder whether anyone beyond the lobby might hear it. The man smiled again and re-seated himself with a shuffle, his eyes instantly reverting to the TV set. Shani stepped back and clasped her hands behind herself, taking in the aesthetic line of the graceful curve on the staircase and the accompanying steel handrail. To her left, a shelf supporting a bunch of grubby plastic flowers forced into a glass vase. She felt as if she were in a time warp – ironically, somewhere in the 1990s.

A door opened behind her, causing her to whirl around. A young girl approached while wiping her hands on a chequered apron. Although plain-looking, the fluidity of her features lent themselves to curiosity. Her fringe touched her eyebrows, and without the ponytail her mousey hair would likely have brushed her shoulders. But there was something about her appearance that just didn't seem to fit the surroundings. A student having to make money, perhaps?

'Hello, I'm Daniela. You are Shani, yes?'

'Yes.' Shani shook the girl's hand.

'I'm delighted to meet you, Shani.'

'Likewise, my meeting you,' said Shani. 'But where, Daniela, did you learn such perfect English?'

'You are very kind.' A quiet smile as Daniela withdrew her hand. 'Mostly, when I lived with my parents in Bucharest. My mother comes from Preston, in the north of England. I visited twice.' The girl shrugged. 'It helped,' she added modestly.

'And now you work here?' asked Shani softly, trying to supress her surprise.

'It's a job.' The coy smile reappeared. 'But today, I earn extra,' said Daniela. 'I am acting as your translator. Shall I introduce you to Serghei now?'

'Please.' Once they reached the landing, Shani decided they must by now be out of earshot of the old man. She wanted to help the girl, although she couldn't explain to herself why she was so keen to do so other than Daniela seemed to be wasting her intellect in such a place. 'You know, Daniela, with your English you could earn a small fortune in Bucharest as a tourist guide – with tips on top, no doubt.'

'Yes, I have considered this. But it is like…umm…how would you say? A closed circuit, yes?'

'Like a club, you mean?'

'Yes. If I tread on someone's territory, then I make problem for myself. It's finding the right opening with good people.' Daniela knocked on the door to the left of the staircase on the second floor before giving Shani a sideways glance. 'It has to be with good people.' She knocked again, above the number 6. 'Serghei, Shani is here.'

The door opened only a few centimetres, leaving Shani's view of the room and its occupant blocked by Daniela.

'You okay? You look tired, Serghei,' Daniela said.

'Yes, yes – okay. Shani?'

'She's here. I said that.'

Shani wondered why Daniela was talking to Serghei as if he were a child or a sick person. But then the door fully opened and Shani was taken aback

– horrified. She found herself facing what looked to be a total down-and-out, in second-hand, if not third-hand, clothes. Rags, basically. His face was pale and gaunt, his lifeless eyes set back – sunken into his skull. He had some hair, not much, just a couple of unkempt sandy-coloured tufts. After a moment of silence, it dawned on Shani that she'd likely been gawping, and she immediately forced a smile through her dismay, wondering what awful life's journey this friend of her parents had trodden over the past twenty-four years.

'Serghei,' she breathed, still collecting herself. 'I am so pleased to meet you.'

Daniela started to translate, but Serghei raised a feeble hand. 'Yes, this I understand.' He lowered his hand to shake Shani's. 'It is…er…right for you, here… To be… Right for you to be, here. Yes? Bless Lucian, bless Zinsa.' A generous smile, laden with stained and chipped teeth. 'And bless Shani.'

'Thank you, Serghei. The privilege, of course, is mine.' Shani turned to Daniela, imagining the latter sentence required translating – which Daniela apparently achieved. They followed Serghei into the room, cell-like and depressing with its brown utility furniture. This man was living a miserable existence. Her immediate thought was that she ought to help him in some way. What would her parents want her to do? A friend of theirs had clearly fallen on difficult times... She was shown to a chair, and Daniela directed with a similar gesture to sit on the bed. Serghei sat at a small table and started to roll a cigarette. Shani wished he wouldn't do that, the room being so small.

Daniela must have had a similar thought because, after speaking to Serghei, she went and opened the window. 'He apologises for smoking, but his nerves are not in good condition. This goes back to when he was in prison in Cluj.' Daniela spoke briefly to Serghei, receiving a nod from him before he lit the cigarette. 'He says it's okay for me to tell you what I know of him. Then he will talk about your parents.'

'Thank you,' said Shani. She noticed that Serghei's fingers were dark yellow with nicotine. Did he drink as well? Probably, although she couldn't see any evidence of alcohol inside the room.

'Not long after your parents died,' said Daniela, 'Serghei was smuggling drugs, here in Timişoara. He was sending the stuff up to Cluj—'

'A city north of here, right?' said Shani.

'Yes. Sort of north-east. That's where he was caught and that's where he served his sentence. He got fifteen years. In those days the prisons were much tougher, and he suffered as a consequence.'

Serghei held up his hand, cigarette burning merrily in contrast to its surroundings. He spoke briefly to Daniela, who again translated.

'He is not proud of his actions and really he has no excuses. Your father warned him and tried to put him on the straight and narrow... This is correct, yes, "straight and narrow"?'

'Yes.' This was the sort of news Shani had hoped to hear: her parents benevolent towards others. 'How did Serghei meet my parents?'

Daniela spoke to Serghei, who carefully put down his cigarette on the edge of a tin ashtray and conversed with her for a couple of minutes, giving Shani time to analyse her observations thus far. She was concerned for Serghei, obviously. And to live one's life in a single room must be torture. How was he managing to pay the owner of the hostel? She had no idea how the benefit system worked in Romania – or whether anything along such lines actually existed.

'Shani...'

Shani swung around from the window to face Daniela.

'You know that your father was an orphan?'

'Yes. So too my mother, of course.'

'There were many orphans in Romania by the time Ceauşescu's reign ended. I have to say it was a terrible time in our history. Serghei's father ran an orphanage and made his money that way. Lucian was left there, presumably by his mother. So, they grew up together and went to the same school. Then your mother arrived, from Africa.'

Serghei briefly interrupted. Daniela nodded.

'From the beginning, Shani, your father always wanted to sit next to Zinsa in class. He was fascinated by her – her skin, in particular. He kept saying to Serghei that he wanted to touch it, but was frightened that if he did so some of the blackness might rub off.'

Shani smiled. An exquisite story beginning to emerge. Lovelier than she'd imagined. So cute! She could picture them sitting together as children in the classroom.

'Then the man who brought Zinsa out of Africa—'

'Andrei,' interrupted Shani. 'He smuggled her out of Séroulé, West Africa. There was a coup.'

'Yes, Andrei. He decided to adopt Lucian, who took Andrei's surname: Bălcescu. So, fascination turned to romance and they married, and then Zinsa fell pregnant with twins – this, a well-known fact across Romania. The nature of what happened to them is written into folklore.'

Serghei suddenly stood up and presented Shani with a black-and-white photograph, creased on one corner. She realised that it was in fact Serghei standing between her parents, his arms across their shoulders. The three of them were laughing at whoever was taking the photograph. She wasn't sure, but her mother looked as if she might be pregnant.

'My treasure,' said Serghei, before adding something more in Romanian to Daniela.

'He wants to give you his treasure, for you to keep,' translated Daniela.

'I could get it copied,' said Shani. 'Then we would have one each.'

As Daniela was relaying this to Serghei, Shani felt herself welling up while gazing into the photograph. Zinsa really was a beautiful woman, with her high cheekbones and spirited smile. Her father wasn't bad looking either, physically strong and lean – athletic. Interrupting his smile was a cigarette. By her reckoning, Zinsa had been exactly twenty years old when she fell pregnant.

Daniela was offering her a tissue from her apron pocket. Shani dabbed her tears away. 'Thank you.' She turned the photograph over. No date, just a smudge of whatever. She showed the photograph to

Daniela. 'I think my mother looks pregnant. What do you think?'

Daniela studied the photograph and nodded. 'I would say so.' She spoke to Serghei, but in response Serghei shrugged his rounded shoulders – before coughing. It was a raw, guttural cough that made him wince. He swallowed back the phlegm and wiped the back of his hand across his lips.

Once he'd settled himself down again, Shani asked, 'I understand my father was a draughtsman for a firm of architects?'

'Yes, he was.' Daniela offered the reply without turning to Serghei.

'When I came here on my last visit – which was my first – I went to the hospital where I was born, and where Zinsa died with my baby brother. The head administrator who talked to me said there were rumours that secret government forces might have been involved. I agreed with him that I found this hard to believe because the footage available on the internet clearly shows a policeman pointing and firing a semi-automatic gun at the car.'

'The rumour still exists,' confirmed Daniela. 'It is nonsense, for the reasons you have explained. Such rumours always appear after this kind of event. Don't you agree?'

Shani nodded and gestured towards Serghei. 'Does Serghei have an opinion?'

Daniela put the question to Serghei, who shook his head before entering into a lengthy discourse.

Shani's interpreter seemed surprised by what he was telling her, frowning occasionally and asking questions. Shani was curious. Daniela started to speak to her, but turned back briefly to Serghei as if to confirm a piece of information he had given her. Finally, Daniela nodded and conveyed to Shani what Serghei had told her.

'This is quite interesting. I knew about the plane, but little else.'

'Plane?' queried Shani. 'What's this about a plane?'

'In 1944, a plane that left America crashed near Timişoara, out in the countryside. Andrei and his future wife witnessed it. Did they not mention this to you?'

'No. Not at all.'

'Well, in the wreckage they found a folder, the material inside looked like it had been written in some sort of code. Andrei must have forgotten about the folder over the years. Your father rediscovered it in the garden shed. He and Serghei took it to a friend they knew called Mario. They knew him from both the orphanage and when they were at school together. Mario was good with crosswords and things like that, so they decided he might be able to…er…'

'"Decipher"?' prompted Shani, fascinated.

'To translate, yes?'

'Yes, translate – I understand.'

'Mario started to do this with some success. So, they left him to carry on. But when your father returned, Mario couldn't be found. Your father felt Mario had stolen the folder from him and was trying to sell it—'

Serghei interrupted. Daniela listened.

'I need to make a correction, Shani,' she said. 'Your father copied the contents of the folder and gave them to Mario, keeping the original for himself.'

'Does Serghei have any idea what the code was about?'

Daniela put the question to Serghei.

'He says that it was to do with world order secrets – this much Mario told them.'

'World order *secrets*,' echoed Shani, bewildered.

'Yes.'

'Has he seen Mario since?'

Serghei answered the question himself. 'No.' He drew heavily on his cigarette. 'He go somewhere. Perhaps much money he get for what Lucian give him.' His voice had become distinctly bitter. 'Two days…I arrest.' He spoke to Daniela.

Daniela said, 'He was arrested by the police two days after your parents died. They asked him about the material your father gave Mario.'

'What is Mario's surname?' Shani asked Serghei.

'Nemescu,' said Serghei. 'Mario Nemescu.'

'No idea where he lives, Serghei?'

'No.'

'So, my father kept the original folder from the plane crash?'

Serghei looked at Daniela, who translated. He nodded.

'I've never seen it,' said Shani. 'I left Romania when I was a baby. I've lived in the Czech Republic ever since, apart from four years in Oxford.'

Daniela quietly shook her head. 'Such a dream city.'

'I don't appreciate it as much as I should,' confessed Shani, before refocussing. 'Going back to this folder that came from the plane crash… When did Lucian come across it? I mean, when he was much younger?'

Daniela put the question to Serghei. The answer surprised Shani.

'Just a couple of weeks *before* that November day?' clarified Shani – the words *secret government forces* resurfacing in her head.

'According to Serghei,' said Daniela.

'Can you ask him if he could try tracking down Mario Nemescu? I will pay any expenses he incurs – and some extra money on top. Perhaps you could help him, Daniela? I'll join in, although my Romanian is non-existent. But if I can help, just ask. What do you think?'

Daniela nodded. 'I will give it a try, Shani.' She spoke to Serghei, who nodded.

'And obviously Mario knew my parents, so I could learn more about them from him.' Shani sat back and thought for a moment. 'Can Serghei expand on what Mario translated? I realise it wasn't the whole text, by the sound of it, and that it was over twenty years ago, but Serghei mentioned *world order*. If he is talking about the "New World Order", I'm very interested. Can he tell us more?'

Daniela relayed the question in Romanian to Serghei, who shrugged. Then he gave a brief reply. Daniela explained.

'The plane that came down was American but had Soviet markings – red stars – on it. The pilot would have been Russian. He remembers Mario showing immediate interest in the folder. It mentioned a group of killers—'

'Killers?' Shani leant forward to make certain she caught every word. 'What sort of killers? Like…mercenaries, or assassins? You know these words? People who are hired to kill people, more often than not political figures.'

Daniela conversed with Serghei, who nodded.

'Yes, like "unit" of assassins,' clarified Daniela. 'But that was just the first page. There were more pages in the folder.'

Serghei started to speak and Daniela listened intently, raising an arched eyebrow before looking at Shani.

'Serghei has just told me that after your parents died, when he was taken to the police station and interrogated, they wanted to know where your father had put the original folder from the plane crash. He couldn't answer them because he didn't know.'

My God, thought Shani. If Serghei was to be believed – and there was no reason to suggest otherwise – then what kind of 'classified' material had her father been playing around with? Facing Daniela, she said, 'Basically, just to summarise, this information was initially written in code inside a folder found in the wreckage of a plane that had flown from America, with the aircrew likely to have been Russian?'

'Yes,' said Daniela.

Neither Andrei nor Rodica had ever uttered a word about a plane crash. But then she supposed they wouldn't, for that would likely reveal the fact she herself was half Romanian as opposed to half Czech.

'I have to say,' Shani told Daniela, 'I would be interested to find this folder. Or even Mario Nemescu's photocopy that my father made for him – unless he sold it to someone. I suppose finding the original folder is too much of a longshot, if not impossible, but finding Mario might just be achievable. As I said earlier, I really would appreciate your help – and, obviously, Serghei's.'

'I see no reason why not, speaking for myself,' said Daniela. 'I'm as curious as you are. I'll work with Serghei. Does he have your mobile phone number?'

'Yes, he does.' Shani began to stand, as did Daniela and Serghei. 'I don't want to tire Serghei any more than I have done. I'm sure over the coming fortnight I'll have countless more questions for him to answer concerning my parents. For now, I'll leave you both.'

Serghei coughed his habitual cough, hunching forward as he did so before he shook Shani's hand. 'Good people, Shani,' he repeated. 'Bless Lucian, and bless Zinsa.'

'Thank you, Serghei.' Shani held up the photograph. 'And thank you for this. I'm so grateful. I too, of course, will treasure it. But I will also make a copy, for you.' She turned to Daniela. 'I'm ready to leave.'

Down in the lobby, the old man was still watching television. Daniela said something to him in Romanian, and without leaving his chair he waved a hand in Shani's direction.

'Is he the owner?' asked Shani.

'Yes. He's absolutely loaded, but I imagine he doesn't charge Serghei much. I really don't know what arrangement they have. There must be one, though.'

Beside the grey double doors, Shani shook Daniela's hand – but felt that wasn't adequate enough, given her assistance, so she dared to embrace her. 'Thank you, Daniela.' To her relief, Daniela responded with equal pressure.

'We are friends,' Daniela said over Shani's shoulder, her arms still wrapped around her. 'This is very good. I will learn more English.'

Shani met Daniela's eyes and smiled with her. 'I'm convinced you can better yourself, but we'll discuss this another time.' She left the step, waved and walked away.

Joining the highway at the end of the street, hoping for a cab, her mind's eye was occupied by a range of images ricocheting off one another, making it hard for her to sift through and evaluate the last hour. On a physical level, she wanted to take a shower – which upset her. Serghei clearly couldn't help the way he lived. Paradoxically, while out in Séroulé, where poverty and hardship were the norm, she'd never felt such a need as she did this minute to wash herself thoroughly.

CHAPTER 11

Shani sat on the bed in her room and called Prague.

'Dusana? Hi, it's me.'

'Darling—'

'How are you feeling? I mean after the break-in at the apartment.'

'The police told me I can make a start on tidying up.'

'But your arm! You've only just had the plaster-cast removed.'

'It'll be good exercise for me, Shani.'

'Okay, I'll take your word for it. But be careful. Don't overdo things.'

'I just want to get it straight, Shani. Like it never happened.'

'I take it the police still haven't any idea as to who might have broken in?'

'No. They don't seem at all interested, since nothing appears to be missing. But they are writing to the management to tell them that CCTV ought to be installed in the lobby. It's in my block. Been in there for years.'

'Well, that's a plus, I suppose. Promise me though, Dusana, you'll just do a little tidying up now and then?'

'Don't worry. One book at a time back on the shelf.'

Shani laughed. 'I'll call you in a couple of days. Love you.'

'Love you too, darling. Any news from the police and I'll be in touch.'

Shani left her phone on the bed and began to undress. Depressing the button on her prosthesis, she detached it from the locking pin on the silicone sock. Out of habit, she massaged the stump. Since meeting Nicolas, she hardly gave her disability a second thought these days. Three months before, on her first visit to Romania and while staying overnight in this very same room, she'd likely cursed her inability to accept what fate had dealt her, while simultaneously accusing herself of being pathetic.

Then came Nicolas.

What happened to you is unfortunate, no question. I'm not trying to trivialise your suffering. I know it's there. I get that. But you can help others, you can give hope to people because of your unique experience. You're a giver, Shani, already I sense this in you. Once you recognise this and act on it, my bet is any self-loathing you still harbour will fade away.

It was a start. Her previous boyfriend had crushed her self-esteem to new depths when she'd found pornographic images of amputees on his laptop.

Shani shook her head. What was she doing thinking about that creep? She showered quickly and, while she was drying herself, a text came through. She took her phone from her jeans: Nicolas, asking if she'd learnt anything new from Serghei. She certainly had. Putting on clean underwear, she adjusted the pillows, leaned back into them and made the call.

'Quite busy,' answered Nicolas to her question. 'I've just completed my first report for mainstream media. Whether they'll accept it remains to be seen.'

'Why shouldn't it be accepted?' asked Shani.

'Because Khamadi and the caretaker government have gone to war with the creditors over the external debt. Khamadi won't go back on his word to the nation. The debt has been manufactured virtually out of thin air, so why shouldn't we print it and put it to good use such as reversing climate change, et cetera?'

'Do you think they will try and sabotage the caretaker government's initiatives?' asked Shani.

'Certain to. The feeling is extremists will be directed towards Séroulé, in addition to utter lies being published about the government and Khamadi's inner circle.'

'Are you suggesting suicide bombers?'

'We can't rule it out, Shani. Border crossings are being strengthened. The northern border has always been quite porous because of the Dendi people. So drones are being deployed to cover as much of it as possible. Did you get to meet Serghei?'

'Yes. It was nothing like I imagined it would be.'

'In what way?'

'He's living in a hostel in quite a poor neighbourhood. Doesn't look at all well. Mind you, the fact he's smoking himself to death isn't helping. But, no, he's really quite a pathetic soul. I feel I should help him in some way. Apparently, my father tried to put him on the straight and narrow. His exact words – or words he gave the interpreter. She was rather nice. Very pleasant. I feel I've made a friend. Her name's Daniela. But there's something odd about her.'

'Odd? In what way?'

'It's hard to put my finger on it. She just seems too bright to be working as a skivvy in such a place.'

'Okay, apart from that, what did you find out?' asked Nicolas.

Shani gave him an approximate account, before mentioning the plane crash and the folder that was found in the wreckage strewn across farmland owned by Andrei's father.

'Where did this plane set off from?' asked Nicolas. 'Did Serghei tell you?'

'America. It was an American plane with Russian markings. Doesn't make sense, does it?'

'Actually, it does. If it was operating under the Lend-Lease Act.'

'Lend-Lease?' frowned Shani. 'What's that, exactly?'

'America was supplying various countries, notably the Soviet Union, with food, oil and materials. But if this plane had Soviet markings, then the greater mystery is what on earth it was doing over Romania. The pilots to my knowledge always used the ALSIB route – Alaska to Siberia, and then dropped down to Moscow, or wherever.'

'Okay, I get that,' said Shani. 'According to Serghei, the person Lucian gave the folder to – or rather a copy of the contents – was Mario something. Nemescu. Mario Nemescu. He decoded some of it and it talked about a group of assassins. I'm left with the impression it had something to do with the New World Order – even back then in 1944.'

'So, what are you planning to do?'

'It's fascinating, but we're talking over twenty years ago. I'm not going to waste time on it. That said, through Serghei I'd like to track down Mario since he knew my parents. Find out what he has to say about them. I'm giving myself a fortnight over here. I can always return at a later date.'

'Serghei doesn't have any idea where Mario might be?'

'No. He went to prison for fifteen years.'

'Prison? You mean Mario?'

'No, Serghei.' Shani detected a note of alarm in Nicolas's voice, but decided to continue since she was against keeping anything from him. 'He was drug-running. Timişoara to Cluj. Threw his life away, basically.'

'Be careful, Shani.'

'He's just a pathetic soul, Nicolas.'

'But maybe the people he associates himself with are not so pathetic.'

'I think he's a loner. But I take your point. Are we still on for your friend's apartment in Cornwall?'

'For sure. Can't wait.'

'Neither can I. Just wish you were here, lying beside me.'

'What's a fortnight?'

'A devil of a long time,' she chuckled, 'that's what a fortnight is. I'm going to wander around the old part of the city, take in a few of the sights.'

'Okay. I'll call you tomorrow, Shani.'

'If you get a moment, Nicolas, can you just run a check on the plane that came down? I'll have a search for it myself, but you're so much better at it than me.'

'I'll give it a go. Love you, Shani.'

'Love you, too, Nicolas. Take care.'

Shani slipped the phone into her shoulder bag, noting the time on its screen to be 16:37. Where had the time gone? She pulled her jeans back on and grabbed a fresh T-shirt.

Facing the mirror above the dresser, she was still in a dilemma over her hair. She lowered the angle on her fringe so that it touched her eyebrows. Hopefully, by the time she hooked up with Nicolas it would no longer be 'pixie' but a definite small bob. She questioned whether the disguise had been worth it after all. Just that one picture of her beside the grave three months ago having made the local paper: long hair, Barbour jacket – crying. And anyway, what did it really matter if someone did identify her as Zinsa's daughter? Three months ago, it was different: General Kuetey was still in power, but now, thank God, he and his vile regime were just a stain on the pages of history.

Reaching for her cotton jacket, Shani decided she would revisit the cemetery at dusk. She was finding it impossible to stay away from her parents and baby brother!

CHAPTER 12

Apart from herself, the only other guests in the breakfast room happened to be an elderly couple seated at a table over by the window with a view of the street. Whenever they spoke, they more or less whispered. So English, thought Shani. In actual fact, they were from Suffolk, so the woman had informed her when they passed each other in the hallway the previous evening.

Her phone vibrated briefly in her jeans. Shani stood and dug it out of her pocket.

I av Mario adres.

Quick work, gauged Shani. She sat back down and poured herself another cup of coffee. Surprisingly quick work, in fact. Had Serghei known all along and baulked from giving it to her for whatever reason? She couldn't scroll down, meaning he hadn't given her the address. She texted him back.

Thanks, Serghei. What is Mario's address?

The owner brought croissants for the elderly couple and then passed by Shani's table.

'Everything good?' he asked.

'Perfect. Thank you.'

Shani finished her coffee, and as she got up from the table the woman from Suffolk gave her a cordial smile – her husband engrossed in spreading jam over a croissant. By the time Shani reached her room, Serghei still hadn't responded to her text. She decided to call him… No answer. Perhaps he'd gone to the washroom. She wished now that she'd taken down Daniela's number. At the time, she hadn't wanted to appear pushy or ask too many favours.

While brushing her teeth, Shani decided she'd get a cab and head back over to the hostel. With luck, this Mario Nemescu character might just fill in more of the gaps. Lucian had evidently known him well enough to have photocopied the contents of the folder for him.

Downstairs in the lobby, amongst its array of various potted plants, Shani called the cab firm she'd used the previous day and left the guest house. She hoped to find Mario in better health than Serghei. She certainly couldn't imagine how he could be in a worse state. While waiting on the pavement for the cab, she spent a moment taking in the street with its lovely trees, the foliage still gleaming from spring. She could picture her parents living in such a street.

The cab arrived and ended her daydream. By chance, it was the same driver. She sat in the front seat, as before. If she had a hang-up, then it was being waited on hand and foot. Assigned a 'scout' as part and parcel of her Fellowship at St Aquinas to deliver her mail and clean her room – including changing her bed linen – was simply too much for her to endure. Apart from receiving pieces of mail, she did everything herself. She'd often suspected that the 'hang-up' stemmed from her disfigurement, and her desire to go unnoticed – the irony, of course, being that by burying herself in academia she had acquired a Fellowship at what was considered to be one of the most prestigious colleges in Europe, if not the wider world.

Spots of rain appeared on the windscreen, the sky thickening over. The driver used the wipers intermittently. Arriving at the double set of grey doors, Shani gave the driver a modest tip and he went on his way. The street looked deserted, no children playing on this occasion. Inside the hostel the television, just as it had been the day before, was switched on but the old man was nowhere to be seen.

'Hello…' called Shani. 'Hello.' She went over to the door from which Daniela had emerged. 'Anyone in there?' She pushed tentatively against the spring on the door. 'Daniela?' The door led into a kitchen; the air filled with the acrid smell of meat being stewed on a filthy stove. Plates, bowls and cups were piled high in the porcelain sink – the tiled floor greasy. It surprised Shani that Daniela didn't keep everything tidier and more hygienic. It seemed out of character. She turned away and the door spring recoiled with a metallic thump.

'Hello? Anyone here?'

Nothing, apart from a stunted echo and a shiver on her spine. It felt as if the place had been abandoned in an instant.

'Hello…?'

Shani decided to go straight on up. Perhaps visitors were allowed to do just that. She started to climb the winding staircase. Approaching the second floor she could hear people talking: a man and a woman, their voices distinctly raised, as if they were arguing. Serghei and Daniela? It didn't sound like Daniela, more like an older woman. She reached Room 6, where the door was ajar. Still they were arguing. Shani pushed open the door.

'Hello—' Her voice caught, her eyes stretched wide by the most horrific sight. Serghei was cross-legged on the bed, propped up against the wall. She hardly noticed the tufts of sandy-coloured hair sticking up, as her focus was at once drawn to his tongue, which dangled not from his mouth but the slit across his throat. Both his wrists were tied by string, balanced in a macabre fashion over his head, so that his limp fingers were level with his misshapen jaw.

The woman stepped forward, frantic. 'No...no! No! No!'

Shani was barely aware of the woman yelling at her, and even less so of her severe obesity.

'We no do! English? *English?*'

Shani found she could hardly breathe, her organs jammed solid – her body and mind terrorised into semi-paralysis. She looked at the woman, and the man frozen behind her with a newspaper crunched up in his left hand.

'We no do!' screamed the woman. 'We no do! We no do...'

Shani ran from the room and straight down the stairs. Blind panic and a torrent of adrenaline propelled her onto the street. It was still raining. She slipped on the cobblestones. Reactions from God knows where caught her from falling. She made it out onto the highway and walked aimlessly along its pavement, oblivious to the people bustling by.

Sergio had been murdered… Correction, slaughtered. Slaughtered like a pig!

His hands, his *tongue*… God Almighty. They must have tortured him first.

We no do! We no do! English?

The woman seemed to have automatically assumed she was English. Or did she happen to select the language because of its international scope? The man hadn't been the old man at the desk she'd seen the previous day. So where had they come from? Were they the actual owners? And where was Daniela? Her day off?

Keep walking, she told herself. *Just keep walking away from that hell. Jesus!*

They must have beaten him around the head first and then cut his throat. Would his tongue just plop out like that or had someone yanked it out through the wound? That image and that of his hands suspended was just so…macabre. How could anyone *do* such a thing?

Shani felt her legs giving way. She came to a café with tables outside under a yellow awning. The café had several customers seated inside. She wanted to be on her own, away from the gaze of people; the shock of what she'd witnessed certain to be on her face. She sat down and leaned forward. She wanted to move on, but couldn't – aside from wanting to throw up, her legs had gone to jelly.

A ritual killing? Had Serghei been the victim of such a thing? It must have happened seconds after she'd sent him the text asking for Mario Nemescu's address because he'd never replied. Shani checked her phone, just in case she'd missed a text from him while in the cab. She hadn't.

Was she involved in some way? By meeting Serghei, had she triggered—

A menu was thrust in front of her. She was so shocked by it that she virtually leapt from the table. Settling herself the best she could, she dismissed the menu and asked for a straight Americano. When the boy left, she wondered whether a large brandy would have been more beneficial.

Shani looked out onto the highway and noticed how busy the traffic was – people going about their day's business, not one of them seeing the ritualistic killing in their mind's eye that she was seeing. What if she was responsible in some way? Could Mario Nemescu be involved? Had he done this to Serghei? Mario…Serghei…her father. Plane…folder…coded information – from America, heading for Russia. And then the *group of assassins* statement that Mario had unearthed in the code – *unit* of assassins, rather. It was too far-fetched, surely?

The coffee arrived, a biscuit in a plain wrapper on its saucer. She wasn't in the least hungry. More weight loss! Security for herself. Get out of the country? She wasn't sure she wanted to return to the guest house, not immediately. The owner would notice a change in her. How could he not? The trauma of it all had scrambled her head. Perhaps for tonight she would use another guest house, detach herself from all that she was presently familiar with while she assessed the situation. She could collect her passport from the Sunrise Guest House tomorrow and then head directly out to the airport... Problem: she would need to hand over her passport at the reception desk at whatever suitable hotel or guest house she came across. There again, the weather was mild enough to spend the night sitting on a park bench. Or perhaps she should collect her passport this minute, inventing some sort of crisis back in the UK and as a consequence was having to cut short her stay in Timişoara. She nodded inwardly. A strategy to aim for, at least!

Shani started on the coffee, which tasted ghastly – beyond bitter. She abandoned the remainder. Perhaps the shock had interfered with her sense of taste…?

What was she thinking! Surely, safer to stay overnight at the airport in the lounge than in a park. God's sake, she needed to be careful, to tame and monitor her impulsive nature. Each and every possible move had to be analysed thoroughly, taking the advantages and disadvantages into account. The fact was her mind had been thrown upside down, nerve endings jangled out of sync along with her ability to process her thoughts constructively. She mustn't make the same mistakes twice. Between Nicolas and the Séroulèse rebels she'd learnt a huge amount when it came to self-preservation: the avoidance of CCTV whenever necessary; phone cloning; how to handle a Walther PPK handgun – and a Steyr pistol, come to that.

She was fairly certain her phone hadn't been cloned. But it might have been hacked into in some ingenious way. She could still phone Nicolas. Why shouldn't she? In fact, it was perfectly normal that she'd do so under the circumstances and tell him everything she'd witnessed. She hadn't done anything wrong, hadn't violated the law in the least… Perhaps she should go to the local police station? Tell them precisely what she had just witnessed?

Shani took the photograph Serghei had given her from her shoulder bag. The three of them, laughing – Serghei in the middle. And now? Hideously mutilated. Why had this happened to him? Was he still involved in trafficking? Had they made an example of him because he'd cheated a drugs baron?

Maybe the people he associates himself with are not so pathetic. Nicolas's comment, after she'd mentioned Serghei had served time in a prison.

She put the photograph away and left the café, feeling a need to keep moving, as if some primitive instinct had kicked in. Fight or flight. She was in *flight* mode, for sure. What if she told Nicolas everything and a journalist had actually hacked into her phone? Expecting information on how the mysterious daughter of Lucian and Zinsa Bălcescu lived her life and the kind of company she kept, he would instead be astonished to hear an altogether different story, one that was many times more compelling. A cold-blooded murder.

There was a taxi rank ahead. She would return immediately to the guest house after all, to shower and change her clothes. Then review her options, such as whether or not to leave immediately for the airport.

She took the cab at the front of the line, and on this occasion opted for the rear seat as she struggled to make sense of the questions inside her head. Why, for instance, hadn't the murder been reported and the street sealed off? *Why?* And why the string tied to his wrists that extended itself over his head? What was the point of it? A feature associated with a specific ritual, like a Mafia killing that combined a warning to others in the neighbourhood? Daniela… If *only* she'd taken her number.

* * *

Arriving at the guest house, Shani found the owner hovering by the reception desk. Just her luck! He started to speak but she cut him short with a smile and a wave as she headed for the stairs. Serghei. Poor soul. No one deserved such a fate as that. She locked the door to her room. He was at peace now. No more suffering – but how he must have suffered during the last minutes of his life. If there was any justice in this damned world then he would be in some sort of paradise now, protected and far removed from all evil. She stripped and showered. She would never wear those clothes again. The cotton jacket had been expensive, but she didn't care. She was going to bundle them up, put them in a carrier bag and dump them in a bin – along with her shoes.

While drying herself, Shani saw the irony in her decision. She was behaving as if *she* had committed the murder, and was now frantically attempting to erase every speck of evidence. Her phone buzzed. She picked it up while putting on her underwear. An email from the Home Bursar at St Thomas Aquinas. For heaven's sake, what did she want? Highlighting some rule she'd breached without knowing, no doubt. She'd heard the Bursar was a stickler for protocol. Shani sat on the bed and opened the email.

Dear Miss Bălcescu,
I trust all is well with you.

No, it bloody well isn't! Shani yelled back. *I've just witnessed the aftermath of a horrific crime, for God's sake!*

Your supervisor, Professor Rothwell, has notified me that you are out of the country on urgent family business.
It is with regret that I have to inform you that it appears your study has been broken into. Your scout, Susan Wilson, reported the damaged lock on the door at ten o'clock this morning. I have inspected the room myself and found a number of books on the floor as if

they have been tossed out of the shelves. I would be grateful if you could inform me as soon as possible whether you might have left your study as I have described before your departure. The bedroom appears untouched. By that, I mean, nothing strewn over the floor.

Additionally, it has come to light that yesterday's duty porter questioned a man at the foot of your staircase as to what he was doing there, this being eleven o'clock in the morning and out of tourist hours. The man claimed he was going to a seminar room, though was unable to identify the room by name or specify its location. However, there happened to be no seminars given by Fellows at that time in College, and besides, the Haverstock Room on your staircase is not available for seminars throughout Hilary and Trinity Terms due to refurbishment.

We do have CCTV footage of the individual in question, though unfortunately, due to Data Protection laws, I am unable to attach an image, or the footage itself. However, on your return, you may look at the footage in my office.

With best wishes,
Miss Harriet Hendon

Home Bursar

Shani leaned forward on the bed, clutching her phone. What was going on in her life? She recalled the news Dusana had given her about Andrei's apartment being broken into. Now this. And Serghei... She couldn't see his eyes. When she'd entered the room, had they been closed or open? The string suspending his hands and his slit throat with his tongue hanging out of the wound, yes. Crystal clear, as in 'high-definition' clear. But his eyes...? A total blank. She imagined they must have been open because he was dead, and dead people's eyes stayed open.

Get out of Romania. That was what she needed to do. Just get away from it all. Prague, en route to Oxford – but she would go straight to Dusana's apartment and stay there rather than Andrei's. Or perhaps Séroulé? She would be with Nicolas and perfectly safe, whether she were being targeted or not, because she would make certain not to leave a trail. But if she was being targeted, *why*? Why the break-ins? Why had they murdered Serghei? Coincidence? *Should* she go to the police? She couldn't speak a word of Romanian beyond basic phrases. What if her account was misinterpreted in some way, even with an interpreter on hand? And if the media got to hear of her being interrogated at a police station, she would never hear the end of it. The gossip in the Fellows Common Room at St Aquinas would be off the Richter scale!

She needed to visit the cemetery. But first she would call Nicolas, just to hear his voice, omitting from the call the day's heinous event in case her phone had in fact been hacked. Without a shot of brandy to hand, she took the water bottle from her backpack and drank what was left in an attempt to shore herself up. Sitting on the bed with her phone, she filled her lungs and made the call.

'Hi, Nicolas…wondering if you had any info on the plane crash?'

'From what Ican gather,' said Nicolas, 'it appears the plane was refuelled at Ernest Harmon Airbase in Newfoundland, and then again at RAF Ballyhalbert, Northern Ireland. It would have been fitted with auxiliary tanks, I imagine, to make the distance across the Atlantic.'

'Oh, right,' said Shani.

'I very much doubt it was heading for Russia. Quite mysterious, really. You okay?'

'Yes, fine.'

'You sound distant.'

'Oh... I'm going to visit the grave, so I probably sound a little emotional.'

'Any news on this Mario character?'

'None as yet. I might pull out of here, Nicolas.'

'Leave Romania? Rather sudden, isn't it? You've only been there a couple of days.'

'I know. It's just I thought it would be nice if we could do this together. And with your research skills, it's likely we would find Mario and other people who knew my parents in half the time.'

'If that's what you want...'

'I think so. In fact, what I really want is to be out there with you.'

'Why not do just that?'

'I'm so tempted.' Shani forced a giggle. 'You can't believe how tempted I am.'

'I'm all for it. But what about your supervisor at St Aquinas?'

'We're coming into the summer break. I can't see it being an issue. Have you finished the article you mentioned?'

'Virtually. Have you checked out my blog?'

'Not since I arrived, but I'll do so this evening.' Shani got up from the bed, fighting off the temptation to mention Serghei. 'Massive love, Nicolas.'

'Likewise. I'll call tomorrow, Shani.'

'Okay – hear from you then.'

Shani sat back down on the bed and wiped her eyes.

Oh, God, she told herself, *what an absolute mess!*

What had the couple been arguing about? How to get rid of the body? If they had committed the act themselves, they would be covered in blood. Or had they murdered Serghei, then changed their clothes…? No, they would change their clothes *after* they had prepared the body for removal from presumably the building itself – wrapping it up in sheets, or whatever. The woman had been quite insistent they'd nothing to do with it. She was bound to say that, though, far from expecting anyone to step into the room. But to make certain of eliminating the possibility, why hadn't they chained the metal gates together at the entrance to the lobby to prevent anyone from entering the hostel? Basic precaution, surely. Or had they, in fact, just discovered the body themselves moments before she entered the room?

Shani searched for flights out of Timişoara and came across a Wizz Air flight at 10:45 to Prague, via Vienna, for the following day. She'd flown with the budget airline before. She really needed to see dearest Dusana, who aside from being Andrei's housekeeper had become a stabilising force in her life. And that was precisely what she needed right now: a stabilising force.

The break-ins at St Aquinas and the Prague apartment had to be in some way tied into Serghei's murder – although she couldn't see how. Too much of a coincidence, otherwise. But why should she be of interest to them, whoever they might be? No sense to it at all... She realised she kept using plural pronouns *them* and *they*. It could, of course, be just an individual orchestrating the entire course of events, though likely to be male rather than female because of the strength required to achieve Serghei's mutilation to such gruesome effect.

Shani bundled the clothes that she'd worn when visiting the hostel into a spare carrier bag, including – with huge reluctance – her cotton jacket. As an alternative, she would use the green Pac-a-Mac tucked inside a side-pocket on her backpack. Before leaving the room, she replied to the Home Bursar's email, stating that she hadn't left her study in the state as found.

While walking up the street and with the cemetery's boundary wall in sight, she came across a virtually empty bin and dumped the carrier bag inside – and felt better for doing so. But if only she could wipe the image of Serghei from her mind as effectively. Not in a million years! She entered the cemetery and headed towards her parents' grave. She didn't care if anyone noticed her and made the connection. She needed to speak to her parents as a matter of urgency.

The sun had started to peek out from the overcast sky as she followed the path away from the domed chapel. What the weather was doing was the least of her concerns. Where was Serghei now? What had they done with his body? Discarded it as if he were a piece of trash? Or had the police finally been called? If so, had her name been mentioned to them? She wanted to go back, in part to see if Daniela was there.

Shani arrived at the grave and knelt, surrounding gravestones concealing her from the administration offices nearby. She started crying and wondered why she hadn't cried at the guest house. There had just been a moment of moisture in her eyes while speaking to Nicolas but now she was sobbing uncontrollably, unable to utter a single word. She found a tissue in her Jhola shoulder bag, the one item she'd been unable to abandon – a graduation gift from the girls she had shared a house with before moving into St Aquinas. She blew her nose, and managed finally to settle herself.

'I never came yesterday. I'm sorry. After walking around the old quarter, I was quite tired. I did meet Serghei, but since then something dreadful has happened.' Shani gave a cautious glance around herself. Reassured that she was quite alone, she turned back to the slightly crooked wooden cross. 'He texted me to say he had found Mario Nemescu's address. I asked him for it, but he didn't respond. So I went to visit him. I don't want to describe the state I found him in, except to say he's dead. I'm in shock. I still don't have Mario's address. On top of all this, Andrei's apartment has been broken into and so has my college study in Oxford. I'm uncertain as to whether everything is connected. I want to tell Nicolas but there's a chance my phone has been hacked.

'I'm having to leave Romania. I'm sorry. I will be back – with Nicolas. You'll get to meet him. You'll be thrilled. He's perfect for me. But there is something that I'm puzzled by. Lucian, I know you gave a copy of the folder's contents that Andrei found in the wreckage of the plane that came down to Mario, in the hope he might decipher it. I believe he did so in part. The question I'm left with is…what happened to the original folder? Is it in any way connected to these recent events? Does someone believe that I might have it? If only you could tell me – or give me a sign – where you left it. I know I sound as if I'm crazy, but I'm clutching at straws. I'm desperate, and very upset. I need to know who is behind all that's going on – unless it *is* just a stream of coincidences. Either way, Serghei has left this world.

'I don't think it will be long before I'm back. I need to find Mario, but I'll have Nicolas helping me. He's a journalist, so we should get to the bottom of things quite quickly.'

Shani stood, kissed the tips of her fingers on her right hand and touched the cross. 'With love, always.'

Walking away from the grave, she decided on the spur of the moment she might sit quietly inside the first church she came to, saddened that she was having to leave Timişoara under such unpleasant circumstances.

Her personal safety was paramount, though.

CHAPTER 13

After more 'topsy-turvy' deliberation throughout the previous afternoon, she chose to stay the night at the guest house. It was comfortable, quiet, and without CCTV as opposed to the airport's lounge. She'd hardly slept, constantly tossing and turning, which came as no surprise to her. Noticing the time to be two o'clock in the morning, she took three paracetamols out of desperation. The effect was minimal, but she had the feeling she might have drifted off for an hour.

Everything was now packed in her backpack, ready for the flight. Breakfast? She wasn't in the least hungry and could grab a coffee at the airport. The strange thing was – as she cast a final glance around the room to check she hadn't left anything – it felt as though the image of Serghei's mutilated body had originated from a film she might have seen rather than from reality, as if her mind were attempting to interpret the horror in a way that made it more 'manageable'.

Taking the key off the dresser, Shani hooked her backpack onto her shoulder, shut the door to the room she would never again occupy and went downstairs. While waiting around at the reception desk for the owner to appear, she told herself that, regardless of how her mind was trying to fix the matter, she was going to have to live with that image for the rest of her life – day in, day out.

She found she still had to keep moving.

Finally, Shani put her head around the breakfast room door. The owner was chatting to the elderly couple from the UK over by the window.

'Ah...' The man came towards her, before noticing her backpack. 'No more days? Three more, no?'

'Sorry, no,' Shani replied. 'Urgent business in England. I will be returning, though. My passport, yes?'

'Of course, Miss Bălcescu... Oh, for you!' The owner took an envelope from inside the passport's frayed cover. 'Came yesterday night.'

Shani took the envelope, instantly curious. Daniela, perhaps? 'Did you see the person?'

'No, no. Letter slot in gate. I find this morning.'

'I see. Thank you.' Shani dropped the envelope and passport into her shoulder bag. She would open the message in the street lest she were about to be hit by another unearthly shock. She extended her hand. 'I will leave now for the airport.'

'Taxi-cab, no?'

'I will walk the street first. Such a pleasant street. All the trees. Very beautiful.'

* * *

Shani made her way up the street, taking the envelope from her bag.

Miss Shani Bălcescu
(RESIDENT)

The writing looked elegant, with a slight flourish. It could only be Daniela, surely? Why hadn't she rung the bell? Perhaps it was late at night or in the early hours when she delivered it. On the other hand, she didn't think she'd mentioned where she was staying – to her, or Serghei. She stopped walking and opened the envelope.

SKID ROW CAFÉ, 11am
What in God's name...?

Her flight was at 10:45. It was now 8:30. Shani swiftly located the café on Google. It was on Strada Mărășești, the opposite end to the Opera House in

Timişoara's main square – the more affordable end of Strada Mărăşeşti, she imagined. It wasn't far away, ten minutes perhaps by cab if there were no hold-ups with the traffic. She would go there straightaway and investigate, find out what the hell the note meant and how the person who delivered it knew where she was staying – the mystery being too arresting for her to dismiss it out of hand.

Reaching the highway, she only had to wait a couple of minutes for a cab. Her guess proved to be virtually on the mark, the journey taking less than a quarter of an hour, despite the rush-hour traffic. Skid Row's entrance proved to be on the corner of Strada Mărăşeşti. Shani paid the driver, swung her backpack onto her left shoulder and didn't move from her vantage point alongside the entrance to a sportswear shop. Nicolas, she was certain, would advise her to scan the area before committing herself. She checked her phone. The café's main window faced a busy street beyond which, according to her app, lay Timişoara's botanical gardens – hidden from view by an assortment of shrubs and trees firing off a medley of deciduous colours. All very interesting, thought Shani, but she hadn't the time to cross the street and take a closer look. Turning back to Strada Mărăşeşti, she watched a perfectly ordinary middle-aged couple enter the café. Moments later, two men and a woman left, different people altogether – the woman smoking a cigarette, chatting away between puffs as they walked past her. Over a period of five minutes, the flow of customers was steady for the time of day. She imagined the owner to be making a reasonable living.

Leaving the sportswear shop, she realised there were no tables or chairs out on the pavement. No immediate escape route, then. Perhaps outdoor furniture wasn't allowed on either street. Whatever, one thing was for certain, she needed to get a move on if she was going to make her flight – and she was desperate to make it!

Inside the café, the unshaven twenty-something man behind the counter gave her a broad smile, not quite a grin. Shani withdrew the slip of paper from the envelope and laid it out on the counter. 'Any ideas?' she asked.

The man stared at it and scratched his head. Turning to a plastic curtain on his left he shouted, '*Victore, te caută cineva!*' Looking at Shani, he started smiling again. 'Where from?'

'Czech Republic,' said Shani.

'Czech Republic?' beamed the man. 'All Czech girls pretty like you?'

Shani avoided rolling her eyes since she wasn't sure of the situation curiosity had drawn her into. She tilted her head at a vacant table. 'I sit.'

'Okay...' said the man with a mournful shrug, before turning back to the plastic curtain. '*Victore!*'

Shani swung her backpack from off her shoulder and sat at the table. It was now 9:15. She put her phone away. An hour and half until she was expected to appear at the Wizz Air check-in desk. She looked around. The majority of the tables were busy. A waitress came from behind her, carrying three croissants on a tray with espresso coffees – a radio or some other device starting up in the background, level in volume with the chitter-chatter. She recognised the song as being *Thunder*, by Imagine Dragons.

'Shani? Yes?'

Shani looked up. The man before her, wearing an apron and smelling of cooking fat and cigarettes, wore a smile not dissimilar to the smile Casanova over by the till had greeted her with. They might even have been brothers.

'I'm Shani,' she said.

'Victor.'

Shani shook the proffered hand and showed him the message. 'Is this something to do with you? If it is, what is the meaning of it? I'm leaving today. Check-in for my flight is in just over an hour—'

'No, no, no. No leave.'

'Pardon?'

'No flight.' Victor's hands gesticulated into life. 'Problem.'

'Problem? What are you talking about?' demanded Shani. 'Thirty seconds to explain before I leave. You understand me?'

Taking a phone from his apron, Victor made a call, speaking rapidly as if agitated for several seconds – before a pause, followed by a calm response from him to whoever it was on the other end. Returning the phone to his apron, he said, 'How much?'

'I'm sorry?' Shani was mystified, yet wholly intrigued.

'How much? Flight... How much?'

'One-seventy. Why do you ask?'

'English money?'

'Yes. English pounds.'

Victor left the table and Shani watched him disappear behind the plastic curtain. Then it was Casanova's turn to visit the table, bringing two coffees. Shani feared he was about to sit down and make suggestive remarks, punctuated by equally suggestive grins, but he veered away instead and returned to the till.

Victor reappeared, presenting her with an envelope.

'Twelve hundred lei. No flight.' With that, he went to the front of the café and looked outside, turning his head frequently from left to right. After a minute of doing this, he then joined the pavement in front of the window. Was he waiting for someone, wondered Shani, or was this just a daily habit?

She turned away and peered inside the envelope. A wad of paper money. What the hell was this about? Why such mystery…? In part, she supposed, that might be due to a lack of communication, which only the presence of an interpreter could fix.

Victor returned, sat at the table and sipped coffee, gesturing for Shani to do the same. 'How you come here?' he asked.

Shani found herself to be suspicious of the coffee and decided she mustn't drink any of it. 'I came by cab.'

'Okay. Your coffee?'

'I hardly drink coffee,' she lied.

'Tea? English tea?'

'I'm fine. Thank you.' Shani tapped the message that had been delivered to the guest house. 'But I want to know what this is about. And why you have reimbursed my flight.' She shook the envelope. 'This money. Why?'

Victor nodded. 'Yes. No flight.' He finished his coffee and motioned for Shani to stand while lifting up her backpack. 'Follow.'

Shani weighed up the risks. The café seemed legit, the people behind and in front of the counter ordinary enough. All the same, as she rose from the chair, she dipped her hand into her shoulder bag and located the bunch of keys for Andrei's apartment. With the longest key now protruding between her clenched fingers, she followed Victor past Casanova, through the plastic curtain and into a kitchen, where the waitress she'd seen moments ago was leaning against a worktop, smoking. Victor said something to her in Romanian. The girl shrugged and carried on smoking. Exiting the kitchen through an archway, Shani followed Victor down a short corridor towards a plain door.

She dropped back slightly. If he threatened her, she would go straight for his eyes with the key – a jab so fast he wouldn't see it coming! Victor opened the door, and Shani found herself stepping into a narrow garage. A blue and white motorbike stood in the middle of it. Her heart lifted and her fingers unconsciously let go of the bunch of keys as she took in the sight, recognising the bike as being a Suzuki 750cc model. Not her dream bike; in the past that had always been the MV Agusta – until recently, when a Norton V4 purchased by a biker friend caught her eye. That aside, she knew this particular specimen took some beating, and from first impressions it looked to be in mint condition. All concerns about her flight evaporated as she keenly ran her hand over the seat and on towards the throttle. She turned to Victor.

'In the UK, I own a six-fifty Kawasaki Ninja.'

Victor nodded. 'Yes. Kawasaki.'

'But why show me this? How do you know I have an interest in bikes?'

Victor gestured that she should follow him over to a workbench. On a piece of paper, he drew an X and pointed at the bike. This he followed with another gesture, asking her to imagine the garage door to be wide open. 'Understand?'

'I think so,' she said. 'But you want me to ride this bike from here – this X – to where?'

Victor returned to the piece of paper, his scribbling resembling the bike being ridden as if losing someone pursuing it. 'Okay?'

'Make sure no one follows me, I'm guessing?'

'No follow. Yes.'

At the far end of the bench glistened a metallic-blue helmet, which Victor handed to Shani.

'But where am I supposed to be riding the bike to?' she asked. 'And for what reason?'

Returning to the bike, Victor tapped an address code into the GPS system. 'But this…' He waved his right hand and scribbled in mid-air, reiterating there was a chance she might pick up a shadow.

'What's at this address?' asked Shani, telling herself an interpreter really should have been made available – although, admittedly, she'd arrived a couple of hours earlier than expected.

'Yes, address,' said Victor.

The fact that she was being offered such a bike dispersed much of her suspicion that she was being set-up in some way, the Suzuki itself a form of security. Impossible as it was to have an in-depth conversation with Victor, he seemed a decent sort of a guy. And he had reimbursed her flight.

'All right,' she agreed. She pointed at her backpack. 'I leave here, okay?'

'Okay,' nodded Victor. 'Passport?'

Shani patted her shoulder bag. 'In here.' She started putting on the helmet. Had she not opted for the pixie hairdo then she imagined it would have been a perfect fit. While adjusting the strap, she watched

Victor proceed with the start-up. No key was required. Instead, the bike used a customised fob ignition system – which duly kicked in. The guttural growl was massive, in part due to the confined space but also, she suspected, the baffles inside the exhaust system having been modified in some way, making the silencer virtually redundant. It made her question whether the machine was street-legal. When Victor blipped the throttle, she felt her internal organs vibrate, the sound alone discharging adrenaline into her bloodstream. Raw paradise!

Shani straddled the Suzuki and took over the throttle from Victor, who ran the wire from the GPS system to the socket on the helmet. She realised it was still in Romanian-mode. She lifted the visor. 'I need English – or Czech.'

Victor gave a nod and reprogrammed the system.

This was becoming so weird, thought Shani. But, hey, to tame this monster of a Suzuki was going to be the equivalent to a rodeo on a spirited mustang. She had no idea where the GPS was going to take her, but more than anything she wanted to head out into the countryside and open up the throttle. She cut down the revs to tick over. 'I need my coat from my backpack,' she shouted. 'And have you gloves?'

Victor's brow creased over.

'Gloves?'

'Yes, yes. And?'

Shani pretended to put on a jacket and pointed to her backpack.

Victor raised a thumb. 'Okay.'

She would have preferred the protection of leathers rather than the Pac-a-Mac Victor was taking from her backpack. But at least she had gloves, and a reasonable fit they were, too. Hitting the tarmac with bare hands was every biker's nightmare.

Victor carefully drew the Pac-a-Mac's zip up under the helmet to her chin before making an OK sign with his thumb and index finger.

Shani nodded and blipped the throttle while anxiously watching the electronic door fold up into the ceiling, her concern intensifying over Victor's gesticulation that she might be under surveillance once she left the garage. Could that be why he'd stood outside the café, watching the street? To seek out signs of her having been followed there?

Whatever! Leaving the matter of 'why' at that, Shani veered across the garage towards Victor, giving him a friendly tap on the shoulder before making her way out onto the street. The GPS system reintroduced her to Strada Gheorghe Dima, which appeared to be more hectic now than when she'd first set eyes on it outside the sportswear shop.

Shani dropped the tinted vizor and blipped the throttle again, now convinced that the exhaust was illegal. If she was pulled aside by the police, what then? She'd have to leg it, confident this beauty could outpace any police car or bike. She flicked up into second gear to drop the revs and swept past the botanical gardens.

Questions abounded... The whole set-up was too bizarre for words. She could have refused, walked away from Skid Row Café, but she rather liked Victor, his nature altogether respectful. For a brief half-hour, Serghei's horrific murder had ebbed from her mind. Whom had Victor spoken to over his phone, though? She tried to join the dots.

1944: Plane crash. Lend-Lease. Folder. Andrei.

1993: Her father, Lucian. Folder rediscovered. Year she was born. Year her parents died.

And now, so far to date, two break-ins, a hideous murder and a journey into the unknown – in more ways than one. Question: did the folder link everything together, recent events in particular? It now seemed pretty clear-cut to her that it did. But surely it had nothing to do with her parents' deaths. A measure of panic combined with probable inexperience on the part of a policeman were to blame, more or less confirmed by footage on both the video she'd discovered in Andrei's safe and what had been uploaded onto social media.

Another five minutes, decided Shani, and she would leave the quiet side roads she'd been riding through and abide by the female stereo voice in her ears. She must have heard 'recalculating' at least fifty or more times. Victor's instruction to avoid a possible tail made her wonder whether she'd been followed from the airport. If so, by whom and for what reason? Did they believe she'd inherited this wretched folder? Had they followed her to the hostel, and by so doing had she given away Serghei's precise location? How did whoever had delivered the note to the guest house know that she was booked in there? Had they found out from some register – a governmental central hub that owners of hotels and so forth were required to send passport details of their guests to by law?

Shani began to obey the instructions coming through the helmet's speakers. She found herself heading west, merging onto a road with tramlines running adjacent on her right. The traffic frustrated her, as she desperately wanted to open up the Suzuki. After several kilometres, she was given the opportunity: a section of dual-carriageway. She climbed through the gears, the initial surge of acceleration giving her a hefty jolt, her arms wanting to extend themselves as she fought against the G-force compressing against her chest and shoulders. She found the bike to be much snappier and yet just as nimble as her Kawasaki back in Oxford. An unexpected series of bends loomed ahead, and as she snaked through them she shifted her weight from side to side to become at one with the balance of the bike. Another stretch of dual-carriageway…

Take the first turning on the left, interrupted the GPS.

Damn it! The Suzuki had virtually freed up her mind from the traumas of the past twenty-four hours. She snicked down from sixth gear, blipping the throttle between each shift – the engine so positive, as if it were teasing her, willing her to give it a caning and take it over two-hundred kilometres an hour. If she'd had a set of leathers she would have been up for it, but now she was back in first gear, running the bike down a clear road, detached suburban houses on either side.

Just as she realised she was heading into a cul-de-sac:

You have now reached your destination.

CHAPTER 14

Shani coasted to a standstill and cut the Suzuki's engine. She looked around. Trees, cultivated front gardens, a man mowing a lawn over on her left while glancing occasionally across at her. She took off the helmet and for a brief moment, believing she still had long hair, shook her head. The sun was out, the sky a passive blue, but Serghei's horrific murder wrecked the feeling of wellbeing she would otherwise have surely felt – despite the all-consuming mystery presented to her at Skid Row Café.

Some hundred metres away, at the base of the cul-de-sac and a small copse of trees, a figure emerged and started to walk towards her. Shirt sleeves rolled up, black slacks and darkish hair – male rather than female, she gauged, by the way he sauntered. A definite confidence about him. Then he stopped and waved her towards himself.

Like hell! He was going to have to come the full distance, decided Shani, with the man mowing the lawn being a possible witness. She secured the strap on the helmet and hooked it onto her forearm, the ignition fob held tightly in her left hand – ready for an immediate retreat.

The gap between them was now reduced to twenty metres, or thereabouts... He was of average height, middle-aged and very lean – a guy who looked after himself. Maybe he worked out, although she imagined he didn't have to, being fortunate enough to have the kind of physique that required little maintenance.

'So...' The man had almost reached her. 'So, here you are, Shani. Shani Bălcescu, right?'

'Right. And you?'

'Oh, just Mario. You have heard of me?' His English was practically flawless.

Shani found herself to be bewildered. 'Mario Nemescu?'

'That's me.'

His teeth were as near perfect as his English, clearly as fortunate with them as he was with his body – or he'd paid for dental work, or perhaps even a costly set of dentures. His cheeks were lightly pockmarked. Nothing he could have done about that, she supposed. 'I was hoping to find you,' she said at length.

'I can understand that. But you're going to have to start trusting me, or are we going to spend the rest of the day confusing that man cutting the lawn? He's a total busybody.'

'How did you find me?'

'Someone trying to bullshit me, that's how.'

Shani bit her bottom lip. Sure, he had a story to tell her. Did he know anything about Serghei's fate? Had he had anything to *do* with it?

'Am I going to have to repeat what I've just—'

'Climb aboard. You live at the end of this road?'

'Yes, I actually do. Okay?'

'Fine,' said Shani, dismissing what she detected as being a trace of sarcasm. 'They should have given me your name at the café.'

Mario hesitated before mounting the bike. 'I told them not to.'

'Why?'

'I wasn't sure what rumours you'd picked up about me.'

'Sounds ominous, I have to say.'

'Ominous or not, the fact remains, I knew your parents – in a good way.'

'I only have your word on that.'

'Then we have to return to where we started. You have to find it in yourself to trust me, agreed?'

'Then climb aboard, for God's sake!' Leaving the helmet hooked on her arm, Shani drifted the bike in first gear down past the copse of trees to a gravel drive, some flowering dandelions showing through. She leaned the bike on its stand alongside a mud-spattered BMW and stood back to survey the house itself with its pale blue brickwork. The design was interesting, not the characterless four-walled buildings with adjoining garages in the road itself, having evidently been built in a different era, possibly pre-war. It perhaps resembled more of a cottage, a vine of some kind climbing in parts up to the first floor.

'How long have you lived here?' Shani asked.

'Here? Ten years, maybe twelve—'

'You know Serghei, don't you? Serghei Sapdaru.'

'Coincidence, really. Had a text from him only two days ago. Of course, in truth I doubt it was from him.'

'What do you mean?'

'Coffee, tea, or perhaps a beer? Let's go for beer—'

'I'm sorry to tell you, he's dead,' said Shani. 'Murdered. I still can't believe it.'

'Serghei Sapdaru, murdered?' There wasn't so much as a flicker of shock in Mario Nemescu's eyes. 'Well, there's a surprise.' He dropped his hands into his trouser pockets and idly drew a semi-circle with the tip of his scuffed shoe in the gravel. 'What a shame,' he said, turning to her, 'that I have no champagne.'

Shani stared at the man, initially speechless – unnerved by his remark. This 'Mario Nemescu' was evidently something else! 'What the hell are you talking about?' she shouted, keeping a firm grip on the ignition fob in her left hand. 'He's dead. I repeat, *murdered*. I witnessed the end result. It was horrific!'

Mario put his hand gently on her shoulder. 'Shani, let's go and have that beer.'

'I don't think so,' reacted Shani. 'I'm not entirely confident about trusting you.'

'That's a shame.'

'Can you blame me? Who do you have in there?'

'No one, apart from a few hens out the back.'

Shani met his eyes, pale blue – and, yes, interesting. Quite soulful, in fact. 'You're asking a lot from me. I mean, why should I trust you? I don't really know you. Just your name—'

'And that I knew Lucian and Zinsa, and that you've met my children.'

'Skid Row Café?'

'Absolutely.'

'Oh…' A measure of calm as Shani recalled 'Casanova' at the till. 'One of them certainly likes to chat up the girls.'

'Cosmin.' Mario shrugged. 'A weakness he has. But a healthy one at his age, you could say. He was impolite?'

'Not at all… You were inviting me inside.'

Shani found the cottage to be rustic but cosy, richly hued fabrics scattered around to give it a Bohemian edge – all of which helped to further calm her nerves. She was taken into the kitchen: a green cooking range, chairs and a mighty oak table that she doubted had been bought from a catalogue. She watched as Mario put pint-sized glasses on the table and reached for the glass jug on the worktop. Answers were going to flow from this man, she hoped, like the beer he was pouring. In fact, they had better – otherwise she would leave. She simply wasn't in the mood to take time-wasting from anyone.

'Have you made that yourself?' she asked.

'Sure have. A by-product of permaculture.'

'Perma…?'

'Culture. I'll show you later. Take a seat.'

'Thank you.' Shani put Victor's helmet on the table and chose a chair with a cushion. 'I have scores of questions. More so now than when I arrived, in point of fact.'

'Of course. But I wanted you to see this place – to see the real me.'

'It's lovely,' warmed Shani. And it was, the décor gentle on the eye. The furniture unpretentious, comfortable. She told Mario so.

'Good. That's how I like my visitors to see it. But we're only staying here tonight. Tomorrow, we're heading back into the city.'

'Why?'

Mario handed her a glass. 'A shade cloudy, but don't concern yourself. It's just the style of the beer.' He sat opposite and began to roll a cigarette, elbows resting on the table. 'Mario Nemescu lives at two addresses. This is my private – *very* private – address.'

Shani nodded attentively. 'Okay…' She watched him lick the slip of paper and complete the cigarette-rolling process with deft fingers. 'I'm listening.'

'Mario Nemescu, the businessman, has an address in town. You see, these days I relish my privacy. In fact, I am immensely protective of it. In the past, the authorities frequently checked me out. Two lives, same person.'

Here we go... Shani felt the growing sense of calmness fall away. The fob was still within reach, on the table in front of her. Serghei had labelled him as being untrustworthy. 'Why should the authorities feel a need to check you out?' she asked.

'I did say *in the past*. Dealing here and there, this and that. Buying low, selling high, as it were...and, on occasion, brushing up against the law.'

'Okay, so why are you telling me this?' Shani noted a distinct pattern emerging: every question answered became two more to be asked. 'Why didn't the GPS direct me to Mario Nemescu's city apartment, or whatever it is you have in town?'

'Because I owe it to your father that I get you to trust me.' Mario lit the cigarette with a plastic lighter and quietly shook his head. 'Plastic,' he muttered soberly. 'Like so much of what we invent, the positive effect frequently becomes a harmful negative, blighting the environment, as a consequence of our inattention.'

'Indeed,' agreed Shani absently. 'You were saying?'

Mario looked up, as if suddenly aware he had company. 'I was saying that from the day Lucian was tragically killed, I've been haunted by the fact that it is likely he believed I had cheated him, that I hawked around the city a document he gave me, hoping to sell it to the highest bidder. It wasn't the case.'

Shani sat up, all ears. 'By document, you mean a photocopy of what was found in the wreckage of the plane that came down in 1944?'

'Yes. Did Lucian's father tell you about the plane crash?'

'No. He never told me anything about Romania. Serghei told me when I visited him two days ago. And while we're on the subject of Serghei, why so much animosity towards him? At least, that's how it came across out there on the drive.'

Mario drank some beer and gestured for Shani to try it. 'Give me your opinion – *honest* opinion.'

Shani took a sip, then another to make certain its palatable effect hadn't deceived her. 'Has something of a Guinness flavour. That's the drink I usually go for if I'm at a pub. It's got body to it.' She took another sip. 'And a kind of quirky bitterness that's not unpleasant. It has depth and makes me want to drink more. Verging on the moreish, in fact. There!'

'Moreish? Not sure I've come across this word.'

'It usually relates to food rather than drink. So very pleasant you just want to continue, regardless.'

'Okay.' Mario twisted his mouth. 'Nevertheless, I sense room for improvement.'

'I'm giving you eight out of ten. The second glass and it could go either side – seven or nine. The chances are, it won't be another eight.'

'You know, you're so like your parents as I remember them. And you have the high cheekbones your mother had.'

'I've been told that before. I never tire of people telling me, though.'

Mario topped up their glasses. 'We need to put structure to this, Shani. Take a thread at a time, if you like. And with luck a clear picture of what has happened and all that's happening now will emerge. As I mentioned, I received a text from Serghei – but I don't believe he sent it. I'll explain in a moment. But I suggest we start with when you first heard from Serghei.'

'It was after I returned to the UK from Séroulé. I was involved in a *coup d'état* out there.'

'Where your mother came from. Yes, I know. It's been in the papers over here that you were involved.'

'That doesn't come as a surprise. Anyway, I received a near indecipherable text from Serghei. I'd never heard of him. But when he said he was close to my parents, then obviously it caught my attention.

The coup and my previous visit to Timişoara meant the wider world had become aware that I was the daughter of Lucian and Zinsa. Someone took my picture at their graveside – an employee of the cemetery, I suspect – and evidently sold it to a newspaper.'

'I read the article,' said Mario. 'The one with the picture.'

'I don't quite know how Serghei got my number. The porters' lodge at St Aquinas College, where I'm a Fellow, might have given it to him, although the porters are not supposed to disclose personal details.'

'And you came to Timişoara on the strength of that?'

'Yes. I saw it as an opportunity to find other people who knew my parents. I mean, I was wary about meeting Serghei. It crossed my mind it might be a journalistic set-up. But as it turned out, it wasn't.'

'So, you met him. Where? At a café?'

'At a hostel in a relatively poor district. There's a girl who works there called Daniela. She acted as interpreter.'

'Was he in good health? I haven't seen or heard from him in over twenty years.'

Shani took a sip of Mario's earthy beer. 'He looked frail. I'm guessing he was around forty-five years old. Same as you, perhaps. Although he looked much older.'

'We were in the same form at school as your parents. I'm forty-four.'

'You've weathered well,' said Shani, and meant it. His face, far from being craggy and lived-in like Serghei's, still projected a semblance of youth within in its angular structure.

'It's taken time to get my health back into shape, but that's another story.' Mario held up the rolled cigarette. 'As you can see, my weakness is tobacco. What did Serghei have to say for himself?'

'He went to prison for fifteen years in Cluj, which I think broke his health.'

'It was well on the way to being broken before he went to prison,' disclosed Mario. 'Of that I can assure you.'

'He talked about my parents, their friendship. He gave me a photograph.' Shani delved into her shoulder bag. 'Here…' She pushed the photograph across the table, watching Mario's face carefully for a reaction, since he'd yet to explain his animosity towards Serghei.

'Happy days,' smiled Mario, and handed back the photograph. 'So, he talked about the plane crash and what Lucian's father found in the wreckage?'

'Yes. At that point he mentioned you, and that my father showed you the folder Andrei found because he and Serghei thought you might be able to decipher the file inside it.'

'They showed me the folder. A few days later – or perhaps even the next day, I can't remember precisely – your father handed me a photocopy of the contents, which I started to work on. It was a relatively easy code to crack – not that I managed to get beyond the first few pages before I was arrested.'

'Arrested?'

'Let's take a break. Freshly baked bread, home-grown salad and some organic chicken. Are you up for that?'

'Actually, Mario,' said Shani, with a sense of candid relief, 'I'm starving.'

CHAPTER 15

The table under the vine at the rear of the cottage was quite rickety but served its purpose. They laid out the food they'd prepared together. The sun shone brightly, and the garden had caught Shani's attention: lots of canes with various leafy plants between narrow paths bristling with intrigue as they wound their way into the distance.

'I'm presuming this to be permaculture?' asked Shani.

'Indeed, precisely that.' Mario took a seat and beckoned for Shani to do the same. 'The principle behind permaculture is to develop ecosystems with sustainability and self-sufficiency in mind. That's the goal. There's no need for these toxic chemicals the multinationals are spewing onto the soil. We've now reached a point whereby the earth has become virtually infertile.'

Shani broke off a piece of bread. 'I've always thought that if nature finds a sore on its skin it will identify the culprit and delete it from evolution. By that, I mean we are that sore.'

'I doubt if anyone with a gram of common sense would argue with that, Shani.'

Shani forked salad leaves and a few slices of tomato onto her plate. 'So, you were in the same form as my parents at school?'

'For a time.' Mario smiled across the table. 'I was thrown out. Not my proudest hour.'

'Why, may I ask?'

'I hit a male teacher, who tried to come on to me – if you get my drift.'

Shani sat back, the sun like a silken wave on her skin. 'Why the animosity over Serghei? Or is it a personal issue?'

'When it comes to you, Shani, nothing is personal. As I mentioned earlier, I owe it to your father that you trust me.' Mario wiped his lips and joined Shani by sitting back in the sun. 'In those days, Serghei was working for me – up to a point. And it was through Serghei that I reconnected with Lucian. I was dealing in this and that.'

'Drugs?' Shani asked, hoping Mario would say 'no'.

'A little. Just weed, as it happened. If harder drugs had come my way at the right price, then I might have been tempted to go down that route, although the dealers were far more vicious. That's the route Serghei took, and came unstuck. He tried – and nearly succeeded – to put the blame on me, blowing open half my network in the process. I managed to secure three alibis by calling in favours. The alibis were, in fact, fake. Thanks to my acquaintances, I avoided prison. And that was the last I heard of Serghei, apart from a rumour that he got arrested and a court up in Cluj threw the book at him. I didn't bother to find out the details.'

'I see... You hate him for what he did. That he was quite prepared to put you in prison rather than himself?'

'Hatred's a negative force, Shani. I simply forgot about him. But you mentioned you visited him again, only to find him dead?'

'It was awful.' Shani returned her glass of beer to the table. 'More than awful. Horrific.'

'Was he expecting you?'

'At the time I left him on the first occasion, we hadn't set a date. He sent me a text yesterday morning, informing me that he had your address. So I asked him for it. When I didn't receive a reply, I decided to visit him. The door to the hostel was open, as it had been the day before. On my first visit there was an old man watching television at the reception desk – if you could call it a desk. More like a foldaway table. He didn't seem to be around yesterday. I called for Daniela. With no answer, I climbed the stairs. As I drew closer to Serghei's room, I heard two people arguing. I went inside…' Shani could barely bring herself to describe what she saw, but did so in as much detail as she could recall with the hope that offloading it might benefit her emotionally.

Mario was noticeably shaken, the roll-up cigarette he'd just lit held in mid-air long enough for it to go out, eyes all the while fixed on Shani, mouth agape. Then, finally: 'I'm sorry you came across such an appalling act of violence.'

'There were no police,' said Shani. 'The street hadn't been sealed off. I'm presuming the couple I saw were the owners. I'm sure they didn't do it. The woman was adamant. I don't recall blood on their clothes.'

'I need the address, Shani.'

Shani scrolled through her phone. 'Here. From Serghei, before I left England.'

Mario took his phone from a trouser pocket and made a brief call, giving the individual the address direct from Shani's phone. 'Before too long, hopefully we'll have an answer as to the couple's role in this.'

'Do you think Serghei was murdered as a consequence of his past catching up with him? Or that he had started drug-running again?'

'No.' Mario put away his phone. 'There are forces at work here. I believe we're both being set up. I doubt whether Serghei would have contacted you had he not been told to do so. Did he ask for money from you?'

'No. No favours at all.'

'I believe he was under pressure to send you those texts. As I think I told you, I received a text from him, giving me the address of where you've been staying.'

'But I'm ninety-nine percent certain I never gave him the address of the guest house.'

'Then you've been followed. We have been brought together for a reason.'

'What precisely *is* the reason, Mario? The folder?'

'Yes. It can only be that, which I have to admit astonishes me. Days before your parents were killed, I was arrested on a false charge of shoplifting. It was easy enough disprove because the school itself supported my claim – that I couldn't have been in two places at the same time. That said, I was still taken to the police station. I was locked up for five days. They wanted me to try and decode the photocopy Lucian gave me, but I lied and told them it was beyond me. My guess has always been that they wanted to take me out of the frame while they watched your father – who he spoke to, and so on. But their operation ended when Lucian was shot on Strada Michelangelo, a bridge that spans the Bega River.'

'Yes, I know. Boulevard Vasile Pârvan is nearby, which gave me the clue when I first saw the footage that they'd died here, in Timișoara.' Shani looked away and gazed into the garden. Birds singing. So heavenly. Maybe this was the answer: to live her life with Nicolas in a similar fashion. She turned back to Mario. 'There's no sense to it. Why such an intricate campaign? We're talking about something that goes back years – nearly eighty years. I mean, what did you learn from the photocopy Lucian handed to you?'

'I only had time to decode a page or two before I was arrested.'

'Serghei mentioned something about a unit of hitmen – or assassins.'

'That was on the first page. I had the impression it was linked directly to Deep State.'

'Deep State?'

'American terminology – although it's used globally these days, and more often than not misinterpreted.'

'Explain.'

'Deep State basically describes a clique of bankers and heads of multinational companies united in forming a world government for global control. By weakening countries with debt, and by instilling immorality and division on every level they can then funnel governments into a programme of perpetual futility.'

Shani lifted a hand. 'Okay, okay, I know what you're talking about. Nicolas, my partner, who is still reporting out in Séroulé, is up to speed on that – as is Khamadi Soglo who led the rebels into crushing General Kuetey's regime.'

Mario nodded. 'I know. I listened to the speech Soglo gave with you sitting alongside him. I like how Soglo is refusing to pay back the country's debt, emphasising that much of it arose through loans coupled to sky-high interest rates formulated by foreign creditors.'

'The external debt will be printed and used to repair environmental damage and to educate people into…' Shani spread her hands. 'What you have here. Permaculture, and variants along that theme. To paraphrase Khamadi Soglo, the banks in Séroulé will no longer be allowed to make money out of thin air, as they do the world over. They'll only receive their finance from modest administrative charges, and nothing more than that.'

'How it should be, of course,' agreed Mario. 'A total rebalancing of the monetary system.'

'Khamadi believes banks will eventually adopt this practise, but only *after* the enslavement of humankind is complete. As it stands, it's impossible to pay off the global debt. When the entrapment, or enslavement, is complete it'll be wiped – according to Khamadi. Our way of thinking is that this debt should be printed immediately, and every cent ploughed into cleaning up the environment and reversing climate change.'

'Agreed, absolutely,' concurred Mario. 'But because Séroulé is attempting to get ahead of the game, as it were, and break the stranglehold, I'm assuming there's now a degree of fear in the country?'

'Oh, yes…fear of suicide bombers and extremists of all kinds being directed towards the country, in addition to mainstream media turning people's opinion against the interim government.' Shani reached for her glass. 'But we're not alone,' she added. 'We now have three other West African countries refusing to hand money over to those same creditors that crippled Séroulé.'

'Good. And, of course, what makes these people who spearhead Deep State all the more depraved than any dictator is that they know how to put it right.'

'To prevent "putting it right" from happening,' completed Shani. 'Correct?'

'Perfectly correct. But we're digressing.'

'Before we continue…' Shani raised her glass and pointed with her left hand towards it. 'Not seven, but nine out of ten.'

'So, still room for improvement?'

'Always room for improvement.'

'You never give a ten?'

'On friendship, I do.'

Mario smiled and relit his cigarette. 'So, I think we can establish we've been set up. For what? Finding the original folder.'

'Well, I can tell you the apartment where I lived with Andrei in Prague has been broken into and searched. So too has my study in Oxford.'

'Is Andrei still alive?'

'No. He died earlier this year. Heart attack. He'd had a couple of small ones before the big one.'

'I see... Well, this unknown force must be quite keen to get their hands on the folder – or rather, the contents of the folder, to put it mildly.'

'It makes me want to get out of the country. I mean, for God's sake, Mario, I don't know where this bloody folder is. Obviously it never went to Prague. Or if it did, there's no trace of it.'

'So it's still here. In Romania.'

'If it concerns Deep State, as you've described it to me, then there's stuff about the perils of globalisation on social media. I'm not into social media myself, but friends have shown me what people put on it.'

'And much of it likely to be inflammatory trash.'

'Then there has to be something about this folder that puts it on another level.'

'Agreed. But I'm truly puzzled by what they did to Serghei. Our unknown force wanted you to see it.'

'To frighten me? But why, Mario? Had I not received the note from you, I would be on my way back to England this minute – via Prague.'

'Why Prague?'

'To check up on the apartment and visit Dusana, Andrei's housekeeper.'

'And she's the one who discovered the break-in?'

'Yes.'

Mario nodded quietly, as if to himself. 'Like you, I don't see how we can find this folder,' he said. 'Did Lucian give it to another person, or what? Who knows? So, we have to go to where Mario Nemescu lives in the city, and wait and see what happens.'

'I'm not so sure I'm brave enough to do that, Mario. Not after seeing what they did to Serghei, assuming everything is connected.'

'Then you shall stay here. Let them believe you've disappeared. I take it you're in regular contact with Nicolas?'

'Yes. In fact, I'm due to call him.'

'You need a clean phone if you're going to discuss any of this with him. Is there an intermediary you can get in touch with in Séroulé?'

'Intermediary?'

'Someone to tell Nicolas to get himself a clean phone?'

'Yes. Monique would be a good choice. Khamadi Soglo's sidekick when it came to the coup.'

'Good. Then that's what you need to do, using the phone I'm going to give you.' Mario reached for her glass. 'Another?'

'Why not. Thank you.'

'The sun's left us. Take a path down the garden and you'll arrive at an arbour. It'll be in the sun. I'll fill these up and join you.'

Shani set off down the garden. Each step she took she instinctively knew that she couldn't stomach academia as a fulltime occupation anymore. Her heart wasn't into it in the least and it felt pointless to continue torturing herself over what she perceived as being an organic correction in her life. This was how she wanted to live: to make the switch from theoretical to practical – literally. She knew without a shadow of a doubt that she could learn much in the way of ingenuity and craftsmanship from the Séroulèse people, not to mention from the likes of Mario here in Romania.

She passed by a bed of baby courgettes, luminous yellow flowers still attached to them. Then, a series of runner beans climbing elegantly up their canes, followed by a shock sufficient enough to make her jump. A hen had seemingly arrived from nowhere at her feet. She reached down, and it allowed her to touch its feathers – smooth as silk.

Shani arrived at the arbour, the chicken having followed her, pecking and sifting through whatever as it did so – remnants of autumn, presumably. She sat on the seat, a wild climber like a clematis with mauve flowers anxious, so it seemed, to envelop the structure. Mario was making his way towards her, through this paradise, and she decided he really was a cool guy who appeared to have his life in perfect order. She stood up to take her glass from him.

'You're a lucky man to have this, Mario,' she said. 'Actually, I suppose the word "lucky" is likely to annoy you, since I'm sure you've put in a huge amount of effort.'

'It didn't come easily, Shani, I have to say.' He sat beside her and stretched out his legs. 'The first half, at least. In a way, it all kicked off with seeing Lucian again. I was something of a no-hoper. I liked Lucian. He had his priorities set in stone. I often think of him when I'm out here in the garden.'

'By priorities you mean Zinsa?'

'Without a doubt. When Lucian came to me with the folder, I was living in a part-basement room, employed as a caretaker at an English teaching school. After six months, I asked them for a pay rise and they refused. So I put it to them that they could give me free English lessons instead. They agreed. But it became more than that…I married the teacher and we had three children.' Mario smiled and turned to Shani. 'And, of course, you've met them. I'm not sure if you saw my daughter.'

'Does she smoke? A waitress there?'

'Yes.'

'Just briefly, as I was being led out the back by Victor to the garage.'

'Victor has a good head for business. Cosmin is wayward in comparison. He can't keep his eyes off the girls.'

Shani chuckled and sipped some beer. There was no denying Mario's words!

'Ana is waiting to go to university. In Bucharest. I'll miss her.'

'But your wife… I can't wait to meet her.'

'I'm afraid that's not possible.'

Shani felt a twinge in her chest. 'You're divorced?'

'No.' Mario glanced across at Shani, meeting her eyes. 'Twelve years ago, we scraped together enough to buy this place. It was a wreck of a building. Simona had a vision from the start, notably with the garden. She wanted to be as self-sufficient as possible. She tamed me, drove common sense into my thick skull.' Mario smiled wistfully. 'Took her a while to do that. But just as it started to sink in, she began to get headaches and double vision. It turned out she had a tumour. Malignant. They operated, but it came back. They operated again, and each time they operated they took something of Simona's personality away from her. Had I fully understood the consequences, I would never have allowed them to operate the second time.'

Without thinking, Shani put her arm around him. 'Enough. No more.' She left her glass on the seat and wiped the moisture from her eyes.

'I'm okay.' Mario cleared his throat of emotion. 'I made a vow…to continue to learn English, so that all Simona taught me wouldn't be wasted. I listen regularly to the BBC World Service, and whenever I'm in town I buy English newspapers.'

'So now, with me here, you can put it all into practice.'

'I did teach English myself for several years after Simona died. On reflection, I think I did so because occasionally it gave me the feeling Simona was at my side… Actually,' stirred Mario, 'I'm wondering if you might be nervous here on your own tomorrow. Yes?'

'It's crossed my mind,' said Shani.

'Then I'll have Victor come over while I try and find out what this unknown force consists of. Whether, for instance, there's a governmental element to it, or whether its roots extend internationally.'

'I like Victor,' said Shani. 'And now I know he's your son, I'm certain to like him more. How old are the boys?'

'They're twins, actually. Twenty years old. Victor has a steady girlfriend, but Cosmin seems to get through one a fortnight.'

'Was it Victor you spoke to about visiting the owners of the hostel?' asked Shani.

'Just to lean on them. Don't worry, there'll be no violence. Can you remember seeing CCTV in the place?'

'No. But I wasn't really looking out for it.'

Mario leaned back on the seat and sipped some beer. 'You're sleeping in the room I usually use,' he said. 'It has an en suite. Miniscule as it is, it does serve its purpose reasonably well.'

CHAPTER 16

The room to which Mario took her overlooked the garden. Shani turned from the window: bare wood furniture, a light shade of green on the walls. On the double bed a folded towel on top of a patchwork quilt. 'This is beautiful, Mario,' she said, her hand on her chest in awe. 'Pastel and bare wood. I love it. So restful on the eye.'

'If you sleep with the window open slightly, as I do, then you wake up to the birds singing. There can be no better way to wake up, in my opinion.'

'I'm with you on that, Mario. Definitely.'

'I'll be sleeping further down the corridor tonight, before reverting to Mario Nemescu's address in town.'

Shani met his eyes, concerned. 'Should we bother with doing this, Mario? I mean, it might endanger your tranquil life here. What then? As things stand, I feel I've made a friend today – a dear friend. I want to visit you, and bring Nicolas with me.'

Mario held up a hand. 'Shani, your emergence from obscurity has opened a can of worms...' He cocked his head. 'This is the correct analogy, yes? A can of worms?'

'I suppose it looks that way,' sighed Shani.

'Someone has gone to great lengths to tempt you over here, do what they did to Serghei, and bring us together. Is this unknown force going to let go?'

Shani nodded reluctantly. 'You have a point. And the break-ins – Prague, and my study.'

'Quite.' Then, interrupting the moment with a smile, Mario said, 'Let's prepare our evening meal. You can mark my homemade wine out of ten.'

* * *

It was to be a vegetable pie. Shani prepared and started to chop the home-grown vegetables: carrots, garlic, courgettes, onions, celery – straight from the garden. It was all making so much sense to her. 'I want to live like you, Mario,' she said aloud.

'The choice is yours, always.'

'Indeed, but I have to think of Nicolas. We need to make the choice together. What herbs do you have in mind to use?'

Mario busily worked the pastry into a ball, kneading it, then rolling it flat. 'Usual. Pepper, salt, fresh sage from the pot over there by the window. I'll add a spoonful of honey and a little butter.'

'Do you have a beehive?'

'Three, actually. There's a saying, from the bees themselves: *When we go, we're taking you all with us.*'

'Because if they disappear there'll be virtually no pollination?'

'Correct.'

'A terrifying scenario.' Shani finished chopping the onions, briefly wiping her eyes with her wrist. 'Bloody multinationals and their poisonous chemicals. Right?'

'Yes.' Mario took a glass bowl from a shelf. 'Now they are involving themselves in geoengineering, making themselves more billions of dollars. Before too long, they'll likely muddle up Earth's ecological systems for good – putting everything, including the seasons, out of sync.'

'Monsters,' said Shani. 'Nicolas is very much into all this. He'd love to talk to you. He's of the opinion we are already living under a world government.'

'That's Deep State. The multinationals are in bed with the moneylenders. Period.' Mario scraped the vegetables off the chopping board and into the bowl. 'The strategy is very simple, Shani. Look at it like a recipe. Firstly, control the monetary system. Secondly, sow seeds of hate. Thirdly, maintain division at all costs. And there you have your global coup d'état.'

'Your recipe reminds me of a quote by Benjamin Disraeli,' said Shani. '"Governments do not govern, but merely control the machinery of government, being themselves controlled by the hidden hand".'

'Benjamin Disraeli?' asked Mario, rolling out the sheet of pastry over the chopped vegetables. 'I've heard the name.'

'British Prime Minister in the 1870's and 80's. I love quotations. They can teach us so much.'

Mario washed his hands over the porcelain sink. 'Fact is, we'd be better off if the predatory fiscal gangsters were exiled to a distant land, leaving them to play their offensive tricks on nobody but themselves, before decaying into feeble dust.'

Shani glanced across at him, surprised by his eloquent use of English. 'You're a poet, Mario.'

'Hardly,' chuckled Mario. Reaching for a green bottle on the worktop, he said, 'I want you to judge this. Elderflower wine.'

'I'm going to be smashed if I drink that after the beer. Honestly.'

'There's little by way of alcoholic content.' Mario placed two glasses on the table. 'It's more of a tonic.'

Shani left the worktop for the cushioned seat where she'd sat before they went into the garden.

While pouring the wine, Mario tilted his head towards the Samsung mobile phone at the far end of the table. 'There's the clean phone for contacting Nicolas. Okay?'

'Yes.' Shani reached down the table for the phone and turned it over in her hands. The screen was scuffed and the casing chipped on two of its corners. As far as mobile phones went, the model verged on antiquity. 'I'll call Monique in Séroulé and get her to tell Nicolas he must use another phone from now on.' Shani left the phone on the table and raised her glass. 'To friendship.'

'Friendship,' echoed Mario. 'The true tonic of life.'

'Absolutely.' Shani took a sip. And then another. 'It's smooth, for sure. Like liquid velvet. Pardon the cliché.'

'Coming up to a year old.' Mario's phone sounded and he looked at the screen. 'It's Victor. Hopefully with news about the hostel.'

While Mario took the call, Shani texted Monique – the rebel she had befriended in Séroulé. Transferring the number from her own phone onto the Samsung, she sent the text, asking her to urgently contact Nicolas, and mentioning that under no circumstances must he use his phone.

'Interesting…' said Mario after speaking to his son.

Shani was about to take another sip of wine. 'Interesting?'

Mario put down his phone. 'They *were* the owners that you saw. Apparently, Serghei slept there just occasionally.'

'Not all the time?'

'It seems not. The owners first got to know of him two months ago.'

'I'm wondering if he got back into drugs in some way.'

'Listen to this… Four days ago, they were told to leave the hostel. They run the place themselves. They don't employ anyone—'

'But the girl, Daniela… And the old man watching television at the reception desk?'

'Nobody has any idea who they were.'

'Who told the owners to leave?' asked Shani, bewildered. 'I mean, how can that be? Were they paid to leave their business?'

'The person who told them to leave had information they'd cheated the tax system for the past fifteen years,' explained Mario. 'The person was also aware of an illegal distillery in the basement. They were instructed not to touch the body until after you arrived. Once you'd seen it and left, then Serghei could be removed from the premises. They told Victor that they wrapped Serghei in a black polythene sheet and dumped him in a skip in another street in the early hours of this morning. Victor walked by the skip moments ago; half of it's full of rubble and wooden panels. Presumably, Serghei's somewhere underneath all that.'

Shani put down her glass. Who the hell was Daniela, then? And the old man at the table? 'Why all the…the theatre?' she asked aloud. 'Why go to such lengths, Mario? What was our unknown force trying to achieve? To scare the living daylights out of me? Well, they succeeded. I was set to leave Romania before I received your note. I'd even booked the flight.'

'They would have drawn you back into the country by some means. A fake message from me, perhaps, giving you my address.' Mario left the table for the range to check on the pie. 'They chose to put the fear of God into you to such an extent that you wouldn't be able to shake it off – a warning that neither of us can escape from.'

'Can't we?' Shani still desperately wanted Mario to arrive at a viable alternative.

'Not unless you want to live your life constantly looking over your shoulder. I know I don't.' Mario sat down again. 'No, we have to find that folder. And to do it, we need to think outside the box, as it were.'

Shani absently toyed with the stem on her glass. 'But I know next to nothing about my father. You know more than I do. Andrei hardly spoke to me about my parents. Obviously, I wanted him to – but he would clam up.'

'Talking of Andrei, did he have a safe anywhere?'

'Yes, in the living room, concealed behind a row of books. But there's no folder inside it. The following day, after he'd passed away, I opened it. There were a couple of brown envelopes, one relating to ownership of the apartment, the other to Séroulé, along with an old-fashioned video showing footage of my parents at the police barrier – possibly recorded from a news report.'

'But no folder in the safe?'

'No. Definitely not. Had there been, we wouldn't have it now because according to Dusana, Andrei's housekeeper, the safe was opened by the intruder.'

'And had that been the case, then it's likely Serghei would still be alive and we wouldn't have met. I'm still of the opinion Serghei was instructed to contact you, that he wouldn't have bothered to have done so of his own accord. He was, after all, from the way you have described the manner in which he was living, a virtual down-and-out. Perhaps he didn't even own a phone.'

'True. But Daniela…she's a mystery all on her own.'

'We'll find answers in the days to come.'

'I can't believe she would be involved in something underhand.' Shani took a sip from her glass and leaned back. 'Rewinding for a moment…you were in the same form as my parents, didn't you say?'

'Yes. And the same orphanage as Lucian and Serghei, but I was with a different group of friends. Lucian and Zinsa always stayed together, Serghei at a desk nearby.'

'Serghei told me his father ran the orphanage.'

'It was a good one – so far as orphanages at that time went. Sponsored to some degree by the

Orthodox Church. I heard later that Serghei's father was cheating the Church, exploiting their aid in some way.'

'What did you do after you were expelled from school?' Shani asked.

'I was kicked out of the orphanage, so I went to Bucharest to make my fortune. Of course, that didn't happen. I lived in the sewers with other kids. It was the only way to keep warm in winter. What I remember most was the camaraderie. We were all in the shit together, you might say.'

Shani smiled with her host.

'But on the other side of the coin there was heavy drug taking, which I managed for the most part to avoid. The subways and Metro stations were the worst. Older kids beating up younger kids, getting them to steal for them. Sadistic. When I witnessed that, I wanted to get back to Timişoara.'

'You helped to set up the twins in business?' asked Shani.

'Yes. I bought the café for them. And I'll pay for Ana at university.'

'Not wishing to be nosey, but what line of business are you in now?'

'Nothing specific. I had some luck a few years back.'

'Tell me. I'm interested.'

'I happened to come across an old acquaintance. He told me to buy Bitcoins. I thought, why not, they might just catch on, and so scraped together enough money to buy twenty. At the time, they were next to nothing. Around forty Romanian leu. Over the next six or seven years, I forgot about them. Then, by chance, I came across the same person. He told me to sell. I looked up the price and couldn't believe my eyes. It was approaching twenty thousand dollars for *each* coin. Obviously, I cashed them in.'

'Well, as I see it, you deserve every dollar, Mario.' Shani pointed at her glass. 'I'm giving you another nine, incidentally, for the wine. What time do you plan to leave tomorrow for Mario Nemescu's town apartment?'

'Around ten o'clock, after the breakfast rush at Skid Row. Victor should arrive by then.'

Shani bowed her head, not wanting Mario to see the look of concern on her face – and if not her face, then the anxiety in her eyes. 'I really don't want you to go.'

'I'm guessing they're not out to harm either of us. They want us to work together to find the folder.'

'But how the hell can we find it?' Out of sheer frustration, Shani slammed a fist onto the table. 'It's impossible. Maybe my father learned of your arrest and so destroyed it. And who are these people? I know we keep asking the question, but *where* could this "unknown force" have come from?'

'That's why I'm leaving for the apartment in the city, Shani. We need an answer to that question.' Mario replenished their glasses and went over to the range.

'How is going to the apartment going to help?'

'Because, as far as the authorities are concerned, that is where Mario Nemescu lives when he's in town.'

Shani quietly sipped elderflower wine, recalling the phone call she'd had with Nicolas at the guest house. 'Mario, what do you know about the plane crash? From the description Serghei gave me, it was an American plane with Russian markings on it. Nicolas thought it likely to have been part of the Lend-Lease Program between America and Russia.'

Mario started spooning out the steaming pie onto plates. 'That's true, and it's been openly documented as such. No secret about that.'

'He said that he was baffled over why it was travelling this far south.'

'Ever since I got to hear of it, I've been mystified by that, too. The planes taking off from Great Falls in

Montana always took a northern route – the ALSIB route.'

'That's what Nicolas said. Alaska – Siberia, and then dropped down to Moscow, or wherever their destination happened to be.' The pie on the plate before her not only looked delicious but also artistic, the vegetables and their deep colours glistening. But Shani found Serghei's mutilated body once again at the forefront of her mind and told Mario so.

'Try to eat. It's important you do so, obviously. Forgive me for saying, a couple of kilos on you would hardly ruin your figure.'

'I've lost several kilos over the past couple of months, mainly as a consequence of the coup.' Shani forked a carrot, then a couple of pieces of celery – the pie loaded with wholesome flavour.

'Going back to 1944, when the plane came down,' said Mario, 'to my knowledge, the crash site is still sealed off. There are signs on the wire netting notifying those who happen to come across it that it's a private nature reserve.'

'Why would they seal it off for such a length of time?'

'There's a persuasive rumour that part of the cargo on that plane was uranium and cadmium sulphate. Concentrated uranium is known to cause kidney disease, while cadmium sulphate can be fatal if inhaled and can cause genetic defects. It might surprise you to know that all the diagrams and materials for the Russian atomic bomb came out of America, under the Lend-Lease Program.'

'That's insane.'

'Since the Cold War, Russian military bases have come to light in such countries as Kazakhstan and Bulgaria,' explained Mario, reaching for the terracotta pepper grinder. 'My bet is that the B-25 was heading for south-east Bulgaria, to the Yugoiztochen Region – much of it heavily restricted in Soviet times. The atomic bomb wasn't constructed there, but there might have been research laboratories linked to it.'

'Do you believe the plane had uranium on board?' Shani was fascinated.

'Yes, I do,' said Mario readily. 'What America sent to Russia via Lend-Lease was recorded in detail by a major called George Racey Jordan, who became concerned about the unusual diplomatic immunity cargo going through Great Falls. After the Program was abandoned, it gave rise to some believing the Cold War was a hoax, designed to divide Europe and generate an arms race to build up global weaponry, in addition to intensifying unrest, mindless hatred, and so on.'

'That takes me back to what you said earlier,' remarked Shani. 'The recipe for a global coup d'état. Control monetary system. Sow seeds of hate. Maintain division at all costs. I really must get you and Nicolas together.'

'We'll make that happen.' Mario began rolling a cigarette, taking the slip of paper and tobacco from a worn tin.

'Going slightly off key,' said Shani, 'or, if you like, returning to our philosophical comments earlier – where do you stand with religion, Mario? Can I ask this question? I'm curious.'

Mario lit the cigarette, waving the smoke away so that it wouldn't reach Shani. 'As I see it, this evil we are having to live with sets faith against faith, as it systematically modifies the evolution of humankind for its own benefit.'

'So the current wave, for example, of anti-Semitism across Europe is part and parcel of this universal attack on religion?'

'By promoting falsehoods and misconceptions, yes.'

'A couple of my friends in Oxford are Jewish.'

'Then you'll likely know that equality and compassion are fundamental Jewish principles, which by itself makes anti-Semitism mindless.'

'My friends are concerned. I don't blame them.'

'Religion to the clique is another tool to fragment society. Another example, you might say, of divide and rule via provocation. Truth is, all the major religions have their merits, they wouldn't have lasted through the ages had they not.'

'And Christ?'

'An enigma, who continues to fascinate – and with good reason.' Mario hesitated in bringing the cigarette back to his lips. 'I think we're being conditioned to loathe Christ, or even made to feel uncomfortable to speak his name in a meaningful way – in part by the Church itself, ironically, with its material wealth and preaching of miracles and such nonsense. It's too theatrical for words. Wasn't it Mark Twain who said: "If Christ were here there is one thing he would not be – a Christian"?'

'I haven't heard that quote before, but can see the significance.' Shani soaked up the last bit of gravy with puff pastry before putting her knife and fork together. 'I like the teachings behind the parables. I found them comforting when I had issues with my prosthesis.'

'Would you like some fruit?'

Shani felt such delight in being able to describe her bygone 'issues' aloud in the past tense. Therapeutic, even. 'An apple would be nice.'

Mario shifted the clay bowl laden with apples and oranges down the table towards her. 'Last year's crop. Too early for apples out there in the garden... When Simona died, I found myself taking a look at Christ's teachings. I remember thinking, "this stuff is dynamite".'

'The Church ought to get back to him – the real Christ.'

'Then it would be in direct conflict with Deep State itself.'

Shani laughed. 'True.' She glanced at the time on her phone. The day had flown by. 'After this apple, I'm going to crash – if that's okay. Here's the fob for the bike.'

'Keep it. I'll be using the car to go into town.'

'How did you know I was a biker?'

'When the photograph of you beside your parents' grave appeared in newspapers, I read up about you. It states you're a keen biker where they list the Fellows on the St Thomas Aquinas website... Is it correct to say that it is a postgraduate college? No students?'

'Yes. Students come to the college for seminars in term time, but that's about it.' Shani finished the apple and stood up. 'I'll help you wash up.'

'No need. You get yourself off. Been a long day.'

'Feels that way, I have to say. What time do you normally rise, Mario?'

'At this time of the year, around six. But rise at a time that suits you.'

'For me, usually around eight. Is that okay?'

'Like I said, when it suits you.'

'I'll say goodnight, then.' Shani started to leave the kitchen, but then turned on impulse. 'Mario, I really meant what I said. I feel I've found a dear friend today.'

'I knew your parents, Shani.' Mario smiled and put out his cigarette. 'How can I stand aside?'

'I know I've said it before, but we could forget about the folder. Couldn't we? What could they do to us?' As she spoke, Shani knew she was talking rubbish. 'On second thoughts, don't bother answering that question.'

CHAPTER 17

The next morning, after Mario had left and Victor had arrived, Shani was surprised to discover Coetzee's *Life and Times of Michael K* on a bookshelf in the living room. Victor seemed to show little concern about what was happening as he sat at the table in the kitchen, absorbed with his laptop. Shani found herself to be worried sick and struggled to settle. The only comfort she could muster was from what Mario had told her: *I'm guessing they're not out to harm either of us. They want us to work as a unit to find the folder.* And if they couldn't find it – and in *her* opinion they hadn't a hope of finding it – then what? Termination, or freedom?

Shani came back into the kitchen with the book. 'Victor?'

Victor looked up from his laptop while reaching for his mug of coffee.

'When you went to the hostel, did you see a young girl there? Her name's Daniela.'

Victor shook his head. 'No, Shani. No girl. Only owner. And wife. I think his wife.'

'Just two people? No old man? He had a distinct limp.'

'Two people...' Victor lit a cigarette. 'You are nervous, I think, Shani.'

Does everyone smoke in Romania? wondered Shani. 'Yes, nervous. I worry for your father. For Mario, I worry. You understand?'

'Do not worry for Mario.'

'I can't help it, Victor.' She sat on a chair, fidgeting with the book. Finally, she put it down on the table. 'He's a good man. You are so lucky to have a father like Mario. If anything happens to him, I will blame myself for eternity.' She absently flicked through the pages of the book. 'You understand what I'm saying?'

'Eternity?'

'Forever. Until my last breath.'

'Calm yourself, Shani.'

'I'm trying to. It's hard.'

'Not your...er, fault. This is true, I think.'

Shani stood up. 'I'll go into the garden and read this book. Leave you in peace.'

Halfway down to the arbour, she was joined by a hen. Shani wasn't sure if it was the same one she'd met the previous day, imagining there would be three or four at least roaming the garden. In fact, hadn't Mario said as much after she'd parked the Suzuki on the driveway? When she sat on the seat under the arbour, the chicken joined her. She stroked its silky-smooth feathers and decided it was the same one. The hen cocked its head, an inquisitive beady eye watching her.

'If only I could be as content as you,' she whispered. She supposed that one day this creature would end up on the kitchen table in some form or another – casserole, or salad. If she could convince Nicolas that this lifestyle was for them, they would have to circumnavigate the slaughter of any creature. She couldn't bear such an act of violence on a defenceless animal. And yet she wasn't vegetarian, which made her something of a hypocrite, she supposed. Her closest friend, Christina, had once told her – lectured her, actually – that moments before it is slaughtered, the fear-ridden animal releases adrenaline into its bloodstream, leaving the meat that ends up on the plate toxic. *You could say the animal has the last laugh*, Christina concluded. She came close to becoming vegetarian there and then. It was still in her mind to give it a go at some point.

Shani stopped stroking the chicken, and it hopped down from the seat, jerking its way along a path to her left. She opened *Life and Times of Michael K*. She'd read it before – twice – but didn't mind doing so for a third time because it was a favourite of hers. She found the storyline consoling, the main reason perhaps being that Michael K had a hare lip and a problematic childhood in South Africa, marked by poverty and apartheid. She'd never had it that bad, but her prosthesis and the fact that she never actually knew her parents spawned empathy with the protagonist.

A sudden buzz in her jeans made her jump. The 'clean' phone, she realised, and dug it out of her pocket. Number withheld. 'Hello?' she said.

'Shani – it's Nicolas. What the hell's going on? Why are we switching phones? Monique's been in contact with me.'

'We have to be cautious, Nicolas.'

'I thought you were leaving Romania. Are you still there?'

'I've found Mario.'

'Shani, explain exactly what is going on.'

Shani did so, just about every detail. By the time she'd finished describing what she'd found on her second visit to the hostel and heard what she thought was a gasp from Nicolas, she realised that perhaps she shouldn't have been so graphic. She just needed to *tell* him – for him to understand what she was going through and for him to comfort her.

'Shani, for Christ's sake, get out of the country!'

'I can't, Nicolas.'

'Why not?'

Shani mentioned the break-ins, Prague and Oxford. 'I'm sure they're linked. That means they can find me wherever I go.'

'Perhaps not here in Séroulé,' responded Nicolas with calm logic.

'But I can't spend the rest of my life hiding from them there, can I? And why should I?'

'I don't like this, Shani. So, you've met Mario?'

Shani explained how that came into being, by a third party – likely to have been the 'unknown force'. 'I'm at his house now. I stayed the night here. He's a wonderful person. You would love—'

'Shani, you barely know him!'

'He's looking after me, Nicolas. Protecting me. Well, his son is at the moment. Mario's gone into town, hoping to try and smoke out whoever's behind all this.'

'Shani! Shani, please! I love you, you know that. This is tearing me into pieces... I think I'd better come out and join you.'

'No, probably not a good idea, Nicolas.'

'Why not?'

'Because if you're here, they might make an example of you like they did to Serghei – to drive home the fear factor.'

'But, Shani, this Mario individual worries me. How do we know that he doesn't have an agenda? That he's not using you, or is in some way part of whatever's going on with these people who murdered Serghei?'

'No, he can't be.'

'That's not good enough, Shani. Not good enough at all, trusting him to the extent that you appear to be doing.'

Shani clamped her eyes shut. She now wished she hadn't answered the call. He was sowing doubts in her head. 'Nicolas,' she said, becoming tearful, 'I'll keep you informed the moment anything happens. I don't want you to worry—'

'Don't be bloody ridiculous. Of course, I'm going to worry!'

'I'm sorry.' Shani wiped a tear from her cheek. 'It's just I can't take any more stress. I still haven't settled down from the coup. Please understand.' She heard a sigh, and then:

'All right, Shani. All right. But you will call me the moment anything happens?'

'I promise, Nicolas… Every day, I'm thinking of our sojourn in Cornwall. It'll be wonderful. I know it will be.'

'Yes, we just have to make sure it's going to go ahead. That both of us actually *arrive* there.'

'We will. Of course, we will. Massive love.' Shani put the phone away in her pocket.

But, Shani, this Mario individual worries me. How do we know that he doesn't have an agenda?

What if Nicolas was right? It couldn't be the case, could it? She had to admit her friendship with Mario had kicked off like clockwork, and had remained that way. Was she in actual fact under 'house arrest'? No! That really was ridiculous. Anyway, she still had the fob to the Suzuki… Although, what if someone had tampered with the bike overnight, isolating the ignition…? *Oh, Nicolas, why did you have to say such things?*

She tried reading and managed three pages. But it was hopeless. Suspicions and scenarios ricocheted off each other inside her head, jamming her mind with what was likely to be utter nonsense. She closed the book and tried to take a logical approach to Mario and their friendship. Would a man who spoke with such wisdom and who tended to such a garden as this, achieving 'permaculture' in the process, and who had raised a family by himself, bought his sons a restaurant and was set to pay for his daughter to go through university in Bucharest, who said he owed it to her father to protect her, would he commit an act of cold-blooded treachery against her?

A movement caught her eye. Shani looked up, shielding the sun from her eyes while seeing Victor heading towards her with his laptop.

'Shani, name of girl at hostel?'

'Daniela,' said Shani. 'Why?'

Victor turned the laptop around. 'Like this?'

'Yes, that's her!' The photograph was black and white, her hair longer than she remembered it, but there was no mistaking the image Victor was holding. 'Why?' repeated Shani. She had a nasty, hollow feeling in the pit of her stomach.

Victor sat beside her. 'Name not Daniela.'

'No?' Shani raised her eyes from the image. 'What then?'

'Mariana. Mariana Tismăneanu. She act.'

'She's an actress?' asked Shani.

Victor tilted his left hand. 'Not every day.'

'Part-time actress?'

'Yes. She finished, Shani. She dead.'

'Dead!' gasped Shani, the weird feeling in her stomach exploding into incredulity. 'How? When?'

Victor held his left hand against his throat, implying strangulation. 'Body found in Beja. Big river in Timişoara. Maybe two days in Beja.'

'Just her, no other body?' asked Shani, recalling the old man behind the table in the lobby. Another actor?

Victor shook his head.

'Have you called Mario?'

'No. Just found on today's news.'

'I think you should call your father, Victor.'

'I will… You okay, Shani?'

'Not really. Big shock.' Shani leaned forward, resting her elbows on her knees. 'You can leave me, just call Mario. I'll be okay.' She watched in a daze as Victor headed back up the garden. So now Daniela, or rather 'Mariana', was dead. God's sake! These people were utterly ruthless. But why would they want to kill her? Because she'd seen something she wasn't supposed to? Or was she a 'dead person walking' before she even entered the hostel? They would have dressed it up in some way. Offered her an irresistible amount of money to play her part, act out her role and, once that was over, simply get rid of her – eliminating any suspicions she might have felt, suspicions arising during and after her meeting with Serghei.

Shani shook her head, trying to clear it of yet another batch of hostile scenarios. She had liked the girl, liked her courtesy. Or had that been part of the act…? No. She was probably an ordinary decent person, in need of some cash. And then these vile bastards got hold of her.

She looked up. Victor was coming down the garden again, without the laptop.

'Shani, Mario coming back.'

'Already? Because of the girl? You told him?'

'Something happen.'

'To Mario?'

'I think. Ana bring him.'

'Oh, God…' She knew she should have tried harder to persuade him not to leave. 'I'll come with you to the house, Victor.'

* * *

The mud-spattered BMW swung onto the driveway. Victor left her by the window in the living room. Ana climbed out of the driver's seat. Yes, it was the same girl she had seen smoking out the back at Skid Row. In comparison to her brothers, she was physically petite, with dyed ash-blonde hair styled into a bob that kissed her shoulders. When she turned as Victor joined her, there was a dash of blue across the bob in the form of a metallic dart. Mario was trying to fend off their concern as he left the passenger seat while simultaneously clutching his upper right arm. Shani left the window and headed into the kitchen since it seemed to be the cottage's central meeting point, the living room itself hardly used in comparison. She wasn't going to call Nicolas. At least, not just yet. Daniela being murdered and now Mario likely to have been wounded would freak him to pieces. She couldn't cope with that on top of everything else.

Mario entered the kitchen, his children squeezing side-by-side through the doorway immediately behind him. His shirt sleeve was covered in blood, his left hand still clutching the wound.

'What the hell happened?' asked Shani. 'Thank God you're safe.'

Mario sat himself down, his daughter dismissing Shani as she went to work on him, unbuttoning his shirt.

Shani sat opposite them at the table. 'Can I do anything?' she asked Ana.

When there was no response from his daughter, Mario looked up. 'Ana, Shani asked you a quest—'

'*Ne aduce probleme!*' shouted Ana, throwing the shirt down on the table. '*Ne aduce probleme tuturor, ascultați-mă!*'

Shani wilted, not knowing where to look. She couldn't translate Ana's response, but judging from Ana's body language she suspected Ana regarded her as a problem – someone who had brought trouble into the family.

Mario spoke. 'Ana, you must apologise—'

'*Nu îmi voi cere scuze.*'

'*Ana!*' shouted Mario, the whole cottage echoing with his booming voice. 'You will apologise to Shani. You understand?'

'*Înțeleg, dar nu îmi voi cere scuze.*' Ana wiped sudden tears off her cheeks, went over to the sink and filled a bowl with water.

'The root cause of this started before Shani was born, Ana,' said Mario. 'It's not her fault.'

Ana whirled round from the sink. '*De ce avem problemele astea acum? Viața mea este liniștită, in afara de placarea mamei.*'

'Shani never had a mama. You know her story?'

'*Știu ceva,*' said Ana, this time without raising her voice. '*Toată lumea din Romania știe ceva.*'

'Victor, you know more. Tell your sister.'

'Ana really doesn't need to apologise,' Shani told Mario across the table. 'She's upset with what's happened to you. Rightly so. I'm upset. I don't blame her. I'm an outsider.'

'No, Shani,' contradicted Mario. 'You are not an outsider. You are a member of this family. I am making you that now.'

Shani felt her eyes well up on hearing those words. She simply couldn't help herself. A family. This beautiful, and somewhat articulate, family.

Still clutching his arm, Mario rolled his eyes. 'Two women in tears. That's all I need.'

'I'm trying not to,' said Shani, 'but what do you expect when you come out with such words?' Taking a tissue from her jeans to wipe her eyes, she asked, 'Victor's told you about the girl I met at the hostel?'

'Yes. Another warning for us, perhaps.'

'Dear God…' breathed Shani. 'I want to go to the police, Mario, for the sake of her family. Tell them all I know.'

'No, Shani. Roll me a cigarette, Victor.' Mario turned again to Shani. 'If you go to the police, you will have to mention Serghei. We don't know the extent of what we are dealing with. It might be authority-based, not necessarily Romanian. When we know more, we can make an informed decision on what to do about the girl.'

Shani nodded dully. It made sense, she supposed. She was in a foreign country, unable to speak the language. One thing was certain: the fear-dimension was ratchetting up – which, no doubt, was the intention of their foe, get them to work harder at finding the goddamned folder. She felt physically sick.

Ana brought the bowl and a pile of tissues over to the table. Victor was still talking to her in Romanian while rolling Mario's cigarette. Shani heard her name mentioned intermittently. Ana, it seemed, showed no signs of retreating from her stance as she stubbornly went to work on her father's wound.

'What happened, Mario?' asked Shani.

'I was being watched. It tells me that Skid Row is under surveillance. I had my suspicion it might be the case, that's why I went to the café. A green Volvo was parked opposite, fifty metres down the street. I drove to the flat, and sure enough the Volvo followed – but then, once it knew the direction I was heading in, it fell right back.'

Victor interrupted. 'You say we close, Papa?'

'Until this is sorted.'

Ana dropped a bloody ball of tissues into the bowl, causing a splash. 'Victor, help Papa. I take Shani into garden.'

Surprised by the urgency of the request, Shani made her second trip of the day down to the arbour, on this occasion sitting alongside Ana – who had yet to say another word since leaving the kitchen. There were bees on the runner beans' red flowers, but no sign of the hen.

'I love Papa,' said Ana as they settled themselves.

'Of course, you do,' said Shani. 'He's a lovely man.'

'I worry for him. Mama gone ten years. He alone. My heart sad for him.'

'I understand, Ana—'

'So, when trouble come I get upset. I want to stop trouble coming, you see?'

'I do see. You want to protect him. It's a natural response.' Shani cast out her hand. 'As natural as this beautiful garden.'

'This is right. You understand. But you, Shani…no Papa, no Mama, from beginning. Die in bad way.' Ana turned to face Shani, tears on her cheeks. 'My sister, Shani. I apologise.'

Any suspicion she might still have harboured from Nicolas's call vanished in that split second. Shani took Ana in her arms, the girl sobbing quietly. 'Don't worry. Mario is going to be with us for many, many years to come.'

'I wish this to be true, Shani. I am frightened.'

'Mario told me they don't want to harm us,' mentioned Shani, while admitting to herself that her honesty was skating on thin ice. 'They just want us to find the folder.'

'And if this is not done?'

'Then...they give up on us.'

Ana straightened herself and took a tissue from her pocket to dab her tears away. 'Maybe it's not folder they want, Shani.'

'There's nothing else in existence – if it still exists – that links me to your father.'

'Okay. I understand. It must be folder. Perhaps, Shani, we do nothing. We take life as normal. They give up. We are free again. Yes?'

Shani was fairly certain Mario hadn't mentioned Serghei's fate to Ana. 'I hope before too long they will leave us alone.' A hen appeared before them, pecking beside their shoes. 'How many are there?'

'Three,' said Ana. 'This one is Café. She belong to me. She's cool. You can touch her.'

'Then it's Café I know. I have touched her. The other two? Don't tell me. Skid, and Row.'

'Yes,' smiled Ana. 'You're clever. I want to visit Oxford. I want to be like you.'

'Then you will visit Oxford. We will arrange for it to happen. Shall we go back?' Shani was keen to hear what exactly happened to Mario once he'd arrived at the apartment.

* * *

He was still seated at the table when Shani returned to the kitchen, a bandage around his upper right arm, secured by a gigantic, cartoonish-looking green safety pin. Shani took a seat opposite. Victor asked her if she wanted a coffee as he was about to make one for himself. She nodded before looking back at Mario, waiting.

'By the time I reached the apartment,' said Mario, 'I could see the Volvo parked down the street. Changing my clothes and wearing a cloth cap, I left through the back entrance, did a small detour so that I came from behind the Volvo. I figured better to go for a challenge – try and get some information. Opening the driver's door, I managed to pull the key from the ignition. But I wasn't fast enough. Simple as that. He pulled a flick-knife.'

Ana came into the kitchen with a fresh shirt. Victor said something to his sister in Romanian. Ana took a card from her bag and put it down on the table.

The card had the letters BCB against a turquoise background with a white dove in the left corner.

Shani found herself staring at the card, and in particular the letters BCB. 'That's a bank card, right?' she asked.

'Banca Comercială Bănăţeană,' said Victor. 'We use bank for business. For Skid Row.'

'Bănăţeană Commercial Bank?' said Shani, turning to Mario.

'Yes. Bănăţeană is the feminine adjective of Banat, a region divided by three countries: ourselves, Serbia and Hungary. Timişoara belongs to Banat. Years ago, Banat was a republic. Why the sudden interest?'

'I'm not quite sure, other than I'm fairly certain a girl I shared a flat with when I first went to Oxford banked with them. Her mother came from Bucharest.' Shani leaned back, perplexed over why the letters BCB should strike such a direct chord with her other than what she'd just mentioned. She shook her head and shrugged off the transitory sensation. As for the present: 'What did the driver look like?'

'Thin face,' said Mario. 'Designer beard, I think you'd call it. Like he hadn't shaved for a week. Black hair. Early forties. Could handle himself, obviously. Nice car.'

'You get number, Papa?' said Ana.

'Stolen plate. I checked it out before you came over. The plate belongs to a Nissan written off three years ago in Constanța.'

Shani took her coffee from Victor. 'So, not the authorities?'

Mario shrugged and put on the clean shirt, the sleeve catching on the oversized safety pin. Ana lent a hand. 'Maybe, maybe not,' said Mario. 'It's not unknown for the authorities to outsource.'

'Don't you need stitches?' asked Shani.

'A few centimetres deep,' said Ana, standing behind her father. 'But small. I think okay.' She put her arm across his shoulders, stooped and quietly hugged him. 'We watch for fiction. Yes, Papa?'

'*Infection*, I think you mean, Ana,' Mario corrected gently as he smiled up at her, perhaps both relieved and proud that his daughter had patched up her differences with Shani. He glanced at Victor, who was scrolling through his phone. 'You need to tell Cosmin to close the café until further notice.'

'I've texted him,' said Victor.

'Can I do anything?' asked Shani.

'Now the sun is not so strong, perhaps do some watering with Ana.'

* * *

That evening, Shani shared Mario's bedroom with Ana. Victor was given the couch in the living room. For Shani, the setting was a dream come true – one that she'd never expected to experience, for she was at the core of a family unit. Cosmin was sleeping wherever he lived, with a girl no doubt that he'd picked up at some point at Skid Row.

Ana was now asleep, her back turned to her, her breathing rhythmic. Shani's prosthesis had caused Ana to blink twice, but she didn't shy away in shock. Shani explained that she'd lost her foot when her parents were killed, the likely cause being a ricochet from a bullet the policeman had fired from the barricade. Once they'd climbed into bed, they talked for another twenty or so minutes, Ana asking questions about Prague and Oxford – mainly Oxford. Shani told her she'd graduated at Corpus Christi and, as luck would have it, a scholarship had given her a four-year Fellowship at St Thomas Aquinas College, where she was expected to complete a thesis, economic history being the subject matter.

Shani sighed to herself. She was going to have to come clean with the college and her supervisor, Harry Rothwell. She imagined questions were already being asked regarding her commitment, since over the past three months she'd spent just a few days in her study

– four days, to be precise. She'd now reached the point whereby she felt embarrassed walking past the porters' lodge and into the front quad. Many an academic would strip their bank account to be offered a Fellowship at such a prestigious college as St Aquinas. But she was tired of sitting at desks and moving a cursor around a screen, typing up theories and what-ifs. She wanted to plant seeds in soil, help the orphans in Séroulé and, above all, be with Nicolas. After years of crucifying herself over her prosthesis, a practical perspective now beckoned.

Shani turned onto her side, away from Ana. Virtually three days had passed since she'd witnessed Serghei's fate. Like a switch tripping out on a fuse board, her mind for the most part still aligned the murder to blood-curdling cinematic fiction. That it never actually happened. But, of course, it *had* happened, and she was now worried sick that some awful tragedy was about to befall this exquisite family. What then?

She clamped her eyes shut and forced an image of Nicolas through her fears, imagining their proposed break in Cornwall, a county she had never before visited. *The apartment overlooks the sea*, he'd mentioned over the phone. And she was looking forward to giving surfing a go.

Finally, her eyes became heavy and her mind by degrees untethered itself from her anxieties.

Dearest Nicolas, she heard a distant voice say, *hold my hand*.

CHAPTER 18

Shani awoke alone, Ana having left the bedroom. It was eight o'clock. Despite everything, she'd slept reasonably well. Perhaps having Ana beside her had subconsciously eased her troubled mind. She dressed, tidied her hair, brushed her teeth and went down into the kitchen. Victor was on his laptop, Ana writing addresses on brown envelopes.

'Morning both,' said Shani. 'Where's Mario?'

'In the garden,' said Ana. 'Croissants and coffee, sister Shani?'

'That would be nice. But I can do that myself. You're busy.'

'It's okay,' said Ana, leaving the table for the worktop.

'What is it you're doing?'

'Advertising Skid Row.'

Shani sat at the table. 'Have we checked on Cosmin?'

'I called him.' Victor lifted his eyes briefly from the laptop. 'Making most of closed Skid Row with girls. I bet bottom dollar.'

Ana spun from the worktop to face them both. 'He will get sickness between his legs! Teach him lesson.'

Shani didn't laugh at Ana's riposte. Instead, she found herself transfixed by the pile of A-5 sized brown envelopes. She recalled the Banca ComercialăBănățeană card that Ana had given Victor the previous evening. There was a link between the two – a tenuous one, perhaps, but a *link* nevertheless. She was certain of it.

Safe, safe, safe. Andrei's dying words to her at Na Homolce Hospital, Prague. And when, in the early hours, it dawned on her what he likely meant… Shani stood up from the table, a clear vision inside her head.

'We need a meeting,' she said. 'I'll go and get Mario.'

Ana put the croissants and a cup of coffee on the table. 'You have idea, sister Shani?'

'Yes – I think so.'

'Then you have breakfast. I will get Papa.'

Victor closed his laptop. 'Good news, Shani?'

'I'm not sure. Maybe.' She took a careful bite out of a glazed croissant, wanting to avoid too many flakes of pastry falling onto the plate. Very buttery, and not altogether sweet – in fact, the best croissant she'd tasted in years. 'This is wonderful.'

'We make them at the café,' Victor said.

'Then you're on a definite winner,' complimented Shani. 'Can you do me a favour, Victor? Find out if Banca Bănăţeană has safe deposit boxes here in Timişoara.'

Mario came in from the garden, his right arm in a sling. 'At the insistence of Ana,' he said.

'He will not rest it,' said Ana from behind him. 'Sometimes, Papa difficult.'

'You wanted a meeting, Shani?' asked Mario.

Shani finished the second croissant. 'I need us together. You remember me telling you yesterday that the safe in Andrei's apartment had been broken into?'

'Yes.' Mario sat with Ana at the table.

'They do have boxes,' interrupted Victor.

'That's good news,' acknowledged Shani, 'but I can't imagine it's going to end in a result for us. Not after twenty-four years and no payments.'

'Shani, explain,' said Mario. 'What's this about?'

'When I opened the safe after Andrei died, I came across a couple of brown envelopes. From the contents of one of them, I discovered my true identity – that I was half Romanian as opposed to half Czech. The other contained documents relating to ownership of the apartment. I can't remember which envelope it was of the two, but I can recall the letters BCB in handwriting on the corner of one of them, and then a number, four or five digits long.'

'You're certain about the letters?' Mario was rapt, as were his children.

'Virtually. As I see it, there are two issues, providing the numbers relate to a safe deposit box at Banca Comercială Bănățeană. The first issue being when Dusana, Andrei's housekeeper, told me that the apartment had been broken into, she mentioned that nothing appeared to be missing. That might not be the case with the envelopes.'

'The second issue?' asked Mario.

'A question of payment to the bank for the safe deposit box.'

'Perhaps Andrei kept up the payments?' Mario blindly rolled himself a cigarette, his eyes not leaving Shani. 'Did he ever mention the bank to you?'

'No. And surely if he had kept up the payments then I would have found paperwork relating toBCB. That it would likely be inside that same envelope.'

'If it's what we hope it is, then I wonder what happened to the documentation inside it?'

'We can only speculate,' said Shani. 'Maybe Andrei dismissed it, having by then moved to the Czech Republic. Or perhaps Lucian took out the documentation from the envelope for whatever reason. I don't think we can answer that question, and in a sense it's irrelevant as long as the number on the envelope relates to a safe deposit box at Banca Bănăţeană.'

'True.' Mario licked along the cigarette paper. 'This could be the breakthrough we've been looking for.'

'I remember thinking at the time, when I took the envelopes from the safe, that the number probably related to Andrei's anthropological cataloguing system, which always seemed haphazard to me. But if the letters BCB are correct, then it'll be too much of a coincidence.'

'We call housekeep woman,' said Ana. 'We get number.'

'We need to be careful,' Mario said. He turned to Shani. 'How do you contact Dusana? Mobile phone?'

'Yes,' said Shani. 'But we can use the clean phone you gave me?'

'Not if Dusana's phone has been cloned or is being hacked into. Does she have a landline?'

'Yes. I have the number on my phone.'

'But she uses her mobile for the majority of her calls?'

'Yes. She finds it cheaper than using her landline.'

'Then use the Samsung to call Dusana's landline. Less of a probability it's been interfered with as opposed to her mobile. But she gives you only the numbers. Not the letters BCB.'

'*If* it is BCB,' reiterated Shani. 'I'm now worried that I'm building up our hopes and it'll come to nothing.'

'What other hopes do we have?' Mario lit his rolled cigarette. 'Let's go back twenty-four years. Your father has this folder, found by Andrei in the wreckage of a plane that came from America during the war. I, personally, can vouch for the fact that the contents had the look of Deep State about them, because they talked of a *unit of assassins*. And that was just on the first page. It's a certainty I would have mentioned this to both your father and Serghei.'

'But then you were arrested,' recalled Shani, 'and they took the photocopy my father made from you. Yes?'

'Correct. That's how it happened. I never got the chance to decipher the rest of it. It's here where I believe Lucian might have decided I was trying to make money from it. He had the original, of course.' Mario drew reflectively on the cigarette. 'But to go to the lengths of organizing a safe deposit box seems extreme. What on earth was going through his mind? Unless…unless it was *Andrei* who decided to use a safe deposit box for a separate reason that has nothing to do with the folder.'

'Forget Andrei,' said Shani. 'I can't see him bothering with a safe deposit box for anything. Maybe Lucian sensed he was being followed. Maybe he was running scared as he got to hear of your arrest. And Zinsa was heavily pregnant, which might have played on his mind in more ways than one.'

Ana interrupted them. 'We call housekeep woman. We think much. We go in circles.'

Shani took her phone from her jeans. 'Ana has a point.' She copied the number for Dusana's landline into Mario's Samsung and leaned back in the chair.

Mario and his children sat watching her in silence, completely focussed on the call.

'Yes? Who is speak—?'

'Hi, Dusana,' answered Shani. 'It's me.'

'Oh Shani, dear. Are you calling from college?'

'No, no. I'm still in Romania, using a different mobile phone. How's your wrist doing?'

'Getting stronger, Shani. I'm still doing the exercises.'

'Good. You must keep doing those. Have you been round to the apartment?'

'I was planning to go tomorrow—'

'Something quite urgent's come up, Dusana.'

'Oh?'

'Yes. It's a number.' Shani hated having to lie, particularly to dear Dusana. But it was for her protection, too. 'Andrei wrote down a number for me. It relates to a professor in Cambridge that I really need to contact. It's a longshot, but I remember seeing a number on one of the brown envelopes I came across in the safe after he died. You remember the day, Dusana? I called you, and you came over. That was when I discovered I was half Romanian.'

'How can I ever forget, Shani!'

'I don't need the initials, just the number.'

'You want the number now?'

'I wouldn't mind.'

'I think both the envelopes are still there. I've by no means cleared the mess up yet.'

'Any news from the police?' asked Shani, trying to keep the call incidental.

'Nothing. That's how it is these days, Shani. A petty crime, to them. Awful. What a world we're living in!'

You can say that again, thought Shani. 'So, I might hear from you in…what, twenty minutes or so?'

'Yes. I'll do my best.'

Shani noticed Mario pointing frantically at the Samsung she was holding, before mouthing 'number'.

'Oh, yes – almost forgot, Dusana. My mobile needs charging. So, from your landline can you call me on this number?'

'The one you're using now?'

'Yes. Has it come up on your phone?'

'Yes, dear. I can copy it down and call you back from Andrei's apartment.'

'Probably best not to use the landline at Andrei's apartment, Dusana. I wouldn't trust it after the break-in. The whole thing could be a consequence of journalists trying to find more information about me.'

'Heavens, Shani! Do you think that's what it's all about?'

'There's every chance. I'll hear from you in a short while, Dusana.'

'All right, darling. Now don't worry yourself.'

'Thanks, Dusana. Love you.'

Shani cut the call with a lengthy sigh, still upset with having to lie. 'Now we wait,' she said to her attentive audience.

'Does she live close to Andrei's apartment?' asked Mario.

'In the next block. Ten minutes from door to door. She's in her seventies, mind.'

'If and when we get the number,' continued Mario, 'we need to act fast, just in case this mobile, or Dusana's landline, happens to be tapped. There are three BCB banks across the city. Victor, find out if all three have safe deposit boxes. Make telephone calls, if necessary – but first check on the laptop.'

'I'll make fresh coffee,' said Ana, leaving the table.

Shani watched Mario put out his cigarette. 'How do we go about this? Am I simply going to go to a receptionist in the bank, give my name and mention that I'm Lucian Bălcescu's daughter, present the safe deposit box's identification number – we hope – and gauge what reaction I get from that?'

'I think that's all we can do, Shani,' said Mario. 'But you need support to keep your nerve, perhaps. Yes?'

'Definitely.'

'Then Ana should go with you. Put on an act of vulnerability, to get as much assistance as possible from them.'

'But if we're on the right track,' said Shani, 'then I find it hard to believe the box still exists. They would have got rid of whatever it contained once the initial payment ran out.'

'If it's no longer at the bank, maybe it's in a storeroom at some other location,' tendered Mario. 'A slim chance, admittedly. That's all we have, chances.'

'Just the one bank,' said Victor, drawing the lid down on the laptop. 'The one we use.'

'Will Ana be recognised?' asked Shani. 'Or doesn't it matter?'

'It's usually Cosmin who banks the week's takings,' said Mario. 'Can't see it being an issue. Besides, all you're doing is making a legitimate enquiry, and Ana is accompanying you to assist with the language barrier.'

The 'clean' Samsung began to take centre stage in the kitchen. Almost twenty minutes had now elapsed since the call. Shani wondered if she might have endangered Dusana's life in some way.

'Perhaps she's being watched,' she said aloud. 'She could be, couldn't she?'

'Doubtful,' reacted Mario. 'Andrei's housekeeper, right? Nothing more?'

'Fourteen years. After Rodica died, like a mother to me – although we didn't see eye-to-eye all the time. She disapproved of my tomboy teens. Riding motorbikes, and what have you.'

Mario smiled. 'Quite the rebel, yes?'

'In some ways. Did you ever get to meet Andrei and Rodica?'

'No. Or if I did, I can't remember.'

The Samsung rang out stridently, almost half an hour having now trickled by. Shani seized it and leapt to her feet. 'Fingers crossed.' Putting the phone to her ear:

'Shani, dear?'

'Yes, Dusana – it's me. Any luck? Just the number. Not the initials.'

'I've got the number, Shani. It's—'

'And you're back in your apartment?'

'Yes, dear. Shall I give you the number? Have you got a pen?'

'I'll remember it. You can give it to me.'

'It's one, six, three, four. Only four numbers, Shani.'

'That's fine. It's an internal number for a college, goes directly to the study of the professor I'm hoping to speak to. I know the preceding numbers that are required.'

'Shall I give you the initials, just in—?'

'No, that's fine, Dusana. I have the professor's name.'

'Are you coming to Prague before returning to college?'

'Yes,' decided Shani, feeling unexpectedly tearful. *You're my surrogate mother.* 'I want to see you. You know I do.'

'Hear from you soon, then, darling.'

'Take care, now, Dusana. Love you, always.' Shani faced her captivated audience. 'We have the number. BCB sixteen, thirty-four.'

'Then let's get the hell going,' said Mario. 'No time to lose.'

CHAPTER 19

Victor found a space to park the BMW in the busy street, Mario sitting beside him. Shani could see the bank through the rear window, Ana having pointed out the building to her as they drove past: blue and white and an excessive amount of chrome, which glistened under the midday sun. Symbolic, thought Shani, because she now shared Nicolas's viewpoint that the usurious-infected monetary system functioned as the primary key for entrapment into the New World Order or, as Mario would likely put it, 'Deep State's' primary key.

'Did the bank use this building twenty-four years ago?' she asked.

'Probably,' said Mario. 'In those days using a bank was a distant concept for me.'

'I'm literally going to be walking in the footsteps of my father,' said Shani, turning from the rear window. 'Incredible.'

'Ana, you're going with Shani,' reaffirmed Mario. 'I'll wait here with Victor. Good luck.'

Shani left the car and walked along the pavement, linking arms with Ana as they closed in on Banca Comercială Bănățeană. Her legs started to weaken. 'My heart's thudding like crazy,' she said.

Ana turned to her as they passed an old man clutching an assortment of helium balloons, a Chihuahua on a lead yapping energetically at his side. 'Thuddin?' she asked. 'What is *thuddin*?'

Shani patted her chest. 'My heart.'

'Ah…okay. Understand, sister Shani.' Then, holding her head high as if in defiance, Ana said, 'We are strong. I will speak for you.'

They climbed several steps, glazed doors opening automatically. Ana led the way to the reception desk. Shani took in the bank's questionable aesthetics. The furniture was angular rather than rounded, and she assumed a total refurbishment had occurred recently, which she deemed a pity. Although maybe the custom-built clock above them, with its silver bird against a blue background, was as original as when Lucian had arrived on that winter's day – *if* indeed the numbers Dusana had given her did relate to a deposit box here at Banca Bănăţeană.

Ana suddenly jolted forward as their turn in the queue came and spoke to the male receptionist, the latter undoubtedly forcing the umpteenth smile of the day. It wasn't long before his bespectacled eyes switched to Shani with a degree of awe. Shani had grown accustomed to such a look, the daughter of Lucian and Zinsa Bălcescu having mysteriously surfaced after twenty-four years. He spoke to Ana, then called a colleague to take over at the desk. Ana stood to one side, beckoning Shani to do the same.

'What's happening?' Shani asked. 'Are we okay?'

'He's gone to get person. Safety person.'

'Safety person?' Shani's pulse skipped a beat. 'You mean someone who deals with the bank's safe deposit boxes? Or security?'

'Boxes. I think this is what I mean,' said Ana. 'We have to wait, sister Shani. Be cool, yes?'

'I guess,' breathed Shani. 'Easier said than done, Ana.'

They didn't have to wait long. A tall man with an athletic physique came over to them and shook their hands, the breast pocket of his blazer sporting the bank's motif: silver bird, blue sky. They were ushered into a side cubicle and took a seat each. The man introduced himself as 'Claudiu' while he fired up the computer on the desk. Working the keyboard, he glanced at Shani, speaking to her in Romanian. Shani gestured that he needed to direct any questions he had to Ana.

'He's asking you for the number,' said Ana.

'Oh…okay. BCB, one, six, three, four,' said Shani, now sensing perspiration on her brow. This was almost too much to bear. For all she knew the police might have heard of her visit to the hostel three days ago and the fact that she'd spoken to part-time actress 'Daniela'. And if suspicions were raised here, would the police be called? The man talked to Ana while his fingers glided over the keyboard. At the first sign of a pause, Shani asked, 'Any news? What's Claudiu saying?'

'He says that after five years with no pay,' relayed Ana, 'the boxes leave building and stored for 'nother five years. Then royed—'

'"Royed"?' interrupted Shani. 'You mean *destroyed*?'

'Yes. With three people.'

'Witnesses, I'd imagine,' said Shani. 'That's what has happened then, surely? Providing the numbers relate to a deposit box.'

Claudiu began frowning at the screen, then more gliding over the keyboard.

'*Ce-i?*' asked Ana.

'*Un moment.*' Claudiu stood up and without another word started to leave the cubicle.

The second he did so, Ana craned her neck to examine the screen. 'Blank,' she said. 'He look serious.'

'We can't be in trouble for this, can we?'

'Maybe bad people who look for folder are government.'

'Ana, don't say that!'

'What you think?' asked Ana.

'I don't know. But I'm feeling anxious.'

'No, no. I mean Claudiu. Good body. Good job. I could go for him, sister Shani.'

'He could be married.'

'I check fingers. No ring.'

Claudiu duly returned. 'You will follow, please.'

'Ana, I'm not sure I like what's going on here.' The jelly-like feeling had returned to Shani's legs. 'Mario will never forgive—'

'Sister Shani, we need to know. We not worry. We are strong.' With that, Ana again wrapped her arm around Shani's as they followed Claudiu into what became a lengthy corridor. 'Next time *I* come here with Skid Row money, not Cosmin,' she whispered. 'I will have problem, and ask for…' She nodded at Claudiu in front of them. '…To help me.'

They arrived at an office in what felt to Shani to be the inner core of the bank. A middle-aged man, stocky and with a comb-over of fair hair, stood up from his desk to greet them, and to Shani's relief did so with a gracious smile.

'I am Cezar Ceauşescu – an unfortunate surname, some might say, though I am not related. Please, be seated. I am the manager of this branch.'

Shani took a seat alongside Ana and crossed her legs. 'I compliment you on your staff and their professionalism, Mr Ceauşescu,' said Shani, seeking to rouse the manager into assisting them beyond the call of duty, if necessary.

'A genuine pleasure to meet you, Miss Bălcescu,' Cezar said. 'That is still your surname, I am presuming?'

'Indeed. And do call me "Shani".' Shani produced her passport. 'Just to confirm.'

The manager flicked through a couple of pages as a matter of course and handed it back. 'Thank you.' He cast his eyes towards Ana. 'And you are…?'

'Ana. Shani my sister.'

'We are not blood related,' stepped in Shani. 'Just the best of friends. Ana came with me today to translate on my behalf, but your English is perfect.'

'It has taken many years, and much hard work – and several holidays in the UK,' explained Cezar. 'Now then, it's quite good news for you, Shani. Your father, Lucian, clearly knew a former employee called Elena Vãduva, and she happens to be the agent, or joint-renter, of the safe deposit box in question. We still have this box on site.'

Shani gasped in unison with Ana, seeing it as a miracle that the number she'd first noticed on a brown envelope in Andrei's safe actually *did* relate to a safe deposit box from twenty-four years ago. 'My goodness…' was all she could say without releasing an expletive.

'It is quite tragic what happened to Elena – must be ten or eleven years ago now. Actually, when I first started, she took me under her wing. A wonderful lady, heart of gold—'

'But you mentioned something awful happened to her?' probed Shani.

'Yes,' nodded Cezar. 'It's not for me to discuss this aspect with you. She will tell you herself, I am sure.'

'I see...' Shani wondered whether this 'tragic event' that came this woman's way had any bearing on the folder. 'You're suggesting I can meet her?'

'Yes. I have spoken to her.' Cezar pushed a slip of paper across the desk. 'Her address.' Then a larger, printed sheet was pushed towards Shani. 'Elena will need to complete this form for you to access the box in question.'

'This is er...result,' said Ana. 'Big result.'

'Absolutely.' Shani gathered herself from the initial shock. 'I can't quite believe it, Mr Ceaușescu.'

'Cezar, please.'

'Yes. Thank you.'

'Again, my pleasure.'

'Mario will be worrying,' Shani said to Ana. 'We'd better leave.' Standing, she extended her hand. 'We will be back, with Elena.'

'I'm not so sure about that,' said Cezar.

The remark took Shani by surprise. 'Pardon?'

'That Elena will want to return to this bank.' Cezar's reassuring smile reemerged. 'I believe she will explain. She is expecting you today.'

* * *

Strada Someș consisted mainly of chocolate-box painted houses and several bungalows, set in a leafy tree-lined street.

'You know,' commented Shani, 'from what I've seen of Timişoara I really like the fact there are trees everywhere.'

'This is a delightful street, I have to say,' said Mario. 'We're not far from the hospital you investigated on your first visit. And just a couple of streets away is the Dan Păltinişanu Stadium.'

'A footballer?' asked Shani.

'Something of a legend in Timişoara. Died very young, though.'

'I support the Bohemians 1905 Football Club, in Prague. You can almost see the stadium from Andrei's apartment.'

'You might consider switching allegiance now you're half Romanian,' quipped Mario, glancing over his shoulder at Shani.

'It'll be tough. I've supported the Bohemians all my life.'

Victor parked outside a magnolia house bordered with railings, behind which an orderly front garden displaying yellow roses and a circular bed of lavender.

'I just can't put my finger on it,' said Mario, 'but the name Elena Văduva does sound familiar to me.'

'Lucian must have known her for her to become the deposit box's joint renter…' Shani became conscious of an inconvenient thought worming its way into her head, and she found herself praying she wasn't about to discover Lucian had been unfaithful to Zinsa.

'I reckon she must have been at the same school as the rest of us,' decided Mario, leaving the BMW – a trigger, it seemed, for a neighbour's dog to start barking. Other dogs in the vicinity immediately followed suit, the raucous din disrupting an otherwise peaceful street.

'Then that's probably how Lucian came to know her,' said Shani above the racket, upset that such a suspicion regarding her father could have evolved in the first place.

'Nice roses,' commented Mario. They walked up the paved path towards a white door. 'Wonder what fertiliser she's using? Hopefully entirely organic.'

The four of them assembled themselves alongside the bed of lavender and Mario rang the bell.

'I'm curious to know why she left the bank,' said Shani. 'The manager certainly made it sound mysterious.'

'Well…' Mario dropped his voice to a whisper when the lock on the door turned. 'We are, I imagine, about to find out.'

They were greeted by a middle-aged woman with blonde hair cut in a short, layered style that immediately caught Shani's attention. Once her hair had grown to a decent length, perhaps she might even have someone replicate such a style for her.

Mario was gawping. '*Elena...tu eşti?*'

'*Eu?*' said the woman, squinting slightly as if she had an issue seeing properly.

'*Mario Nemescu. Am fost colegi de şcoală, îţi aminteşti?*'

'*Oh... Oh, Mario... Doamne Dumnezeule!*'

'I have Zinsa's daughter with me.'

'Oh, yes. Shani... Please, you are all welcome. I have cake and coffee for you.'

Shani sat with Ana on the settee, Mario in an armchair, while a wooden chair from the small dining table in the corner of the room was brought over for Victor to sit on. Bare of framed photographs on side tables or the mantelpiece in front of them, the room suggested that Elena lived alone. Through the patio doors, the garden appeared to be in full bloom with a cheerful mix of pastel colours.

The elders had entered into a lively discussion in Romanian, catching up on the thirty-odd years that had elapsed since the day Mario was expelled. Then, quite abruptly, a spell of despair from Elena, who shook her head several times before Mario turned away to look across the room.

'Shani, Elena has just explained to me what happened, why she left the bank. It wasn't her choice.' Mario asked their host a brief question, and was given a reply, to which he nodded, and then continued. 'Twelve years ago, Elena was leaving the bank for lunch when masked gunmen came in spraying acid in people's faces. She caught it first, and if it hadn't been for the quick-thinking of a passer-by who happened to be carrying a large bottle of orange juice, she might have been permanently blinded.'

'That's appalling!' cried Shani. 'Please, Mario, you must convey to Elena my sorrow.'

'Elena has about seventy percent vision,' added Mario. 'Glasses are of little use to her. She had to leave her job at the bank because she could hardly read the words on the computer screen. She hasn't been back since. She does still have the keys to the deposit box—'

'Your father did not take key, Shani,' interrupted Elena. 'He left bank without key. I can't remember why. Maybe he in hurry.'

'Do you remember that day, twenty-four years ago?' asked Shani. 'I understand if you do not want to recall it because of what happened to you—'

'Yes, I remember, Shani,' said Elena softly, while clasping Mario's proffered hand. 'A couple of days later came the tragedy at the protest march. I was upset. I thought of Zinsa and her babies. Then, I learn boy was gone. Only girl live. And now…' Elena wiped a tear away, '…here is that girl. Zinsa's beautiful girl.'

'Thank you.' Shani felt compelled to leave the settee and kneel beside this brave woman. A woman who was literally carrying her scars with utmost dignity. 'Please, Elena, tell me about that day.'

Elena let go of Mario's hand and settled back into the armchair. 'I remember the receptionist calling me over the phone. It was your father. He was…er…the word is missing. Like…tight. His body tight.'

'*Anxious*, perhaps?' asked Mario.

'Yes, anxious – that is the word I look for,' agreed Elena. 'Babies close to birth, Shani. This perhaps why Lucian anxious. He said he would bring them to the bank to show me. It is clear to me what he said.'

'And he wanted a safe deposit box?' prompted Shani.

'Yes. But not enough money.'

'Did he mention what he wanted to put in the box?'

'Personal item only. I might have said keep it safe at home. But he wanted box. I felt sorry for Lucian. He was, as Mario say, anxious.'

Shani touched Elena's knee, tears welling up in her eyes. She was sure that this lovely woman was living a life of loneliness. And she didn't damn well deserve it. 'Don't worry yourself, Elena. You can stop whenever you want.'

Elena shook her head. 'No. You must learn everything... So, I say to Lucian, I will become agent. No cost to me as staff of bank, and no cost to Lucian. This is how we did it.' Elena crossed the room to the dining table and handed Shani two keys. 'For the box, Shani.'

'You never looked inside it after the tragedy?'

'No. Too upset. I tried to contact parents. But disappear.'

'Yes. To the Czech Republic. Long story, Elena. But I will tell you another day.'

'Well,' said Elena, still standing, 'coffee and cake.'

Shani handed Elena the form she'd been given at the bank. 'Just this to sign, Elena, when you are ready.'

'I will do this now, Shani,' said Elena, taking the form from her.

* * *

During tea, Shani found herself studying Mario's body language and the animated way he spoke to Elena, who reciprocated in a similar fashion. Years of catching up, perhaps. But there was explicit fascination, too. Ana nudged Shani discreetly with her foot, evidently equally intrigued. When the last piece of gingerbread loaf went to Victor after everyone else declared they were full, Mario announced that Elena was going to show him around the garden and, despite Elena's utterances to the contrary, they were to take the plates and cups into the kitchen and wash and dry everything up.

Mario had hardly left the patio with Elena before Ana turned on her heel to Shani. 'Tell me what you think?'

'There was much going on between them, Ana.' Shani looked at Victor, seeking the man's perspective. 'You agree?'

'I agree,' said Victor, stacking the plates carefully.

'Shani, this is the news we want. Papa so alone. Many years. You have done this for Papa.'

'I have?' said Shani, leading the way into the kitchen.

'Without you, without the bank, this would not happen.'

'Ana speak the truth, Shani,' interjected Victor. 'We have wanted this for him.'

'But we don't know for certain,' said Shani.

'I will not leave until date has been set for them to meet up,' announced Ana. 'It will be done, sister Shani.'

* * *

Unsurprisingly, the return journey to the bank was dominated by Ana's impatience to know the details of Mario's tour of Elena's garden.

'We talked of the past,' said Mario. 'Obviously.'

'A date has been done?' persisted Ana, leaning forward from the rear seat.

'Yes. Okay?' Mario swung round to Shani. 'As you can see, my life would not be worth living had I not done so.'

'I'm with Ana,' said Shani. She itched to reach the bank and the contents of the safe deposit box. 'Elena strikes me as being a kind and altogether lovely person. A person who has lived with sadness in her life, and not through her doing. The same can be said for you.'

'True,' remarked Mario, facing the screen and the build-up of afternoon traffic. 'I did enjoy Elena's company, and that's why she's coming over to stay a few days at the end of the month.'

'Papa!' cried Ana. 'Am I dreaming? Tell me.'

'You're not dreaming, Ana. Elena wants to see permaculture in action, meaning we share common interests.'

* * *

Cezar Ceauşescu walked the length of a corridor to arrive at a large, circular metal door, Shani and Ana at his side. To the left of the door, a panel of switches. The moment the orange button was pressed, a whirring sound came from the door's gigantic hinges and, by degrees, it began to open.

'This is all very different to when your father banked with us,' the manager said to Shani. 'This vault did not exist.'

The door looked to be a metre thick, and now that it was three-quarters open, its whirring had stopped. Ahead of them was a corridor lined with stainless-steel safe deposit boxes as high as the ceiling, gleaming against the harsh lighting. As she stepped through the circular entrance, Shani likened it to a threshold into the next century. At the end of the corridor, a capacious area, again packed with boxes apart from two curtained cubicles and a desk, incorporated into which a flat screen and a keyboard.

The manager ran his fingers over the keyboard, and Shani heard a click from the bank of deposit boxes immediately to her right.

'All done,' said the manager with a note of gratification. 'Everything as it should be.' Lowering the outer panel with the number 1634 on its facia, he extracted a black box and took it over to the nearest cubicle, leaving it on a shelf inside. 'You can look, or take whatever you find away with you,' he told Shani. 'Draw the curtain. Your friend can, of course, accompany you.'

Ana straightaway followed Shani into the cubicle.

Shani drew the curtain. 'I'm nervous,' she whispered. 'Twenty-four years...'

'I'm with you,' spoke Ana. 'Remember, we are strong.'

Shani took one of the two keys Elena had given her from her jeans. 'You've got the carrier bag Victor gave you?'

'Yes. Folded in pocket.'

'Okay, here goes.' Shani inserted the key into the lock at the third attempt, her fingers shaking as never before. After she'd turned it there was a moment's awkwardness until she realised the box could only slide out from its outer casing to the right and not to the left... And *there* it actually lay! Shani breathed a sigh of relief. The folder was black, its cover torn down the centre. 'This has to be it,' she whispered. 'The thing that's caused all this trouble.'

'Yes,' agreed Ana, unfolding the carrier bag.

'Just think…my father was the last person to touch this.' She lifted it from the box – and froze.

'*Sfinte Sisoe!*' breathed Ana.

'Oh, my God!' uttered Shani, her eyes fixed on the handgun and the handful of bullets. 'This cannot be true.'

'Shhh!' interjected Ana, signalling with a tilt of her head, reminding Shani of the manager outside. 'We take.' Reopening the carrier bag: 'Put inside.'

Shani took the gun from the box and carefully placed it with the folder inside the bag. Then came a thought. 'Detection? When we leave the bank.'

'Not airport, sister Shani.'

'Okay, we just have to hope.' Shani scooped up the bullets and put them in her jeans rather than the bag. It would be just their luck if one of them slid out of a small hole as they made their way across the foyer. 'Let's go.'

'Now I worry,' said Ana, frowning.

'Worry?'

'About gun. Should we leave in box?'

'Because of detection?'

'Maybe.'

Shani put the last bullet in her jeans. 'No. We take the risk. I don't want to come back here again.' Reaching for the carrier bag, she said, 'I'll hold onto this. If something happens, you know nothing about what's inside it. Clear?'

Ana nodded. 'Yes. Papa go crazy.'

Shani hadn't thought of that aspect. 'You think so?'

'I calm him. It's okay. We go. I need cigarette.'

Shani left the cubicle in front of Ana. The manager stood several feet away, beside the desk. Shani smiled, but the trauma of finding a gun in the box made her want to dash for the exit. 'There wasn't much,' she mentioned, surprised she could muster a note of indifference. 'I really don't know why my father went to all the trouble.'

'A premonition, perhaps?' offered the manager, leaving the desk.

'Well, yes.' Shani sensed perspiration once again on her brow, her throat parched to an almost painful degree. 'You could be right. Something we'll never know, I suppose.'

Ana suddenly threaded her arm under Shani's, the signal to leave the bank unmistakeable. *Talk about partners in crime*, thought Shani, before she explained to the manager that they were in quite a hurry – so would it be all right if they proceeded towards the foyer, leaving him to do the 'locking up'?

'I'll need to come with you,' he replied.

Damn! reacted Shani privately.

'There are two doors where I need to use my pass,' explained the manager as the huge circular door began to close at a snail's pace.

Shani looked at Ana. Whether the strain they were under had something to do with it wasn't clear, but Ana seemed prettier than ever before: perfect skin tone; her emerald eyes vivacious, while her upright bearing accentuated the theme by conveying palpable vitality. A catch for any intelligent male, Shani imagined. And *intelligent* he would have to be, with a hefty measure of mercurial wit thrown in!

The manager took off down the corridor, Shani finding herself eager to follow his stride. Pass one…done. Then another corridor, partially glazed doors to offices on both sides. Pass two. Now the foyer and the shaking of hands, followed by good wishes and smiles. The foyer seemed busier, queues here and there.

'Just our luck the bag splits open,' Shani whispered out of the corner of her mouth to Ana, who still had her arm wrapped around hers.

'We are good news,' responded Ana. 'We have result.'

Fresh air. *Heavenly* fresh air. And now down the steps and onto the pavement. 'I think we've done it,' said Shani. The BMW was still parked adjacent to a kiosk selling popcorn.

The moment she sat on the back seat with Ana, Shani said, 'Drive. Just get away from here.'

Mario swung round. 'Problems?'

'Better you don't know. That way, if we're stopped I can take the blame.'

'But you have the folder? Was it there, in the box?'

'*A* folder, yes. Whether it's the one in question remains to be seen.' Shani leaned forward. 'Victor, I suggest you make a few false turns in case we have a tail.'

CHAPTER 20

They sat around the kitchen table, cups of coffee and curiosity in equal measures. Shani guessed that Ana was having a hard time containing herself. She began with the black ring folder, producing it from the carrier bag.

'I know this is likely to sound ridiculous,' she said, 'but the last person to touch this was my father. I'd like to keep it that way. But not what it contains, obviously. I don't know how long fingerprints last. I imagine a long time in stable conditions – such as a safe deposit box.'

'Nothing ridiculous about that, Shani,' concurred Mario. 'It's your property, remember. Now, open it.'

Shani did so. A page of typed letters inside a square, with columns of numbers marked 1 to 5 to the left and above. Below the square, seven rows of numbers.

Mario came and looked over her shoulder. 'That's it. As I remember it – what Lucian showed me twenty-four years ago.'

'What bearing do the rows of numbers have?' asked Shani. 'Are they the clues to lift the encryptor's words from the square, so to speak?'

'Yes.' Mario returned to his chair. 'You know, that day is becoming quite vivid to me now. A few days later, Lucian gave me the photocopy of what you are now holding.'

Shani raised the folder slightly and turned it around for Ana and Victor's benefit. 'What are we going to do, Mario?' she asked. 'Can we put the contents inside another folder before handing over this material to these people? I can then keep this folder.'

'I don't see any reason as to why not. I'm not sure quite how we're going to contact them. Perhaps take the folder to Skid Row and see if anything happens, like the Volvo putting in another appearance.' Mario reached for his tobacco tin. 'But as you say, Shani, first we need to make copies. We can do that here. I have a scanner and I can put the material on a memory stick for you.'

'How long do you imagine it will take to decipher?' Shani asked.

Mario shrugged. 'As I recall…' Leaning forward and looking at the top sheet, he nodded to himself. 'Yes, the code is fairly basic. Based on the Polybius Square. In fact, if it really does concern Deep State, then the simplicity of the code used surprises me.'

Ana pointed at the sheet of encrypted material. 'Papa, why I/J together?'

'Because the modern-day English alphabet has twenty-six letters, which cannot make a square, so it's rounded down to the next figure. Sometimes the coder chooses to miss out a letter, usually Z. Polybius was Greek, so he didn't have that problem – the Greek alphabet having only twenty-four letters. All he did was leave one square blank, making an overall square of five by five.'

'Who was Polybius?' asked Victor.

'A Greek historian, a hundred and fifty years or so before Christ.' Mario put down the freshly rolled cigarette and leant over the table. 'A thought has just occurred to me. I need to turn the pages, Shani.'

'Of course. You might as well remove them from the folder if we're going to scan them.'

Mario slid the handful of pages carefully off the folder's rings. Sitting back down, he flipped through the pages. 'Yes, I thought so. I remember now…'

'Remember what?' asked Shani.

'When your father delivered the photocopy, I discovered that only the first two pages are set using the Polybius Square. The programmer, as if realising the code might be broken, decided to switch to the more intricate Playfair Square. But these days, that in itself is relatively insecure, due to applications that can be harnessed to computers.'

'But can you crack it?'

'Oh, yes.' Mario lit the cigarette he'd just rolled. 'Without such an app, it'll just be more laborious.'

'As keen as I am to know what it's about, Mario,' said Shani, 'that's not the main issue right now. We need to get this wretched 'unknown force' off our backs.'

'Yes,' said Victor, reaching for his father's tobacco tin. 'We want Skid Row open. No good losing business.'

Mario finished his coffee. He seemed pensive, and consequently drew everyone's attention.

'What is it?' asked Shani.

'Something's always puzzled me about all this.'

'What way, Papa?' asked Ana.

'How did the police know I had the document? Once they had me down at the station on a charge of shoplifting, which was proven to be false by the principal of the language school since I couldn't have been in two places at once, they suddenly mentioned the document. Someone went back to the room I was living in, found it and brought it to the police station.'

'Lucian wouldn't have told them, would he?' asked Shani. 'I mean, to our knowledge he was never arrested.'

'The only other person who knew, apart from Lucian's parents, providing Lucian had told them he'd handed me a photocopy, was Serghei. But I can't see him trotting off to the police over anything. Quite the opposite.'

'It baffles me why Lucian wasn't arrested at the same time as you?' considered Shani.

'Maybe they couldn't find anything to hang on him. Besides, Andrei would have paid out for a lawyer. He had the resources. It could have turned into a public affair, resulting in these documents being returned to some agency in America. I imagine this doubtless corrupt cell of officers wanted to decode the photocopy to see whether the original had any value. And if it had, then presumably they would have come up with a scheme to take it from Lucian.'

'When I saw Serghei the other day, before…well, when I saw him,' debated Shani, certain Mario hadn't told Ana of Serghei's horrific fate, 'he mentioned that he was arrested two days after my parents were killed.

He was asked about the folder and seemed puzzled as to how the police knew about it.'

'I didn't know he'd been arrested,' said Mario. 'Or if I did, I'd forgotten.'

'He seemed as bitter about you as you are about him,' said Shani, curious as to how Mario might react to that remark. There was something that wasn't clear in her own head and she couldn't quite pin down the reason.

'He would be,' said Mario bluntly, 'because of his prison sentence. Remember what I told you before? That he tried to get me to take the blame for his illegal dealings. But I had my fabricated alibis – favours that I called in, basically.' Mario unexpectedly met her eyes directly and held his gaze. 'Shani…Shani, be honest…do you doubt me? Think I might be up to something when it comes to this folder?'

'No.' She thought more about her knee-jerk reply. 'Some doubt at first, maybe.'

'Who can blame you for that?'

'But getting to know Ana and Victor and the manner in which you have brought them up has removed all such doubt. It's just that there are loose ends and I'm finding that frustrating.'

'We're talking twenty-four years ago, Shani.'

'I know—'

'Maybe...' interrupted Ana, pointing at the carrier bag on the table. 'Perhaps it help Papa to give answers.'

Shani nodded and stood up from the table. 'Apart from the folder, these items were also in the safe deposit box.' Extracting the bullets from her jeans, she left them on the table before exhibiting the gun from the carrier bag.

'Jesus,' muttered Mario.

'Wow,' breathed Victor. 'You find this with folder?'

'Yes,' said Ana. 'We find. And bullets.'

'Well...' Mario reached for the gun, turning it in his hands. 'I believe I can tell you where Lucian found this, along with the bullets. He took them from me.'

'Papa,' cried Ana. 'You had *this*?'

'Yes. It was a side-line. I was buying deactivated guns. Guns that were made harmless for collectors to keep. Only, I was reactivating them by drilling and filing, then selling them on. Of course, your mother made me stop this particular pastime.'

'So, what can this gun tell us?' asked Shani.

'I can remember hiding the others the moment I saw the police appear on the driveway of the school where I worked. At the time, perhaps I suspected Serghei had taken this Beretta from me.' Mario stubbed out the rolled cigarette. 'Okay, so the question we need to ask ourselves is this: why would Lucian go to all the trouble of going to the bank to keep the folder safe?'

'Because he regarded it as valuable,' said Shani.

'By itself, that's not enough. He could have kept it at home, as Elena suggested he might do when he turned up at the bank. It's the gun – this reactivated Beretta – that's the clue. No, Lucian sensed, or realised, he was being targeted. Surely, that is the truth of the matter.'

'I get the feeling,' said Shani, 'that my emergence from obscurity has reawakened this same force that concerned my father. Don't you think?'

'Certainly appears that way,' agreed Mario. 'Lucian must have come over to the school, where I was living as the live-in caretaker, to tell me that he suspected he was being followed...' He sighed and lifted his hands, as if in despair. 'Alternatively, of course, though it saddens me to say it, he came over to retrieve the photocopy because he had doubts over my honesty.'

'You really had no intention of selling it on, given your character in those days?' asked Shani.

'No. I liked Lucian. More than I did Serghei, in fact. I dare say I thought that this was a good opportunity to get to know him better. I looked up to him. His decency, you know. I'm sure he tried to get Serghei away from taking drugs.'

'Serghei said as much to me,' confirmed Shani.

'So, going back twenty-four years, perhaps only days before you were born, Shani, we can say that for some reason Lucian became fearful. He saw the gun at my place and took it.' Mario reached for a bullet and then shook his head quietly. 'Oh, Lucian…' he murmured, as if Lucian was sitting at the table with them.

'What is it?' asked Shani.

'These bullets don't go with this gun. No doubt he took them at the same time, but they correspond with a different make of gun. If he had tried one of these bullets in this Beretta, it would likely have blown up in his hand.'

'Okay,' agreed Shani, 'what you've said regarding the fear factor makes sense. Except, why would he put the gun in the box with the folder? Surely he would want to keep the gun in case he needed to use it?'

Mario leaned back in the chair. 'Lucian was quite a straight sort of guy,' he said gently. 'I think that's why I respected him to the point of envy – wanted, if you like, to be like him. I suspect that it lay uncomfortably with his conscience that he was now in possession of a gun. And Zinsa was about to give birth, remember. What an object to have lying around at such a time. That's my view – how I would likely have felt, had I been in his shoes.'

'But he could have hidden it,' argued Shani.

'Yes, but perhaps he'd already considered going to the bank with the folder, putting it safely under lock and key. The two items combined swayed his decision to use a deposit box. He could still have withdrawn the gun from the bank whenever, in a matter of minutes. And, remember, it didn't cost Lucian a cent. Thanks to Elena, he got it for nothing.'

'Okay…' Shani picked up the gun, guessing her fingers were touching her father's prints from over two decades ago. The Beretta felt surprisingly heavy for its size. 'What are you going to do with this?' she asked.

'You must break it, Papa,' insisted Ana. 'Guns not good.'

'You don't want it?' Mario asked Shani. 'Something your father touched.'

'No. I have the folder – which I can get through customs.'

'You could keep the gun here in Romania. You're going to visit us, are you not?'

'Of course she will, Papa,' said Victor, taking a closer look at the gun.

'She come often,' said Ana. 'Shani come to see her sister.'

Shani smiled and met Mario's eyes across the table. 'There you are, they have answered for me. No, as Ana has said, better to destroy it. How can you do that?'

'I'll use the welding equipment out the back and the grinder I have in the garage.'

'The English school where you worked,' said Shani, 'is it still an English school?'

'That I don't know. I haven't been back since I got married.'

'Do you think we could drive over there tomorrow?'

'I'll take you there after breakfast,' said Mario. 'Then we'll head over to Skid Row and see if by chance the green Volvo happens to be parked up nearby.'

'Dinner, Papa?' asked Ana.

'We'll have beef stew. You and Victor can start preparing it. Shani can find the vegetables you need in the garden. I'll be in the back room if you want me, scanning these pages.'

CHAPTER 21

The following day, after they had dressed, Ana sat down on the bed.

'Sister Shani, I am sad. Don't go.'

'I have to, Ana.' Shani tucked the few clothes she had left into her backpack, having stuffed the rest into a bin near the Sunrise Guest House. She really didn't know how she was going to come to terms with finding Serghei murdered. The horror kept repeating itself inside her head, flashing onto her inner screen when least expected. Whoever had done it had to be mentally deranged, with a definite penchant for dispensing cruelty. 'I need to go to Prague and then England to meet Nicolas,' she explained.

'Boyfriend. You have picture?'

Shani sat on the bed beside Ana. 'On my phone.' She scrolled through reams of pictures, many of them now irrelevant to her.

'Stop!' said Ana. 'Oxford?'

'Yes. My college.'

'Wow. Old.'

'Very.'

'One day, I come. Please.'

'Of course, you will. I insist. With Papa, and the boys if they want to.'

'Boys not understand culture.' Ana tilted her hand. 'Maybe Victor. Not Cosmin. Only girls Cosmin understand. And not very well, I tell you.'

Shani laughed, seeing Ana as quite a character, who wouldn't put up with any nonsense from her brothers. 'Here he is. This is Nicolas.'

Ana took the phone from Shani and studied the picture of a man with tousled blond hair and a strong, almost chiselled, facial structure. 'Good-looking guy. Cool. English?'

'No, French,' said Shani. 'And, yes, he's a cool guy. Helped me to come to terms with – to accept – my prosthesis.'

'Thesis?'

Shani tapped her left ankle.

'Oh, yes. Sorry.'

Shani stood and finished packing.

'I will try not to be sad.'

'Good,' said Shani. 'I never want to see you sad, Ana.'

'I want boyfriend, like you.'

'When you go to university in Bucharest, you will have to fight them off.'

Ana rolled her eyes. 'Boys. Nine from ten stupid. Always drinking. Always showing…er…'

'Showing off?'

'Yes.'

'Just their age, Ana.' Shani hooked her backpack onto her left shoulder. 'We'd better go downstairs. Mario's called us twice for breakfast.'

* * *

Shani tucked into a freshly baked croissant. 'You must show me the recipe.' She glanced at Mario. 'Delicious. As was the beef stew last night. I could vastly improve my culinary endeavours by watching you. All of you, in fact.'

'It becomes part and parcel of permaculture,' replied Mario, sitting down at the table with a mug of coffee. 'If you grow food, then you tend to respect to a greater extent how you prepare and use it. You never waste anything. That which is inedible is composted – unless it's diseased, in which case it is burnt and the ashes spread on the land. All perfectly logical.'

'I want to come, Papa,' said Ana, 'to where you take Shani.'

'I will take you another time, Ana. I need you to go with Victor on the Suzuki and open the café with Cosmin. Everything must be as normal.'

'If you say so, Papa. But Shani will come to Skid Row with you? You will not take her to airport before I see her?'

'Correct.'

'Your arm,' pointed out Victor. 'You can drive with it?'

'It's fine. The blade went into muscle. Another week or two and I'll be as good as new.'

'I'm still distraught over what happened to Daniela,' said Shani, putting her coffee cup down. 'Or rather Mariana. I can't see myself ever getting over it. What must her parents be going through?'

'Absolute hell, I'd imagine. And I know what you're about to say. That we should go to the police and tell them what we know.'

'Precisely that, Mario. Maybe the information we have will give them a lead to catching her killer.'

'A possibility, of course. But I have to say my central point remains unchanged: that our foe might be authority-related and, if so, unlikely to be Romanian in origin.'

'Meaning Deep State?'

'As dramatic as that sounds, yes. If we go to the police then there is no knowing what could happen – what triggers might be activated. Having said that, and returning to the situation with Mariana's parents, a solution of sorts has crossed my mind – where we don't involve ourselves directly.'

'The solution being?' asked Shani.

'That a neighbour in the street describes the goings-on at the hostel. The neighbour being, of course, too fearful to state his name. And that our fictitious neighbour, having briefly passed the time of day with her, realises the girl who entered the hostel matches a picture of Mariana he's seen in a newspaper. We can even mention that he witnessed the dumping of a body at night into a skip.'

'Skip in different street,' interrupted Victor.

Mario hesitated while reaching for his tobacco tin. 'I forgot. Okay, I'll change that to *saw* the removal of what looked to be a body from the hostel. Should a team of forensic scientists be called to the hostel they will soon discover overwhelming evidence of a murder having occurred – a very *recent* murder. Serghei's death should put them on the road to discovering Mariana's killer.'

Shani agreed. 'A good idea.' Mario's scenario began to ease her conscience. Under the circumstances, it was perhaps all she could hope for. 'But the old man at the reception desk,' she mentioned aloud. 'I wonder what's happened to him?'

Mario shrugged. 'Maybe they didn't see him as a threat in the way they did with Mariana and let him go. Did you feel you got on with Mariana?'

'Yes, I would say so. But, Mario, do you really believe that Deep State could be involved? That it, or part of it, believes we are searching for the folder?'

'In my heart of hearts, no,' said Mario. 'I think their approach would be subtler.'

'It could have been outsourced to criminals, as you previously suggested.'

'I doubt if they would trust it going to amateurs of any description.'

'You regard what we have witnessed so far as having an amateurish edge?'

'Some aspects. I think the break-ins, for instance, would have gone unnoticed, avoiding scrutiny.' Mario got up from his chair. 'We still need to assume Deep State *could* be involved. To dismiss the possibility outright would be foolish in my opinion.'

* * *

Mario pointed straight ahead before turning into a side road. 'Timişoara has a zoo, further on up that way. And an open-air village museum, covering the Banat eras. There were two such eras. I'll explain further and take you there when we have more time.'

'I saw the sign to the zoo,' said Shani. 'Is it a big zoo?'

'Quite big. I took the children there years ago. The area's become quite industrial now, lots of factories going up. And as you can see, a number of these houses we're coming to have fallen into disrepair. All very different to how it was,' reflected Mario.

'I love Baroque architecture,' said Shani. 'I know it's quite theatrical, but I just love it. Far from mundane. I never tire of Prague.'

'The house I'm looking for is more Art Deco and should be on our right…'

'I'm starting to feel nervous about the handover, Mario,' Shani said, and meant it – her stomach verging on somersaults.

'That's if it happens. It's the only way I know that we can make contact with them.' Mario parked outside one of the houses. 'Meanwhile, we're here. This is going to bring back some memories.'

'Oh, Mario!' Shani instinctively put a hand on his arm. 'I should have realised. This is where you met your wife.'

'Correct. But it's okay. I'm curious, actually. There seems to be building work going on. Refurbishment to some degree. Nice to see, I guess. Preserving it.'

Shani noted the long drive lined with sycamores.

'Let's go and take a closer look,' said Mario.

Shani left the BMW. 'My father must have walked up this driveway.'

'With Serghei. On the first occasion, anyway.'

'This is how you remember it, Mario?'

Mario nodded as they walked over gravel, peppered with weeds. 'Yes.'

'But my father came in November. With autumn turning to winter it's likely there would be no leaves on these trees.'

'Yes, it would have been like that. The trees bare of leaves.'

'I can't believe I'm actually walking in his footsteps. I wonder what he was thinking?'

'Probably hoping I could decipher the contents of the folder he was carrying.'

They came to a workman sitting on a carpenter's trestle, idly smoking a cigarette. Mario spoke to him, and the workman waved an airy hand.

'We can take a look around,' said Mario. 'The only place of any significance, really, is the room where I lived.'

They made their way over to the right of the building, towards scaffolding that rose up in a rectangular tower against a chimney breast.

'Did Serghei visit you often?' asked Shani.

'For a period of time. I was buying cigarettes and other stuff for next to nothing, passing some of it onto him. He did quite well with the cigarettes, I recall.'

'And then you met Simona, right here.'

'Just as well. I'm quite sure I would have ended up in prison.' Mario chuckled. 'Probably sharing a cell with Serghei.' He pointed in front of them. 'I'm certain there was a wooden gate here. In fact, here's the post for it.'

'Quite rotten now.'

'This path leads to the back garden.' Mario stepped over a pile of rubble and then under the scaffolding to push on a door, which creaked on hinges caked in rust. 'Here we go. This is it…where I lived for about three years.'

Shani entered the windowless room and smelt the damp immediately. It seemed to be full of wardrobes and other pieces of utility furniture, with an old porcelain sink to her left, partially covered with cobwebs.

'Incredible!' roared Mario.

'What is it?' Shani caught up with him between the furniture.

'I think this is the actual mattress that I slept on. I had it in a corner over there.'

Shani cast her eyes over the mattress, upright between two wardrobes. It looked filthy. 'I don't know how you managed to live here for three years, Mario.'

'I was young. No rent to pay. It wasn't an issue.'

'So, Lucian stood in this very same room all those years ago?'

'I can see him now, handing me the folder. Zinsa would likely have been at home, about to give birth to you.'

'And my brother.'

'Of course.'

Without warning, Shani felt her eyes prickle.

'We'll leave. Yes?'

She took a tissue from her jeans and dabbed her eyes. 'I think so. Life can be so bloody cruel.' She met Mario's eyes. 'I don't have to tell you that, do I?'

'No. Come on, let's get away from here.'

Outside on the drive, Mario waved his thanks to the workman, still sitting on the trestle.

'You don't know the house where they lived, do you?' said Shani. 'I think I asked you. I should have asked Serghei. Because of their age I imagine they were likely to still be living with Andrei and Rodica.'

'Serghei would have known. It'll be documented somewhere where they lived.'

Shani waited for Mario to unlock the BMW's passenger door, taking one last look at the building they'd just visited. A November day, bare sycamore trees and a pebbled drive, and her father walking away from her towards a wooden gate separating the rear from the front. She wanted him to turn around and wave to her. But he didn't. He simply carried on, walking up the drive.

* * *

At Skid Row Café, Mario instructed Shani to sit at a table reserved for them over by the window that looked out across the street.

Shani put the plastic bag she'd been carrying under the table, the original material from the plane crash now inside an authentic-looking dog-eared green folder Mario had found. After speaking to Ana, working the till, Mario sat opposite and handed her the menu card. They'd hit lunch hour. Cosmin was busily taking orders; Victor presumably somewhere out the back – cooking, assumed Shani.

'Do you think they'll show?' she asked.

'It's our only hope to get them off our backs. The fact we've reopened the café is a signal to them. Have you chosen?'

'Cheese salad in a baguette.' Shani looked out onto the street; cars, buses and the occasional tram sweeping by. 'If we get an image of him, I can then send it to my college and see if it's the same person who entered the staircase to my study.'

'Interesting to know,' agreed Mario.

'Although I don't see how it can be. The break-in in Oxford virtually coincides with what happened to Serghei in the hostel.'

Mario gave the order to Cosmin, asking him something in Romanian.

When Cosmin replied, his father rolled his eyes.

While Cosmin strode towards the kitchen, Shani asked, 'What did you say to him? Your expression looked altogether comical.'

'I asked him why he wasn't wearing a tie. He said he'd left it at some girl's address.'

Despite the mounting tension, Shani found she had no difficulty in smiling. 'You're only young once, remember. And he is good-looking, Mario.' She noted the camera above them, pointing at the street rather than the café's interior. 'If he comes, then I'm out there with you.'

'I'd rather you were not.'

'He's not going to try anything on such a busy street.'

'I wouldn't be so sure.'

'We're giving him the document. I want to see this bastard's face close up. If he stabbed you in the arm, then he might well have strangled Mariana before dumping her body in the river.' Shani leaned back, making room for Cosmin to deliver the baguette she'd ordered. Mario was having beans on toast.

'My favourite,' he said. 'Ever since I can remember.'

'Excellent protein,' remarked Shani. She gazed down at her baguette. 'This looks beautifully prepared, but I have to say I'm not particularly hungry.'

Mario reached for his knife and fork. 'Shani, I'm going to say something here.'

'Go ahead. About food, I'm guessing.'

'You're quite thin. Not desperately thin. I think I mentioned to you the other day that you could do with putting on a few kilos. It won't ruin your figure.'

'I know.' Shani sliced the baguette in half. 'I suppose my weight loss started when Andrei died, which was then followed by the coup in Séroulé. It really took it out of me. I felt like I was on a rollercoaster of fear for the most part, operating completely outside my comfort zone.'

'I can imagine.' Mario tucked into his beans on toast. 'So, what happens now? You return to your studies in Oxford? Are you going to set up home there with Nicolas?'

'No.' Shani made a start on the baguette. It tasted gorgeously fresh, the bread still warm. 'Compliments to the chef, I would say.'

'I'll tell Victor. The answer to my question?'

'I don't think Oxford would suit Nicolas. He would find it claustrophobic. It would be like a prison for him. He wouldn't fit in. He's happiest when he's in the field, as it were.'

'War zones?'

'In that vein, unfortunately.'

'And you?'

'I'm leaving academia. Actually, I made that decision in your garden. I came across Café on one of the paths. The friendly hen that belongs to Ana. Café allowed me to touch her feathers.'

'She's rather cute, I agree.'

'I couldn't kill her.'

'I have three. Café will die from natural causes, being Ana's favourite. The other two...well, unfortunately for them I'm not vegetarian. The best way is to hypnotise them first.'

Cosmin came and interrupted them, speaking to Mario – who nodded.

Shani could see a swathe of tension on Ana's face over by the till. She looked across the street. A green Volvo had pulled up.

'He's parked in front of the entrance to the Botanical Park,' said Mario.

'Might that be significant?' asked Shani.

'Can't see how,' said Mario, abandoning the few beans left on his plate. 'Okay, let's get this over with.'

Shani reached for the bag. 'Do you think that guy's been parking opposite for days on end?'

'Since they hooked us up together, at a guess.' He gave her a hard stare. 'I really don't want you out there.'

'The contents of the folder belong to me. Right?'

'I'm sure there's a loophole, like it belongs to some ruling elite banker or corporate chief in the US.'

'They'd be dead by now,' reacted Shani, her tone unequivocal. 'Fact is, Mario, we haven't time to argue the point, have we?'

Mario sighed heavily. 'Come on, then.' They stepped out onto the pavement together. 'Remember not to block the path of the camera, if possible.'

'I could use the camera on my phone,' said Shani.

'He might not like that.'

'I suppose not.' Shani watched as the Volvo remained beside the curb. 'He's expecting us to cross the road.'

'If we do, then we're not going to get an image of him. He – or the people he's working for – want this material. And from what we've learnt about them, they'll do anything to get hold of it.' Mario's phone began to chime. He took it from his pocket, answered it and promptly cursed. 'He's called the café. He's saying we have to cross the road.'

'Let's just do it, Mario,' urged Shani. 'As you say – get them off our backs so we can return to living our lives. We've scanned the sheets.'

Mario nodded reluctantly. 'There's a crossing up by the lights.'

They walked towards it. 'What about me taking a picture on my phone, then?' asked Shani. 'We no longer have the camera in the café.'

'I still don't like the idea, Shani.'

'Why?'

'Because the chances are he won't be alone.' They waited for the lights to change. 'Sure, he's alone in the car. But there could well be an accomplice watching the proceedings. Perhaps that's why he pulled up outside the park. Plenty of trees and bushes for cover.' Mario looked across at her. 'Give me the folder.'

'No,' said Shani decisively. She'd half expected him to ask her to hand it over. The lights changed and they crossed the road, all the while closing in on the green Volvo. 'I want to get a good look at his face.'

'I've noticed you can be bloody stubborn at times,' commented Mario. They were now twenty metres from the Volvo. 'I can't recall Zinsa being this stubborn. Nor Lucian, come to that.'

Shani stopped beside the Volvo, the driver's window descending smoothly into the door. There was nothing on the rear or front passenger seats, nothing that could give her a clue as to the identity or habits of the driver. As for the driver, he had a thin, unshaven weasel-like face and a full head of black hair. She thought she could detect a faint scar on his chin, about a centimetre in length and at an angle of thirty-five or so degrees.

'You speak English?' she asked.

The driver shrugged indifferently and gestured for her to hand over the folder.

She did so. Then temptation latched onto her like a bull shark on an open wound – seeing before her a perfect opportunity. She put everything she had into it, her fist connecting with the side of his face. Blood jetted from his nose. 'For Mariana, you sick bastard!'

Mario dragged her away, preventing her from throwing a second punch. He quickly raised a hand in a non-combative gesture when it looked as if the driver was about to step out of the car. The man muttered something at Mario, who didn't respond and instead frogmarched Shani along the pavement.

'Hell,' said Mario, 'I didn't know you were going to do that.'

Shani looked across at him, and then over her shoulder, seeing the Volvo filter into the traffic down the street. 'The least I could have done. You can let go of me now. Put your arm around my shoulders instead. I could do with a fatherly hug.'

Mario drew her to himself.

Shani relaxed, liking the moment. Her father might have clinched her in such a caring way. Ana was so fortunate.

Mario turned to look at her as they waited at the crossing. 'I have to say, that was an immaculate right hook. Correct word, *immaculate*? Yes?'

'I recognise the correlation,' said Shani. 'Was it the same man who stabbed you?'

'Yes. No question. An ugly-looking shit, really.'

'If only we could find out who he's working for.'

The lights changed and they crossed the road. 'It's history now, Shani – in more ways than one.'

'But you're going to work at cracking the code on the scanned sheets?' asked Shani.

'Definitely. Probably make a start this evening. By the way, when is your new family going to meet Nicolas?'

'Soon. After the vacation he's fixed up in Cornwall.' Shani glanced at her right hand. Despite the fact it had begun to sting, outwardly there was no change – no blemishes on the skin whatsoever.

The second they entered Skid Row, Ana rushed up to them. 'It's done?'

'He's gone away with a nose-bleed, thanks to this one,' said Mario, tilting his head towards Shani.

'But he has folder?'

'Yes.'

Ana made a fist and looked at Shani. 'You give him this?'

'I did.' Shani examined her hand again. 'It probably hurt me as much as it did him.'

'What time do you need to be at the airport?' Mario asked.

'I should be making tracks. The flight's in an hour and a half.'

'Papa,' interrupted Ana, 'I want to come to airport with sister Shani. Lunch finished.'

'Then go and get changed,' said Mario.

Out the back, in the kitchen area, Shani said her goodbyes with hugs to Cosmin and Victor. 'That Suzuki,' she said to Victor, 'when I'm back next month, can I borrow it?'

'It will happen this way,' said Victor. 'You are our sister. What we have is yours to share. Always.'

PART 3

A SNAKE IN THE GRASS

CHAPTER 22

Dusana had clearly done some tidying up after the break-in. Books were no longer strewn across the floor, as described over the phone by Dusana to Shani on her arrival in Romania, but were instead stacked neatly on the dining table, ready to be returned to their original order on the shelves – not that such a task could ever be accurately achieved; only Andrei would have known their specific sequence. The safe, a flimsy sheet-metal affair, lay on a cloth on the table beside the books, its feeble lock having been wrenched open. Brown A4 envelopes lay next to it, the top one revealing the numbers relating to the safe deposit box at Banca Comercială Bănăţeana, Timişoara. BCB 1634.

Shani put down the empty ring folder and off-loaded her backpack. Picking up the envelope, she sat on the settee. Now that she found herself scrutinising the lettering, she realised it wasn't Andrei's near illegible scrawl – the letters and numbers, in fact, quite tidily written, the handwriting perhaps that of a draughtsman. So, was she staring at her father's handwriting from over two decades ago? Perhaps even Zinsa's? To what extent had her mother been involved when it came to the folder? Or had she been wholly preoccupied with the pregnancy? Shani caressed the folder, wondering again at the cause of the tear virtually the length of the cover. Did it happen when the plane came down? If ever a folder had an air of intrigue about it, then for sure it was this one.

She took her mobile phone from her pocket and called Dusana, who lived a matter of minutes away in the same street.

'Hi Dusana, I've arrived. But I'm whacked out, so I'm going to take a shower, put on my PJs and relax for the rest of the evening. Probably go to bed, in fact. Can we meet tomorrow morning?'

'Of course, darling,' said Dusana, her tone maternal. 'You must rest. These past three months you've been dashing about from country to country.'

'It has been rather like that.'

'Time to get back to your studies.'

'Yes,' said Shani distantly, knowing that wasn't going to happen, but hardly in the mood to enter into a debate with Dusana over her decision. 'So, I'll see you tomorrow, Dusana. I'm going to take that shower.'

She took the charger from a side-pocket on her backpack and charged her phone, then showered and put on her PJs. She felt fresher, her skin tingling with the mint shower gel that she'd bought after trying Nicolas's in Paris. Lying across the settee with a mug of hot chocolate, she called him on her usual phone. Although Mario had asked her to keep the clean phone on the off-chance of a 'development', she couldn't see any reason to use it when calling Nicolas now that they'd handed over the document.

'Hi,' she said the moment the connection was made after a short delay, which seemed to be a typical feature when trying to reach Séroulé. 'Where are you?'

'On my way to the airport. I'll be in Paris by this evening, but I'm going straight through to the UK.

I'm not staying overnight. You've said your goodbyes to Mario?'

'Yes.' Shani gazed at her backpack and wondered what Mario might be doing this precise minute. Working on deciphering the code, perhaps. 'I'm here now, in Prague. Tomorrow I'm seeing Dusana, then I'll leave for London and make my way down to Cornwall. Can't wait.'

'Likewise,' crackled Nicolas through some static. 'I feel I haven't seen you for months.'

'Weird, isn't it? I'm the same. I looked up the place where we're staying, Trebarwith Strand. It's quite remote. Do you want me to bring my bike?'

'It'll be a long journey from Oxford. We'll hire a car. I'll fix that, Shani. Just get to the nearest rail station, wherever that'll be, and I'll collect you.'

'Okay. Have a safe flight, Nicolas!'

No sooner had she ended the call than the 'clean' phone sounded inside her backpack. It could only be Mario. Perhaps he'd tried to get through while she was talking to Nicolas. She dug out the phone. He could have left a message, she told herself. Probably just wanted to make sure she'd arrived safely. Hearing a voice was so much nicer than a text.

'Hi-ya, Mario.'

'Shani – we have a crisis.'

'Crisis? Like what?'

'They want the folder. Straightaway.'

'The folder? What—?'

'You're going to have to come back with it, Shani. Tomorrow at the latest—'

'*Mario*, what on earth is going on?' cried Shani, sitting forward on the settee, bewildered. 'What use is the folder to them? They have the original document it contained. I can't see why they would want it.'

'Shani, they messaged the café--—'

'It's the only thing I have that I know for certain my father actually touched, apart from the gun. Nothing else. Nothing from Zinsa.'

'Shani, they will destroy the café if I do not deliver that folder within forty-eight hours. And after that, it's going to be my children they'll target. I told Victor to close the café and packed the three of them off to Cluj. That's how seriously I'm taking this. Remember what they did to Serghei? Not to mention the actress.'

'Mariana...' Shani started to pace the room. Were they *ever* going to be able to extract themselves from this perverse nightmare! 'Of what interest could having the folder be to them? It's basically trash.'

'I've no idea, Shani. I know it's of great sentimental value to you, but you've got to return to Timişoara with it. I'm sorry—'

'Mario, listen, don't worry.' Shani sat back down on the settee. 'Of course, I'll return to Timişoara with it. I'm just totally mystified.'

'Let me know the flight schedule and I'll pick you up at the airport.'

'Okay. I'll look for one right away.'

Before doing so, she called Nicolas – hoping he was still in range. As luck would have it, he was.

'Nicolas, change of plan. God only knows what's going down in Romania.'

'Explain.'

'I've got to head back there and deliver the folder.'

'Hold on a sec, I need to negotiate some heavy traffic. I'm at the airport.'

Shani waited for him to reconnect, wishing she was in Séroulé and both of them were driving *away* from an airport – into the life they had more or less mapped out together.

'I'm back now, Shani. I thought you had given them the folder?'

'No. I wanted to keep the original folder for sentimental reasons. We gave them the actual contents and Mario found another folder to put them in. But now Mario's just called me and wants me to return to Timişoara with the original folder.'

'No, no, no, Shani. You're not doing that.'

'I have to, Nicolas. These people have made threats to Mario, threats against his children and the café they run. I have to go back.'

'The folder will be returned.'

'How?'

'I'll divert from Paris and join you in Prague. We'll fly together but come off the plane separately – and I'll be carrying the folder. Right?'

Shani nodded slowly to herself as Nicolas's strategy sunk in. 'I'll call Mario back and explain how we're going to do it.'

'Make sure he doesn't try and change anything.'

'I don't think he will. Sounds rock solid to me. A good plan, Nicolas. And…just can't wait to see you, to be in your arms.'

'A matter of hours.'

'Then I'll say it again, Nicolas. Have a safe flight – or rather, flights.'

She remembered the hot chocolate drink and sipped it pensively. *Bastards!* What the hell could they want with the folder? Putting down the mug, she called Mario and explained Nicolas's plan. Mario agreed to it without hesitation. Shani could only imagine what he was going through, having had his family threatened. She thought of Ana, and her first explosive meeting with her in Mario's kitchen. If anything happened to Mario, there was a chance Ana would judge her to be the cause – and this time around her accusation might just stick. Ana had grown on her to the point that she, too, felt that fate had presented her with a sister. And she wanted to keep it that way.

Shani reached for the empty folder. What could be so unusual about it? Might it be destined for someone obsessed with World War Two memorabilia? That sounded too insane for words, to go to such lengths – including murder. Or was it? On occasion, a collector would pop up in the media, having paid a ridiculous amount of money for an artifact, particularly if there was an intriguing story attached to it. For all she knew the contents combined with the folder could be worth an absolute fortune.

Shani put the folder down and yawned. Tomorrow was going to be hectic, no question – starting with Dusana coming around. It would be nice to see her. She always emanated stability. And, right now, she felt that was precisely what she needed. A chunk of wholesome stability.

* * *

Shani awoke in the night with a possible alteration to her flight schedule. By morning, it still had a degree of common sense about it. After a breakfast of porridge, since that was the only cereal left in the cupboard, made more tasteless by the fact she had no fruit to stir into it, Shani called Mario on the clean phone while sipping coffee.

'Mario, all is going smoothly. Nicolas is in London and set to board a flight to Prague.'

'That's such a relief, Shani. I can hardly put it into words.'

'He should be here in about three hours. I just wanted to mention, Mario, in the night a thought came to me. If this is being conducted by some authority-based offshoot, so to speak, then these people will have the wherewithal to monitor passengers arriving at Timişoara. Because we've been given forty-eight hours, they will check the lists for that period of time. So should we fly to Bucharest, or Cluj, and take the train to Timişoara so we can meet up at a location other than the airport?'

'Good point, but—'

'If I can't change my ticket, I'll just get another.'

'Shani, make it Timişoara and I'll collect you. These people could alter the timeline, or find the location of my children in Cluj, despite the fact I've told them to move around. Apparently, the café window was smashed in the early hours.'

'Oh, no,' gasped Shani.

'Anybody's guess as to who did it—'

'These people are evil, Mario.'

'No question about that.'

'Okay, I'll call you before we board the plane with the precise time of arrival.'

Shani left the living room to brush her teeth, then repacked her backpack with clean underwear, spare jeans and the same routine toiletries as before. As she was battening down the straps, she heard Dusana enter the apartment, using her housekeeping key.

'Dusana!' she cried, cutting across the living room to throw her arms around her. 'I've missed you.'

Dusana reciprocated and then stood back. A brief but intense study of Shani resulted in a judgmental shake of her head. 'You're thin, darling.'

'I know, I know, but only by a few kilos. I'll soon put those back on.' Shani watched as Dusana unbuttoned her summer coat which, like the winter one she wore, had oversized buttons. Her grey hair was drawn back into a bun as always, her general appearance giving the impression of being someone with an austere personality – which wasn't quite true. For sure, Dusana could fight her corner effectively, as

Shani knew only too well. One memorable occasion happened to be when Dusana caught her riding a neighbour's motorbike in the street. But, bless her, after a severe telling-off and embarrassing her in front of the boy, Dusana never mentioned the incident to Andrei.

'So, am I taking you to dinner this evening?' asked Dusana.

'Coffee?'

'Please.'

'Raincheck, I'm afraid, Dusana. Something's come up. I'll explain in a moment. Come into the kitchen while I make your coffee.'

Dusana inspected the plant on the sill by the sink and snipped off a couple of feeble-looking leaves.

Shani filled the kettle. 'How's your wrist?'

'Back to normal, I would say.'

'Good. Next winter, I want you to come out to Séroulé. That way, you'll avoid the ice.'

'Darling, I'm seventy-two.' Dusana put the pinched-off leaves in the bin under the sink. 'I haven't been out of the country for years, and that was only to see an aunt in Hungary for a couple of days.'

'Dusana, hasn't anyone told you? Seventy is the new fifty.'

'Don't be silly.'

'It's true.' Shani brought the coffees over to the kitchen table, a solid oak affair that she had insisted Andrei kept when the kitchen was refurbished. 'I have to leave for the airport in a couple of hours. Return to Romania. Long story. I'm meeting Nicolas at the airport. I imagine we'll only be there for a few days. So, on the way back to the UK, we'll call in here and you can take us both to dinner and get to meet Nicolas at the same time.'

Dusana sat at the table and met Shani's eyes. 'This is the one?'

'Definitely. I've never felt this way about – or been so committed to – anyone in my entire life. He's perfect for me. It's not going to happen for a while, but I want a family with him.'

'Finally,' sighed Dusana.

'I'm only twenty-four, Dusana.'

'But the years go by so quickly, Shani.' Dusana sipped her coffee. 'What's this about Romania and a long story? Did you find out anything about your birth parents?'

'A few things,' said Shani, just as an image of Serghei propped up on the bed with his throat cut ghosted itself in front of Dusana. 'I met and got to know one of their schoolfriends. A lovely person called Mario.'

'But you have to go back today?'

'He's unearthed more information. Really exciting.'

'Can't he tell you over the phone?'

'It's a folder of information. Photographs, I believe, too.'

'And Nicolas is flying all this way?'

Shani felt her cheeks starting to glow. She'd often thought Dusana would have made a first-rate detective – comparable to 'Miss Marple'. 'We're just desperate to see each other, and I want to show him my parents' grave. After calling in here on the way back, we're heading down to Cornwall in the southwest of England. We're going to spend a week there. Nicolas is going to teach me to surf.'

'What about your studies?' asked Dusana, finishing her coffee.

'Well…we're coming into the summer break.'

'But all this rushing about, darling?'

'I know,' agreed Shani, scrambling around inside her head for a convincing response. 'It's ever since Andrei died, and what I discovered about myself and my birth parents. But it's all going to settle back down again. I promise you, Dusana.'

CHAPTER 23

Shani took the coach for the half-hour journey to Václav Havel, Prague's international airport, not for one second letting go of the folder in its Wizz Air carrier bag. She'd found some notes relating to her Master's degree, which she'd popped inside, just to make everything authentic in the unlikely event of being detained by customs officers. Had she not done so, she imagined it might have appeared altogether peculiar to be carrying a folder fit for the trash can, and little else – except, of course, to her it had become her most treasured possession to date. And now it was about to disappear from her life forever. Sickening!

On the upside, she was minutes away from hooking up with Nicolas. Despite it being little more than a fortnight ago, it felt like an age since she'd last kissed him, while waiting for her propeller-driven

Séroulé Airlines plane to take her to Senegal for the flight to London, and from there to Oxford and the Stated General Meeting at St Thomas Aquinas. A meeting she was not expected to shun, come what may.

The coach began crossing the Vltava, its waters in calm contrast to her emotions. *Harry Rothwell...* Every time the UK surfaced in her head so, too, would her supervisor. That said, it was now all perfectly clear to her: she was leaving the college after having been there barely four months, of which little more than a couple of days had been spent at her desk – and even less time working on her thesis, in between her daydreaming. Dusana would almost certainly go ballistic, but Harry, hopefully, would be philosophical, shake her hand and wish her safe journeys ahead. Nicolas's reaction? That, she was about to find out.

The coach pulled into a parking area opposite the main concourse, and she waited for the passengers behind her to leave, giving her room to struggle with her backpack from the overhead cord-woven rack. She'd managed to book a direct flight for two with Wizz Air to Timişoara and prayed she hadn't already picked up a tail. Depending on how 'global' their foe was, she wondered if they had photographs of Nicolas and whether he was already under surveillance, a tail having perhaps latched onto him in Paris.

Whatever, she was still broken-hearted with having to hand over the folder – and relinquishing in the process traces of her father's fingerprints, no matter how faint they might now be.

* * *

He was there, standing beside a closed Lufthansa check-in desk. He must have seen her first because he had that magical grin on his face that she liked to believe was reserved only for her. She reciprocated, and before she knew it she was in his arms. An awkward moment, until she'd released herself from her backpack and the carrier bag.

'Not exactly how I imagined we would be reunited,' Nicolas told her. 'Really thought it would be Cornwall.'

She'd never been one for kissing intimately in public, but this was different – tearful, in fact, after the stresses of the past few days.

'Hey, there's no need for that, surely?' said Nicolas, gently running his fingers over her lips.

'You don't know the half of it,' disclosed Shani, using a tissue.

'Then let's go to the cafeteria, and you can tell me. Don't know about you, but I'm starving.'

Nicolas went for a full English breakfast; she opting for a refreshing ham salad. They chose a table overlooking a flight path, a Finnair Airbus taxiing away from them.

'You've lost more weight?' enquired Nicolas, settling himself before reaching for his glass of orange juice. 'I'd say you have.'

'A little. It's been difficult. An upsetting time, Nicolas.'

'I get that, Shani. Just promise me you'll put a couple of kilos back on before the end of the month.'

'You're going to treat me to gorgeous meals, then?'

'If I have to. But there are no underlying issues that I should know about, right?'

'None at all. Promise. It's just I'm one of those people that when stuff kicks off, I rely on coffee and little else. If you think about it, the last three months, what with the coup and its complications, I've hardly had a break from feeling anxious over something or other, to put it mildly.'

'We can still head for Cornwall after this,' reassured Nicolas. He started to butter the bread roll handed to him on a side plate. 'You're going to love it. The tiny flat I've been lucky enough to borrow overlooks the sea.'

'Sex while watching the waves roll in,' winked Shani.

'You're ahead of me.'

'I don't believe that for one moment, Nicolas.'

They laughed and tucked into their meals. Shani found herself to be somewhat perturbed that Nicolas had picked up on her weight loss. Was it really so conspicuous? Three people – or was it four? – had now made the same comment. Physically, she'd never felt healthier: everything functioning as it should, and in her heart of hearts oodles of happiness. Decisions about her career had been made and a stable relationship was evolving merrily of its own accord.

'So, show me this folder that's attracted so much attention,' said Nicolas, putting down his knife and fork.

Shani lifted the carrier bag over the table. 'I fail to see a reason why they would want it. They have the original script.'

'And that was in some form of code?'

'Yes.'

Nicolas peered inside the bag. 'I know it has sentimental value, but quite honestly if that wasn't the case you would throw it out, wouldn't you? I mean, there's a tear down the front of it.'

'I'm so annoyed, Nicolas,' said Shani. 'I'm sure it still has my father's fingerprints on it. That makes it worth the world to me.'

'What's in it now? I can see pages of something?'

'A few notes I had lying around relating to my Master's, just in case customs officers detained us. It would be a disaster if they became suspicious and held onto it.'

'How's this Mario guy going to hand it over to them?'

While finishing her salad, Shani explained about Skid Row, the location chosen by their foe to hand over the script. 'I imagine Mario will go through the same routine with the folder,' she said. 'During the handover, I gave the bastard a smack in the face. He was sitting behind the wheel of his car.'

'Mario had kittens, did he?'

'He pulled me away.'

'Tell me about Serghei.'

They ordered coffees and Shani read the time on her phone: twenty minutes before check-in. 'Serghei was basically a down-and-out, but he was a close friend of my parents. What they did to him was absolutely horrific. Then there was Daniela…'

'Daniela?'

'Not her true name.' Shani explained and, as she did so, realised she probably ought to have mentioned it sooner in a phone call. 'I didn't want to worry you. You were thousands of miles away. What could you have done?'

'Boarded a plane, that's what.' Nicolas opened a sachet of demerara as the coffee arrived. 'And you've no idea who's behind this?'

Shani shook her head. 'No. By no, I mean we can't fathom whether this *unknown force* – the title we seem to have given them – is authority related, or…well, a private enterprise of some description. But promise me, Nicolas, you're not going to have a go at Mario. He's kept me away from danger the best he could.'

'But he also kept you in the zone, didn't he?' Nicolas sighed and shook his head, stirring his coffee. 'He should have put you on a plane, goddammit.'

'Nicolas, I would have refused. You know how wretchedly stubborn I can be. I wanted to stay with him and his family. They're lovely people. Truly.'

'Okay, okay…'

'So, you're going to promise?'

'I promise.'

'It's important to me that you get on. Actually, you have much in common with Mario.' She finished her coffee and leaned on the table, her elbows forming a pyramid with her hands. 'What's the news on Séroulé? Khamadi and Monique in good spirits? I mean, they're optimistic, right?'

'Five countries now have stated that they are refusing to pay off their external debts to creditors, and that the money will be printed and used to repair environmental damage. The multinational corporations, of course, being the major villains.'

'That's terrific news. The policy is spreading—'

Nicolas raised a cautionary hand. 'As expected, the mainstream media is largely keeping a lid on it.'

'They would,' said Shani, and sensed Mario would say the same, and with as much animosity. 'But the danger is suicide bombers infiltrating the country, yes?'

'Unfortunately. The powers that be are obviously going to try and sabotage the policy. By not paying back the external debt we have broken free of their shackles. They will rubbish the country through the media, and in fact have started doing so – inventing stories regarding abuse of human rights, torture and the mounting concern of genocide. Ridiculous, of course.'

'Why can't they just leave Séroulé alone?' fumed Shani. In her next breath she shook her head, because she knew why. 'Mario calls this world government shit and the heinous clique at the core of it "Deep State".'

Nicolas looked up, evidently taken aback. 'If he's using phrases like *Deep State*, I'm almost certain to get along with him.'

'They're the closest thing I have to a family, so it's important to me that you do.'

'Don't worry. Anyway, going back to Séroulé and the countries that are following suit... Deep State, if you like, will obviously manoeuvre all the crazies and religious fanatics into West Africa in an attempt to destabilise the region. But the Dendi people in the north have started to patrol the border up there. It's going to be interesting. We've even received words of encouragement from prominent economists on a global level – Canada, Australia, New Zealand, even China. From what I hear, New Zealand is showing more interest than any other country outside the African Continent.'

'Then this really could have legs, as they say.'

'Optimism is still outweighing pessimism. We've just got to keep it that way.' Nicolas glanced at his wristwatch. 'I guess we'd better head for check-in.' He started to stand. 'Talking of economists, have you made a final decision?'

'I'm leaving St Aquinas,' said Shani, her tone matter-of-fact. She was that positive.

'Abandoning your thesis?'

'Yes. Harry wants me to continue with it and reckons I could stitch the whole thing up in eighteen months by simply expanding my Master's.'

'I'm with Harry.'

Shani stared at him, stunned. She couldn't help herself, hardly expecting him to be so direct. 'Nicolas, don't say that.' She took a thousand koruna note from her purse to pay for the meal. 'You don't know how much I've been wrestling with this.'

'Wait, listen…' Nicolas picked up the carrier bag with the folder. 'You're a Fellow of St Aquinas. But you want to leave. Fine, do that. You'll always be connected to the college, and therefore to the University. You'll forever be…what's the word? It's Latin they use, I'm sure.'

'You mean, *quondam*.'

'That's it. So, you'll have that connection. If Harry made it possible for you to complete your thesis in Séroulé, would you do it then?'

'I don't know if that's possible,' said Shani, handing over the money to the waitress who had served them. 'But if it is, then I might reconsider. You have to realise, my prosthesis held me back on so many fronts. So, what did I do? I buried myself in academia. Now, largely thanks to you, I'm experiencing liberty like I've never known it to be before.'

'Shani Bălcescu, unleashed!' quipped Nicolas, laughing. Putting his arm around her: 'Hell, I'm uncertain over how alarmed I should be.'

'I want to involve myself more with Mother Nature. A harmless, but a practical and worthwhile pursuit, surely?' Shani took her passport from her shoulder bag and they started to leave the cafeteria. 'Although I really don't want to disappoint Harry. You might just have found a way to avoid that from happening, Nicolas. That said, after four years and with several of my friends having graduated and left, I'm definitely through with Oxford.'

CHAPTER 24

Shani began preparing the table that had now become perfectly familiar to her. While Mario busily sliced up a pre-cooked chicken on the worktop, she laid out the cutlery and assembled the dishes of various salads. Cruets went to the right of the folder, presently in the centre of the table. She debated whether to put it to one side, but since it was the main topic of their discussions she decided to leave it.

'Mario, are you sure it's all right for us to use your bedroom?' she asked. 'I feel we're imposing. Nicolas or myself could sleep on the couch in the living room.'

Mario turned briefly from the worktop. 'Wouldn't hear of it.'

'Nicolas will be down in a minute. After he's showered.' Shani rearranged a couple of dishes. The drive from the airport had gone well. Mario had asked

Nicolas a number of questions, the majority of which related to journalism. At one point, the conversation resembled a father vetting a possible son-in-law, and she couldn't help but turn to the window with a blissful smile. 'I was thinking, Mario…'

'Go on.'

'Well, it's a bit cheeky of me to ask, but can I tell you what my perfect Christmas would be?'

Mario turned from the worktop, on this occasion with the carving knife. 'I'm all ears.'

'That I had Christmas dinner with you all, around this table. With Nicolas, of course. Ana, Victor, Cosmin. It would just be out of this world for me.'

'And Elena, I'm guessing.'

Shani looked up in surprise. 'Wow. Perfect upon perfect. Ana will be ecstatic, as I will be. I'm telling you!'

'We'll make that happen. Okay? And we'll be honoured to have you at our table.'

'Thank you, Mario. Means so much to me.'

Nicolas walked into the kitchen.

'Feeling fresher?' asked Shani.

'A whole lot better.'

'I'd be dead to the world after all that flying,' said Shani, putting out the plates. 'You're so lucky you can sleep on flights. I'm useless at it. Never works for me.'

Mario brought over the chicken. Shani took up her seat opposite Nicolas, with Mario at the 'head' of the table. Predictably, the conversation reverted to the folder, and in particular that September evening in 1944 when the B-25 Mitchell came down on land owned by Andrei Bălcescu's father.

'For a time, I studied Lend-Lease,' said Nicolas. 'In fact, I'm still fascinated by it. The amount of gear shipped out of the US to the Soviet Union was mind-blowing. Over four and half billion dollars in munitions, and much the same figure in other materials. In today's money, somewhere around a hundred and forty billion dollars. That's why some theorists call the Cold War a total hoax, since America basically armed and rebuilt the Soviet Union.'

'But can it be true that materials and diagrams for the atomic bomb were also shipped out?' asked Shani.

'Flown out, mostly,' Mario said. 'Through Great Falls, Montana. Right, Nicolas?'

'Yes. Everything was thoroughly documented by a major called George Racey Jordan, a 're-tread', as he called himself from the First World War.'

'Mario has mentioned his name to me,' said Shani.

'Jordan was assigned as a Liaison Officer for Lend-Lease at the Gore Field Airbase, and was initially puzzled and then astonished by what was being loaded onto the planes.' Nicolas accepted a glass of red wine from Mario before continuing. 'Although he didn't know it at the time, Jordan documented materials typically required to make an atomic bomb – such as uranium 92, for the transmutation into plutonium. Also, cobalt nitrate, thorium and deuterium oxide – better known as heavy water, which is used as a moderator to slow down the speed of neutrons in nuclear reactions.'

Mario looked up from his plate, a slice of home-grown cucumber on his fork. 'And all this came under the Manhattan Engineering District, right?'

'The pre-cursor of the infamous Manhattan Project. The Lend-Lease aspect was headed up by a somewhat shadowy guy called Harry Hopkins, a trusted confidant of Roosevelt. Now, of course, some folk say Hopkins was a communist. But I would argue that he was a trusted confidant of Deep State. A matter of opinion, obviously.'

'A controversial figure for sure,' reflected Mario.

'Jordan talked about what he called the "push-button system". Whenever the US military didn't give the Soviets precisely what they'd asked for, Harry Hopkins would overrule everyone.'

'But going back to when the plane came down,' interjected Shani. 'You've both said the planes never went south – that they travelled over Alaska and Siberia. So what was this plane doing coming south? Where do you think it was heading?'

'Something of a mystery,' agreed Nicolas. Then, looking at Mario: 'When did the Soviet Union invade Romania? That same year?'

'Yes. September 1944. They invaded Bulgaria at just about the same time. It was a difficult time for Romania. We had, after all, assisted Hitler in the invasion of the USSR. That aside, unlike the Bulgarians, we are not Slavs and have few ethnic or cultural ties with the Russians, which in itself caused conflict – but that's another story. My bet has always been that plane was heading for the Yugoiztochen Region. By then, the Soviets had already started to construct secret military bases, ready for what we now know as the Cold War.'

'But where does the Cold War fit in with Deep State?' asked Shani. 'What was the purpose – apart from putting fear into the hearts of people?'

'The Cold War really began before World War Two ended,' said Nicolas, 'with evidence pointing to

Deep State at the controls.' He reached for a chunk of baguette. 'Before Europe could be carved up Russia needed to have an opposing ideology, hence the Bolshevik Revolution and the promotion of communism. The next stage was to modernise its infrastructure to make it a credible foe against the West, the Lend-Lease Act being the main source for the material framework. When the Yalta Conference took place in 'forty-five, Churchill and Roosevelt told Stalin that the West had the atomic bomb. Stalin, by all accounts, turned to them and said simply, "So have I"'. Nicolas leaned back, taking his glass of wine with him. 'Deep State operates by the most basic of strategies: divide and rule, at every level.'

'That's why migrancy has reached epidemic proportions in today's world,' said Mario. 'Migrancy generates paranoia, guaranteed, not to mention the anguish endured by the poor souls driven by fear and poverty out of their homeland.'

'Nicolas and I have witnessed such fear in Séroulé,' said Shani. 'The West fed General Kuetey with weapons in return for plundering the country of its minerals, without so much as a whisper of protestation against Kuetey's abysmal record when it came to human rights.'

'Migrancy is but one of many distractions,' agreed Nicolas, 'while the New World Order is rolled out. The strategy is blatant enough: a country bombs another country – usually a poor country – or sells weapons to another country to obliterate the infrastructure of that poor country to get people to flee for their lives. In the case of invading Libya, it gave those migrating the African continent a relatively short crossing into Europe – the removal of Gaddafi giving the invasion an air of legitimacy.'

'And that would have been the route the Séroulèse would have taken had we not trounced the Kuetey regime,' said Shani. 'So, we come back to this folder in front of us and what it might tell us. Mario only managed to decipher the first couple of pages before the police arrested him.'

Mario leaned back in the chair. 'It talked of a *unit of assassins*. As I recall, I drew Lucian's attention to the probability that this unit was created for the purpose of getting rid of the likes of Kennedy, or any such dignitary who opposed the ruling elite.'

'By "ruling elite" you mean the faction that is Deep State?' asked Shani.

'Yes.'

'And your view now?'

'Much the same,' shrugged Mario. 'That's if this unit existed. I suppose the question is if it *did* exist, does it still exist today?'

'Perhaps no longer a unit as such,' said Nicolas. 'I'm quite sure they can and would call upon the services of an assassin to remove a political figure who, for whatever reason, obstructed their mission to enslave humanity. Assassination would be a last resort if removal could not be achieved by other means – by the stain of corruption, for example. And let's face it, the majority of world leaders are pre-stained for such insurance purposes before being voted in.'

Shani put down her glass. 'I know I keep repeating myself, but I'm really upset that we are going to have to hand over this folder. Why do they want it? They have the original documents that were inside.'

'I don't understand why myself,' said Nicolas. 'Any ideas, Mario?'

'No.' Mario replenished their glasses. 'The only thing I can come up with, and to me it sounds ridiculous, is that there's a collector out there who wanted not only the encrypted eight pages but the full package. Beyond that, I can offer no further explanation.' He sat down again. 'But we have to give it to these people, Shani. I'm sorry.'

'I understand that, Mario,' accepted Shani. 'This whole affair is blighting our lives. I want it gone.'

'What's the procedure?' asked Nicolas.

'We go to the café tomorrow,' said Mario. 'I would imagine that the green Volvo will park on the opposite side of the road, as before. We simply cross the road with the folder and hand it over. That's it.'

'I'm tempted to hit him again,' Shani said. 'Truthfully.'

'Probably not a good idea,' said Mario. 'We've got a copy of the document.'

'How long might it take you to decipher?' asked Nicolas.

'If I could find a relevant program for the PC, then not long at all. If I have to do it manually, then several days of solid work. The encoder used the Polybius Square for the first couple of pages, but then switches to the more intricate Playfair Square.'

Shani began to clear the table and noticed as dusk began to descend that it had stopped raining. 'I want to show Nicolas the garden tomorrow, Mario,' she said.

* * *

Shani sat on the bed and was about to disengage the locking pin on her prosthesis when Nicolas emerged from the cramped en suite, a towel around his middle. Naked from the waist up herself, she left the bed.

'You look gorgeous,' he said, and put his arms around her. 'Over dinner, I couldn't stop glancing across at you and thinking how lucky I am.' He kissed her neck, drifting quietly towards her lips. 'I've missed everything about you. Your smile, your words, your bodily perfume. Everything.'

'I'll times that by ten,' she said, his chest against her breasts driving her to near distraction. 'Let's get on the bed!'

Nicolas threw off the towel and yanked back the duvet. 'Can't wait to take you back to Africa. It's my belief that's where you belong.'

She detached her prosthesis, her body tingling and coming alive by the minute. 'Do my sock for me, Nicolas.'

Nicolas rolled down the silicone-like sock with its locking pin.

'And my knickers.'

'You need to ask?'

She giggled as he made her totally naked. Then she swung herself onto the mattress and reached up to him.

'Where's Mario's room?' he whispered.

'Along the corridor.'

'How far along the corridor?'

'Is this a health and safety questionnaire?'

'Can't make too much of a noise, can we?'

Shani bit into a corner on the pillow case. 'Satisfied?' she mumbled.

'I'm not sure why, but that looks incredibly erotic!'

She made herself available to him. 'Don't let's bother with too much foreplay.'

'What's your ultimate fantasy? I keep meaning to ask.'

'More questions?'

'Tell me.'

'Aren't we supposed to keep our fantasies secret?'

'Not to one's partner.'

'I don't know…'

'Yes, you do.'

Shani twisted her mouth, unsure whether to tell him. It would perhaps sound altogether weird if she said it out aloud! 'Well…if you really want to know, naked while riding a powerful motorbike. A Norton V4, actually. There!'

'On a beach?'

'Could be.'

'Know what, I reckon I'll share that fantasy with you.'

'I imagined that might be the case!'

'Make it a reality at Trebarwith when we hit Cornwall. It's a long beach when the tide's out. Nice if there was a full moon.'

'You've got me thinking,' said Shani, 'you'd have to be the passenger.' She reached down to him to make her point, surprised by how ready he was to take her. 'It wouldn't be as much fun the other way around, would it?'

Nicolas smiled with her, and then came in close.

She'd never have guessed she could ever be this hungry for his physical contact. No past boyfriend had fired up her body and influenced her conscious being to this extent. After years of horrid anguish, it dawned on her that the near-perfect life she'd decided could only exist in her dreams appeared to be actually heading her way. And as far as she was concerned, she damn well deserved every minute of it!

CHAPTER 25

Shani awoke without Nicolas beside her. She assumed he was in the en suite bathroom until she heard voices downstairs. She looked at the time on her phone. 8:20. A reasonable night's sleep. After they'd made love, Nicolas had fallen asleep virtually straightaway – which hardly surprised her given that twenty-four hours earlier he'd been in West Africa. What kept her awake was a measure of guilt. It caused her to cry a little, because she'd just achieved gratification while the part-time actress, Mariana Tismăneanu, lay in a mortuary somewhere not so far away. And then, of course, there was the hideous image of Serghei and the indescribable fear he'd undoubtedly endured during the last minutes of his life. Had the man she'd punched in the face murdered both of them? If so, one major question remained unanswered: *for whom?*

She left the bed, washed and dressed and realised that for the first time in a while she was actually looking forward to breakfast rather than approaching it out of necessity.

Arriving in the kitchen, she was confronted by a curious sight. Mario was lightly running his fingertips over the back of the folder.

'You're right,' he said to Nicolas.

'What are you doing?' Shani asked.

'I thought of something in the night,' said Nicolas. 'Pick up the folder and run your fingers gently over the back of it.'

Shani did as asked. She detected a slight bump. 'Excess buckram, probably.'

'Excess what?' Nicolas put down his coffee cup.

'Buckram. They bound everything in it back in the day. Books, folders, you name it.'

Mario left the table. 'Shani, you want cereal?'

'Please. I'm actually quite hungry.'

'Delighted to hear it,' said Mario. 'Take a seat. I'll bring a bowl over.'

Shani opened the folder. 'This is definitely buckram. When I was at Corpus Christi, a librarian from another college gave a lecture on bookbinding. I can't remember why I attended. I think Christina, whom I shared a house with, wanted to go and I tagged along.' She took the bowl of muesli topped with fresh blueberries from Mario. 'Underneath the buckram it's likely to be strawboard – which is quite acidic, giving bookbinders a hard time when it comes to restoration.'

'But the fact remains,' said Nicolas, 'why do these people want this folder – *empty* folder? Any ideas?'

'That's what we can't—'

'Because it's not empty, Shani.'

She held her spoon in mid-air, eyes fixed on Nicolas. 'Not empty? It looks empty. You can't deny that.'

'A case of looks can be deceiving.'

'You're saying something might be between the buckram and strawboard?'

'It's all I can think of, unless we go with Mario's suggestion that a collector will do anything to get his hands on it.'

'It was a ridiculous suggestion, if you remember,' said Mario, sitting back down at the table and rolling a cigarette. 'I feel we can rule it out. The replacement folder has been rejected, so I'm with Nicolas, which means we need to carefully slice it along the edge and lift the buckram material.'

'Then let's do that.' Shani moved the folder away from her. 'I'm not going to see it again, am I?'

'It's likely they don't know the actual condition of the folder,' reasoned Nicolas. 'How could they? It was Andrei who found it. All they know is that something might be concealed inside the binding. A consequence of a rumour, perhaps. Meaning, you could keep a piece of buckram for yourself.'

'I suppose I could.' Shani's disinterested tone took her by surprise before she realised why. 'To be honest, it's caused so much trouble that I really don't think I want to keep any part of it. There's an envelope back in Prague that I believe might have my father's handwriting on it. The number of the safe deposit box that introduced us to this folder – or in Mario's case, *re*introduced.'

'Mario,' said Nicolas, 'have you something along the lines of a scalpel, or a very sharp knife?'

Mario opened a drawer under the worktop. 'Try this.' He handed over a peeling knife.

Nicolas took it and Shani watched with renewed interest as he ran the blade delicately along the edge of the folder.

'A little more,' said Mario. 'Make it at least twenty centimetres.'

Nicolas slid the blade further and then carefully lifted the material. 'Ah-ha, bingo!'

'What is it?' Shani leapt from her chair to look over Nicolas's shoulder. 'What can you see, for God's sake?'

'It's pretty tight. An envelope, I think. It's stuck down.'

'Held in by the acidic strawboard, no doubt,' speculated Shani. 'Hopefully whatever's inside the envelope isn't damaged.'

'Mario, do you have any pincers – like tweezers?' Nicolas looked up. 'If not, pointed pliers?'

'Give me a moment,' said Mario. 'Ana has tweezers upstairs in the bathroom.'

Shani reached over the table for her bowl of cereal. 'It's got to be important, hasn't it? Worth a lot of money, perhaps.' She rubbed Nicolas's back, proud of him. 'Well done.'

'Maybe Lucian put it in the bank because he guessed it might be worth something,' considered Nicolas. 'Enough to set himself and Zinsa up in a house of their own, if they hadn't already started to do so.'

'Do you think?' Shani liked it when people brought her parents to life for her – however speculatively.

'It can only ever be a guess,' emphasised Nicolas, as if aware of Shani's unbridled imagination when it came to her parents. 'But the fact that he put it in a safe deposit box says something.'

'Unless he found himself to be unnerved for whatever reason. I still feel that's the more likely scenario, because of the gun. And what with Zinsa about to give birth to twins, his mind was probably hyper and all over the place with worry.'

Nicolas gave Shani a reflective nod. 'There's that, too.'

Mario returned to the kitchen with a pair of gold-coloured tweezers. Nicolas took them from him. After a couple of hesitant tugs, he managed to extract the envelope, which had a yellowish stain across the left corner.

'That'll be the acid,' said Shani, pointing. The envelope was approximately fifteen by twenty centimetres in size. 'It might have got damp at some point, which would have accelerated the process.'

'How are we going to open it?' asked Nicolas. 'It's sealed down pretty tight.'

'We need a lamp,' decided Shani. 'We might be able to see through it.'

Without a word, Mario left the kitchen and returned almost immediately with a vintage Anglepoise desk lamp. He put it on the table and plugged it in.

Nicolas switched it on and raised the envelope. 'Paper's too thick. Can't see anything. I think I know what it might be, though.'

'What?' demanded Shani. 'I've never been so curious.'

'I'm going to carefully slice it open,' said Nicolas. 'Everyone in agreement?'

'Totally,' nodded Shani. 'Only thing is, what about our foe if we do? They'll know we've been inside it.'

'They're not going to bother us over an opened envelope,' judged Mario, 'so long as they get their hands on the contents.'

Nicolas positioned the tip of the blade under the flap. 'If it's what I think it is, we're going to need a scanner, not that it's likely to benefit us a great deal.'

'I have one,' said Mario.

'A piece of cloth, or a tissue, one of you?' Nicolas asked.

Shani rummaged in her shoulder bag and located a pack of tissues. 'What do you think it is then?'

'I'll show you.' Nicolas plucked a couple from the pack, using one of them to protect the envelope's contents from the tweezers.

'Microfilm,' breathed Mario as Nicolas extracted a transparent sheet that had a blue tint to it from the stained envelope. 'Amazing. I wasn't expecting that.'

'What's it made from?' asked Shani. 'Plastic?'

'Silver gelatin's often used,' said Nicolas. 'That's about all I know.'

'Do you think there's lots of information on it?'

'With any luck.' Nicolas held the sheet up to the light. 'Appears to be.'

'Can you read anything off it?'

'The print's far too small.' Nicolas carefully laid down the film on a separate tissue. 'I don't think a code of any kind has been used. Mario, we need the scanner.'

'I'll fetch it,' said Mario, already leaving the kitchen.

'I wonder if my father had any idea there was microfilm hidden in the folder?' considered Shani, finishing her cereal.

'I doubt it.' Nicolas stood up, stretching his legs. 'That film hasn't seen the light of day since at least 1944.'

Shani took her empty bowl over to the sink. 'But what are we going to do with it, Nicolas?'

'How do you mean?'

'These people clearly know what they are expecting to find. If they don't find it, then Mario and his family, if not ourselves, are going to run the risk of them turning violent. And I mean violent.' Shani rinsed the bowl and left it to dry on the wooden rack.

'We'll have to go for second best.'

'Meaning?'

'Try and print a copy from it. I doubt we'll be able to achieve that via the scanner, in all honesty. But we'll try. We haven't the time to get hold of a suitable projector.'

Mario came back into the room with the scanner. 'It belongs in a museum by today's standards, but it might just do the job.'

It took several minutes to set up the equipment on the kitchen table. As they did so, Mario twice went over to the window to look out onto the front.

'Mario, are you getting paranoid?' quipped Shani.

'I thought I heard someone on the gravel.'

'That's it,' said Nicolas. 'We're done.'

'I don't think the magnification is going to be powerful enough,' said Mario.

Nicolas increased the magnification on the computer. 'This part's readable. Looks like an overview.'

Shani moved her chair closer to the laptop's screen and leaned forward to read the typed script.

MAPPING OF WORLD ORDER

Annihilation of religion through scandal, mockery and the rapacious desire for materialism. For the most part, all related buildings and symbols will be razed and ground back into the earth from whence they came. This will be achieved by means of decay and retaliatory reprisals from rival extremist groups that we are now in the process of cultivating.

Middle East will be thrown into irresolvable chaos. This will be achieved by concentrated and prolonged ineptitude on all external governments and corporations involved. Their desire for oil and the selling of weaponry to pay for it will be the root cause.

A unit of assassins to cover the globe is now required, each unknown to the other, and each having no understanding of who we are. Occasionally, a leader will slip through the net and talk about us. Such a leader will need to be dealt with instantly. Solution? Immediate removal. Nothing less will do.

When hostilities cease between the Axis powers and the Allies, our focus will be the United Nations. Our operatives will attend the UN Conference on

International Organisation in April, 1945, for which delegates from over fifty nations have signed up, in addition to non-governmental organisations. To all intents and purposes, those who believe they are in control of the United Nations will only see our operatives holding in their left hand the dove of peace, not the butcher's cleaver in their right hand.

<u>A rapid decline</u> in natural resources as the stronger nations plunder the weaker ones, unwittingly assisting in an escalation of social conflict and fragmentation resulting from constant flows of migration and the rise of nationalism. Our operatives will issue protestations, but that is all. At this stage, our operatives must ensure the United Nations to be regarded as a relatively ineffectual organisation. When the time is ripe, the superpowers will implode as simultaneously as is deemed possible: trade and economic wars and the Federal Reserve presently the favoured triggers. Dry runs will be introduced periodically over the coming decades.

<u>By the next century,</u> besides achieving the unthinkable by inflicting starvation on Europe as a consequence of mismanagement and economic collapse implemented by the external governments, anarchy

and migration will appear to be incontrollable, the engineered illusion of peace for the completion of the World Order made available once all armies have fallen under the patronage of our operatives. They will be directed accordingly to quell the multitude of factions by brutal means, this specific moment being our opportunity to complete the programme of depopulation. The ones who are left will be fearful, and therefore wholly subservient, their once intrinsic resolve to rebel forever broken and entirely extinguished by means of brainwashing within three generations thereafter. All beings will appreciate what has been achieved for them, after studying the foolishness of the external governments over the past centuries who, by the end of the next century, will be nothing more, or less, than obedient stewards of predesignated sectors.

Shani leaned back, physically weakened. Why did it have to be this way? A planet capable of relative unification amongst its peoples disfigured by ludicrous systems to obtain and enhance a fantastical concentration of greed and dominance. She supposed by asking the question of *Why?* she was being naïve, but nevertheless... 'It's like a countdown to Armageddon,' she said aloud.

'It's been mooted in different formats for years by conspiracy theorists,' said Nicolas. 'Like myself and Mario.'

'Not so much in way of theory these days,' Mario remarked soberly.

'I know.' Shani toyed absently with the Suzuki's ignition fob on the table in front of her. 'But to see it on microfilm…it just turns my stomach over. It's both clinical and merciless. Downright senseless, by any standards.'

'Proves the point,' said Nicolas. 'Evil never sleeps, while the rest of us sleepwalk into enslavement.'

'I loathe the concept of hate,' Shani said. 'As Mario pointed out to me, it's such a negative energy. But what other emotion can you apply to these people? I haven't a hope of forgiving them, not after witnessing what they've done to Séroulé via General Kuetey. This godforsaken clique, or whatever, hasn't just got blood on its hands, it's swimming in it.'

'Then that should be the basis of your thesis,' said Mario 'How it took hold via a corrupt monetary system.'

'Maybe,' considered Shani. 'For months now, I've had it in mind to open the thesis with a quote from William Paterson, one of the founders of the Bank of England.'

Nicolas looked up from the laptop. 'The quote being?'

'The bank hath benefit of interest on all monies which it creates out of nothing.'

'By itself, it explains a great deal,' responded Nicolas. 'Looking at this stuff makes you wonder how many false flags there've been since the Second World War.'

'"False flags"?' queried Shani. 'What are they?'

'Covert operations directed against their own people,' said Nicolas. 'Some believe to varying degrees that 9/11 was a false flag, that elements within the US government supressed information that an attack was imminent. Wouldn't be the first time. Pearl Harbour: vital intercepts delivered to officials in Washington were apparently never passed on to Army and Navy Commanders stationed in the North Pacific, with Admiral Husband Kimmel finding himself the main scapegoat.'

'But why?' argued Shani. 'If at all true, what was the point?'

'Aside from drawing America into the Second World War,' said Nicolas, 'Pearl Harbour itself culminated in an excuse to drop two atomic bombs, not as a test in some desert location but onto the cities of Hiroshima and Nagasaki. Much information regarding the extent of infrastructure obliteration, et cetera, would have been gleaned from those detonations. In the case of 9/11, provoking an ongoing conflict between the West and Islamic nations. You agree, Mario?'

'Fits in with the routine pattern of things,' nodded Mario. 'Human beings are not designed to hate one another, quite the opposite. That's why, because they are flying in the face of nature and the natural world, it is taking these vile people centuries of deceit and aggression to achieve their endgame.'

'And you think they will?' asked Shani. 'Achieve their endgame?'

Mario shrugged. 'A politician's primary objective should be to protect us from all evil, so judge for yourself.'

Shani reached for her coffee. 'If we had the proper equipment, we could view the details.'

'Not enough time,' said Mario. 'We have an hour left until the deadline I was given. It's going to take twenty minutes to reach the café.'

'And there's no way this equipment can make a copy?' asked Shani.

'Not a hope,' said Mario.

'Shame we can't make a copy,' reflected Nicolas. 'We could have put it on social media, although it's doubtful even if it went viral that it would harm them. It needs a media organisation.'

'Mainstream media?' queried Mario. 'Impossible.'

'Journalists like myself are favouring Loran Communications these days, in California. It's owned by a media old-timer by the name of Joshua Waldo. He would be our best hope. But I have to agree with you, Mario, it's a faint hope that he would do anything significant with it.'

'Not that it helps us much,' said Shani, 'but whoever put the words onto this microfilm wasn't American.'

'How can you tell?' asked Mario.

'Favoured, for one example, has a "u". An American wouldn't spell it that way. And the word organisation has an "s", not a "z". Also, an American would likely use the word *un*controllable rather than *in*controllable.' Shani glanced from Mario to Nicolas. 'Would you say that a subtle coup of sorts has befallen the UN? Or even a coup that began a while ago, and is still in progress today?'

Nicolas carefully returned the film to the envelope. 'One wonders, at times…'

Shani's hearing swung her attention away from Nicolas to the front of the house.

'Shhh,' she hissed. Then, in a whisper: 'Mario, I think I just heard someone on the gravel.' She faced the windows with Nicolas, Mario having already left his chair, heading for the front door.

Shani crossed the kitchen to the largest of the three windows that fronted the drive, seeing only the BMW and the Suzuki parked next to each other – until a leather-clad figure wearing a green crash helmet shot up from beneath the window. She screamed. A tinkle of glass, and a round object skimmed past her before there was a deafening thunderclap, the object simultaneously releasing a jet of smoke as it jumped in the air. Disorientated, she staggered back, another stun grenade detonating itself elsewhere in the cottage.

Two full-helmeted figures appeared out of the haze of acrid smoke in the kitchen, the green-helmeted one shoving Mario back through the doorway, a gun in his left hand. Shani didn't know whether instructions were being issued behind the heavily tinted visors. She couldn't hear a sound against the enormous pain, akin to the violent earaches she'd suffered in childhood. She now feared there might be a more terrifying outcome: partial or permanent deafness.

The gun veered towards her, directing her to sit down – then the same aggressive gesture to Mario, and Nicolas. Shani prayed neither of them would be tempted to resist. Their captors looked mean, as if they'd been dispatched by 'Deep State'. With the three of them now seated, the one with the green helmet handed the gun to his accomplice. At the worktop, he rifled through drawers, throwing utensils onto the floor.

What the hell was he looking for? Shani yearned to massage the back of her jaw to try and soothe her eardrums. She saw Nicolas rubbing his ears, which gave her the confidence to raise her hands and do the same. She noted that Mario didn't appear to be particularly concerned, presumably resigned to the situation. What *could* they do? Nothing. Nothing at all!

It had to have been the airport. Shani felt certain about that. She and Nicolas had been detected as soon as they came off the plane. Mario should have accepted her suggestion that they fly to Cluj, or Bucharest. Anywhere but Timişoara. From either city, they could have lost a tail by taking a coach or train. Or better still, hired a car or motorbike. But if their present location had been discovered the previous day, why hadn't the attack happened at night-time, while everyone was asleep?

It was string. That's what the green-helmeted thug had been looking for. They were going to tie them to the chairs. Shani found partial relief in that it appeared violence was not going to be meted out, or worse. String and gun were exchanged between them, the latter promptly directed at her, the possible ringleader of the two indicating he wanted her tied first. She thought that to be strange; of the three of them, she was physically the least threatening. Not that it made the slightest difference. The gun alone could eliminate any attempt at retaliation in a fraction of a second.

She had to think, and fast. The individual with the ball of string removed his gloves – *his* because there were black hairs across the backs of his hands. She tried to swell her wrists by keeping her hands clenched behind herself, knuckles together. There didn't appear to be any objection to her doing this. A centimetre was all that was required, she imagined – infuriated she could no longer massage her ears. They were burning now, and she was still perfectly deaf. Had the detonation really affected her hearing? God's sake, she'd barely come to terms with her prosthesis after years of mental anguish. And music? She was now hooked on So Kalmery and Manu Dibango, and several other African-born musicians.

Three or four times he wrapped the string around her wrists, but throughout the process she managed to maintain that vital gap. The string itself felt coarse, the fibres loosely entwined. She imagined Mario used it in the garden. The uprights, though, that formed the back of the chair couldn't have been smoother, the friction between wood and string virtually absent. But there was no alternative. It was her only hope – that, combined with the impetus of the utter cruelty doled out on Serghei and Mariana.

Shani made a start when the man went to Nicolas, knowing she had to keep her shoulder blades motionless to the point of rigidity. She glanced at the one with the green helmet, the gun now directed solely at Mario, who sat staring ahead, between herself and Nicolas. Had he a plan? Or was he unruffled because he knew the score, that at some point these intruders were going to leave?

She kept up with the 'sawing'. She could hear a little now: the scuffing of footsteps on the rustic tiled floor. Her eardrums – or perhaps it was her estuation tubes – had begun to itch. A sign of recovery, perhaps? She made the string taut, and as she did so unexpectedly discovered an imperfection in one of the struts – a knot in the wood that was marginally abrasive. She looked up from the table, and realised it was Nicolas who was talking.

'…Your hearing?'

'It's coming back,' Shani told him. Her voice sounded weirdly ethereal, as if she had a double speaking on her behalf from another room. Their talking didn't appear to annoy their captors, so she made the most of it. 'They're going to take it, aren't they?' she said, her eyes swerving towards the stained envelope.

'No question, I'm afraid.'

Shani continued sawing, before a strand abruptly snapped. She couldn't believe her luck, until the one with the gun glanced directly at her. She wondered if the slight jolt on her shoulders had aroused suspicion. She held her breath. 'Why tie us up?' she asked.

She was ignored.

'At a guess he doesn't understand English,' said Nicolas. 'They need time to get away.'

The red-helmeted assailant left Mario and took the gun from his colleague. Everything seemed well organised, Shani realised. Or was it? They'd forgotten to bring string, or cable ties, with them. The other 'biker' leaned over the table and took the envelope, just as another strand gave way. With a realistic chance of freeing herself, the question now was how to maximise the stroke of luck? On a shelf to the right of the worktop lay the gun her father had placed inside the deposit box, the bullets nearby. But Mario had said that the gun and bullets didn't match up.

The green-helmeted man started going through the drawers again. Producing a tall lidded jar, he carefully rolled the microfilm as if to avoid creasing it and slid it inside. Screwing the lid back on the jar, he took the folder from the table and tore away much of the buckram material. *You bastard!* railed Shani. As if to vex her further, he threw the 'precious' folder onto the floor and seconds later kicked it aside.

Convinced there was enough room to extract her right hand from the final loop of string, Shani watched as the intruders abruptly exited the kitchen. Her eyes immediately focussed on the Suzuki's ignition fob. Timing was going to be crucial. Ironically, Nicolas was now a threat to her, *providing* she untied him first.

Certain they'd left the cottage, Shani anticipated another stun grenade being tossed through the window at any second. It didn't happen. Instead, running feet on the gravel. Shani stood up from the chair.

'Christ, Shani!' cried Mario. 'Brilliant! We'll get the BMW. Quick. Get a knife.'

Shani took a knife from the worktop. With Nicolas being nearest to her, she started to cut him free – *almost*, leaving him more to do in order to gain time on him. Then she grabbed the ignition fob and a helmet from a series of hooks on the wall.

'No, Shani!' shouted Nicolas, half-standing with the chair still attached to him. 'No! Don't do this to me!'

Shani swung round, seeing him striving to set himself free. 'They murdered two people. Serghei was a friend of my parents. And they murdered Mariana. If I don't do this, we'll lose them.'

'No, Shani! *No!*'

She sensed Nicolas wouldn't be far behind her as she sprinted across the gravel. She fired up the Suzuki and settled herself on the seat. In her mirrors, she saw that he'd already left the cottage and was now hurtling towards her. A red mist had fallen. She could cope with him being mad at her, but not Mariana dumped in a river after serving her purpose.

That was just evil.

CHAPTER 26

Shani caught a glimpse of a bike taking a left out of the cul-de-sac, away from Timişoara and into open country. Fast and furious, she predicted. Better that way than trying to pursue them in side streets unfamiliar to her. She looked for Mario's BMW in her mirrors. It wasn't there. Had it been, she might have changed her mind and joined them. Leaving the cul-de-sac, she piled up the revs and snicked through the gears, keeping tabs on the bike in the distance as it weaved around some traffic.

Unless they'd taken a good look at the Suzuki on the driveway, it was doubtful the rider would recognise her in his mirrors. Something of an advantage, then. Besides, she was still tied to a chair in Mario Nemescu's kitchen, wasn't she?

Shani closed in: a hundred metres down to a gap of seventy, thereabouts – settling for a cushion of fifty metres. The one with the green helmet was the rider. He'd given her the impression he was in charge back at Mario's cottage – the bastard who tore apart the folder. They were travelling at between eighty and ninety kilometres an hour. No great speed. All the same, the wind was tearing into her t-shirt, making her chest ache. And she hadn't the luxury of gloves – that nightmare for any biker. No gloves, bare skin hitting the tarmac.

She drifted in further. There were few cars, ideal for what she had in mind. She recognised the bike in front of her as being a Yamaha 700 Tracer. She knew just by looking at it that it could pack a punch. To her right and left, vast expanses of what looked to be sweet corn. Reasonable protection, she figured, should she part company with the Suzuki – unless she was tossed onto the road itself. God forbid!

The Suzuki's fairing barely kept the draught off her hands. Before long, she wouldn't have the control required, her fingers already beginning to numb over. Influenced by the thought of having to abandon the pursuit, she decided to make her entrance. Pulling out of the Yamaha's slipstream, she drew up alongside and kicked out at the passenger – and missed by as much as half a metre. She hadn't gone in deep enough. A feeble attempt, in truth. Pathetic! They both glanced at her, their visors masking their expressions of doubtless alarm – the element of surprise nevertheless wasted in a single moment. She dived in again, before seeing a gun in the passenger's right hand.

Shani dropped straight back, slotting in directly behind them. Too dangerous, by far. And she now questioned whether she had the required strength. No sooner had she processed the probability of a flawed strategy than the Yamaha braked sharply, cutting its speed by half. The Suzuki's front forks compacted in response to her reactions to avoid a collision – doing so by millimetres, the Suzuki briefly overtaking the Yamaha. Her spine tingled at the thought of a bullet smacking into it. She tried to settle herself. Impossible, because this had now become a desperate situation, and she cursed the feral mist back at the cottage that had triggered her impulsive nature.

An open sports car cut past them both at speed. The Yamaha latched onto it, as if the rider aimed to get a tow in its slipstream and shake her off. Seeing the bike gaining ground reignited her outrage, the girl who'd translated Serghei's words for her doing the rest. It had to be done! The BMW was still nowhere in her mirrors. They would never find them again. The Yamaha undoubtedly had either been stolen or had a false registration plate. Questions needed to be answered!

Shani nailed down the power and hit sixth gear. The Suzuki responded beautifully, caterwauling up a slight gradient like a wily feline tearing in on its prey. *Make or break*, she told herself, before her hands failed her.

This is for you, Mariana, she insisted. *And for you, Serghei.*

Hitting the crest, she dropped a gear to keep the Suzuki as responsive and as stable as possible – and then immediately sold the Yamaha rider a dummy, dipping to the right, switching to the left. Like a missile unleashed, she dived in, and kicked out with her right leg, striking something metallic as opposed to leather padding. The bikes separated and she had to fight off a tank-slapper, the Suzuki snaking towards the kerb until her reflexes and a hefty measure of luck redirected the bike into the road. With an expletive out of sheer fright on her lips, Shani cast a glance in her mirrors – the Yamaha nowhere to be seen. She snicked back down through the gears and swung the bike around. Still no sign of the Yamaha. Some cars went by, drivers and passengers seemingly unperturbed. She rode the bike onto the grass verge, killed the engine and took her mobile from her jeans.

'God sake!' yelled Nicolas. 'God's bloody sake! You idiot.'

She'd expected it. In fact, she would have been upset with him had he not sounded off at her. It was love, nothing less. 'Nicolas—'

'Where the hell are you? We're in the BMW.'

'I'm on the main highway out of Timişoara.'

'So are we. Are you safe? *Tell* me you're safe!'

'At the moment, yes. I think so. It's weird. They've vanished.'

'He's got a gun, Shani! Head back into town. We're certain to see you.'

'I can't. I'll have to go past them. They could be hiding in a field. I'm surrounded by fields of corn.'

'What the hell happened?'

'I think I knocked them off the bike – unbalanced them.'

'Look out for us.'

Shani headed another hundred metres further up the road and swung the Suzuki into a U-turn, the rear tyre throwing up dirt from the verge. She didn't like the idea that they were out of view and somewhere in the cornfield. Presumably, they still had a gun between them. A trickle of cars passed by and she wondered if it was a Sunday. That would account for the low level of traffic. Unsurprisingly, she'd managed to lose track of the days. She lifted her visor and looked down the road, waiting. Poor Nicolas. He was right, of course. She really needed to curb her reckless behaviour. Whenever such an 'eruption' occurred, it often shocked even her on reflection!

Finally, a white BMW travelling at what seemed a leisurely pace trundled over the crest in the distance. Shani unstrapped and lifted off the helmet. Leaving the Suzuki, she flagged them down with both arms aloft – Mario at the wheel. Nicolas was first out of the car.

'*Mon Dieu!* I'm livid—'

'Nicolas, not now—'

'I could have bloody lost you. That was selfish, Shani!'

'I'm sorry…' Tears sprang and coursed her cheeks. She leaned into him, allowing him to put his arms around her. She'd put their future together at risk. 'I need to stop being impulsive,' she mumbled into his shoulder.

'Well…not quite with everything,' said Nicolas, his tone unexpectedly soothing.

Shani looked up, meeting his eyes, her vision a squishy blur. 'Not everything?'

'The sex. I can handle you being impulsive when it comes to sex. But not when it comes to this. I'll be a wreck with a wiped-out nervous system before I'm thirty, I'm telling you.'

A pistol shot rang out and Shani jumped. She looked across to her right; Mario aiming the gun in his hand at the ground. Wiping her eyes: 'Mario, you might have warned us.'

'Sorry.' Mario disengaged the clip from the Beretta. 'Just checking it out.'

'Is that the gun my father took from you?' Shani asked.

Mario started to feed bullets into the clip. 'Sure is.'

'I thought you said they didn't fit. That they were the wrong ones.'

'They were,' confirmed Mario. 'These bullets are different. I've had them in a kitchen drawer for ages. I use them for weights on the scales when I'm measuring out herbs.'

'How far down the road did they disappear from sight?' asked Nicolas.

'Couple of hundred metres,' said Shani, keeping her arm around Nicolas. 'More or less at the foot of the hill.'

'Okay, let's go.' Mario climbed behind the BMW's wheel.

Shani got in the back. Nicolas returned to the front passenger seat and took the gun from Mario. Traffic was still sparse. A blessing, but then a thought came to Shani and she leaned forward. 'Do you think we ought to call the police? Get them to flush them out?'

Mario made a U-turn. 'We want answers. If all this is related to some authority, we'll never get those answers. Right, Nicolas?'

'No question.' Nicolas looked across the road to his left as they advanced towards the hill. 'That's sweet corn, isn't it? Never seen so much in my life.'

'Grows like weeds out here,' mentioned Mario before his eyes darted from the road ahead. 'Hey, this must be it.'

They'd arrived at a swathe cut through the cornfield, evidently fashioned by the wayward Yamaha.

'Might have done a reasonable job there,' Shani remarked.

'Situation's still dangerous,' said Nicolas. 'One of them is armed, remember. If not the other one, too.'

'How are we going to do this?' pondered Mario. 'They could be anywhere in that field by now. Plants have got to be coming up to a couple of metres tall.'

'I'll keep the gun,' Nicolas said. 'You two keep in tight behind me.'

'Disagree,' said Mario. 'I'll hold onto the gun. You two stay in the car and take it back to where we found Shani.'

'No.' Shani came forward again. 'The three of us go in. And if we waste any more time, the further away they'll get from us. Right?' With that, she opened the door.

'Has she always been so obstinate?' asked Mario.

'This is nothing,' retorted Nicolas. 'Should have seen her during the coup in Séroulé.'

'I'm thinking of Serghei and Mariana and what they did to them.' Shani found she wasn't in the mood for jibes. 'They're bastards, and if they're not suffering now then they're going to suffer – and for a long time to come.'

With Mario in front, they tentatively followed the swathe of damaged corn.

'Nicolas, you look to your right, I'll look to my left,' suggested Mario. 'Shani, just keep your eyes wide – checking behind us.'

Nicolas noticed it first, the red-helmeted figure face-down in a hollow several metres inside the field.

'That's the passenger,' Shani whispered loudly, before glancing across at the Yamaha, lying like a maimed animal on its side.

'Looks fairly incapacitated,' weighed Nicolas.

'Leave him,' said Mario. 'We need the one with the green helmet. He looked like the leader out of the pair to me. The one who will have the most information.'

The swathe came to an end where the bike lay, the air heavy with the stench of spilt petrol. Ahead of them, visible signs that leaves had been freshly torn away on some of the corn stems.

'Should we divide up?' suggested Shani. It seemed the next logical step. 'Spread ourselves and widen the net?'

Mario shook his head and raised the Beretta. 'This way the three of us have some protection.'

Just at that moment, Shani detected something to the left of Mario that definitely wasn't vegetation. It was hard to define at first because of its colour, but now she could clearly recognise a green helmet. She nudged Nicolas and pointed. Mario caught sight of her gesture.

Shani closed in with them, seeing a figure on its side a couple of metres from the helmet. In her peripheral vision, she noticed Mario's left hand had joined his right hand on the Beretta to keep the gun perfectly steady. The man said something in Romanian. A plea, of sorts, judging by the stifled cry, which she was certain included Mario's name.

'I don't believe this,' muttered Mario.

'What?' demanded Shani, nervously craning her neck around Mario to get a better view of the prostrate figure. 'Believe what?'

Mario rolled the figure onto his back with his foot. 'Serghei bloody Sapdaru.'

'No!' The statement was outrageous. 'You're wrong, Mario. You *have* to be!' Shani stared down at the man. She had to admit there was a definite resemblance to the man she'd seen back at the hostel. His right shoulder, though, was now pushed back from his neck. Dislocated, she suspected. Or perhaps broken in some way. Whatever, she wanted him to be in agony – to pay the price! But how the hell could it possibly be Serghei Sapdaru?

Nicolas squatted and went through the man's pockets. When he rolled him back onto his side the man shrieked in pain, before muttering a likely expletive in Romanian. Nicolas extracted his wallet and the jar containing the microfilm. He handed the wallet to Mario. 'See what you can find in that.'

Mario drew an ID card with a picture of the man from one of the pouches. 'A traffic cop in Cluj. A greed-ridden twisted one at that, who had all the resources he needed to hand. My details, no doubt. And those of the owners of the hostel.' He turned to

Shani, his eyes a ferocious glare. 'You want proof. There's his name. I bet he never even went to prison. Did some sort of deal with a crooked official.'

Shani stared at the card, disbelieving. 'But who was that I saw on my second visit to the hostel?'

Mario dropped to his knees. 'That's what I'm going to find out.' He spoke to the man, now known to them as Serghei Sapdaru who, in the past – if not the present – had a penchant for taking 'mainline' narcotics. With no answer's forthcoming to his questions, Mario shoved the Beretta into Serghei's neck.

Serghei spat at him.

'Piece of shit!' swore Nicolas, before applying pressure on the distorted shoulder blade with his foot.

That got Mario a full response, in Romanian.

Mario looked up at Shani. 'They came across a down-and-out lookalike and set everything up the way you found it. I get it now…the aim was to distract you and the owners into believing it was this murderous idiot we have here, driving the fear factor home in the process to get you to look for the folder.' Mario asked more questions, and on a couple of occasions gestured to Nicolas to rest his foot on the deformed shoulder blade.

It shocked Shani to see Nicolas do such a thing, having never imagined he was capable of dispensing pain – quite the opposite. But in a sense, he was doing it for her. For all of them. Questions *needed* to be answered. The fact remained, though: she simply couldn't accept that this repulsive wretch had been a close, if not *the* closest, friend of her parents.

Mario stood up. 'I don't think he's lying. He had an uncle in the police. That's how he got the job in Cluj. I remember his uncle. He gave a lecture at school, on how to be good little boys and girls. A guy with a limp, an injury from some shootout. I think that's why I remember him. It made for an interesting story for us kids. But more than that, for the first time in twenty-four years I get why I was asked at the station to decipher the pages I'd received from Lucian. Because he'd told his uncle there was a chance I could do it.'

'The old man watching television at the hostel…' recalled Shani. 'He had a limp. I bet that was his uncle!'

Mario returned to interrogating Serghei. Whenever Serghei decided on reticence, Mario would shake him viciously. This went on for several minutes before Mario turned to Shani. 'He was in need of drugs when your parents were alive. He told his uncle about the folder. His uncle discovered it had been documented that a folder was missing from the wreckage of the plane, because several other folders were intact in a box that had partially split open. It was rumoured that the one that was missing was the most important, which we can vouch for.'

'Because of the microfilm?' asked Shani.

'And the encrypted information inside.'

'So he actually snitched on my father – to get money from his uncle for drugs?'

'It's why I was put inside a cell for a week, isolating me from Lucian in the hope I could translate the photocopy, to see whether it was worth getting the original off Lucian. The charge against me, after it was proven I hadn't shoplifted, was one of conspiracy to undermine the United States Government. But the charge was dropped after Lucian and Zinsa were killed. I never saw his uncle at the station, so I'm guessing a couple of colleagues he worked with were in on it.'

Mario asked another series of questions, the only hesitations from Serghei Sapdaru arising when the pain from his shoulder caught his breath.

'What's he saying to you?' interrupted Shani.

'I want to know more about his uncle,' said Mario before listening to Serghei's reply. Mario duly looked back at Shani. 'He's now saying his uncle came across a rumour that microfilm had been concealed inside the folder. He drove Andrei and his wife to the hospital after your parents were shot, and then together they searched the house to see if they could find the folder. Then nothing for twenty-four years, until you appeared on the scene a few months ago.'

'And so they teamed up again?' said Shani.

'They planned to sell the microfilm and encoded material to the authorities in America, making a fortune from it.'

'Naïve on their part, I would say,' cut in Nicolas. 'I haven't met his uncle, but I doubt either of them have the contacts or the aptitude to pull it off with their lives remaining intact.'

'Bastard…' muttered Shani. She looked directly into Serghei Sapdaru's eyes, his face crunched up with pain. 'You total bastard!' she screamed, suppressing a desire to kick the hell out of him. 'Ask him who broke into Andrei's apartment in Prague, and my study in Oxford?'

Mario asked the question, the response surprisingly obliging. 'His accomplice did Prague, and for Oxford his accomplice contacted someone who lives in the city.'

Shani stooped over the man, to maintain eye contact with him. He'd started sweating badly, his face glistening all over. 'You're goddamned evil, Serghei Sapdaru!' she shouted. 'Evil, I tell you.'

Serghei glared back at her, unblinking, until his eyes widened in apparent trepidation. There was a rustle from behind and, as they turned, the startling crack of a pistol shot before it echoed out into the distance. The accomplice, still helmeted, briefly muttered something in Romanian.

Serghei Sapdaru lay with a bullet between his eyes, a rivulet of blood meandering from his brow. Shani swung back to the helmeted figure, her mouth drying up as her pulse soared.

'What did he just say to you?' she shouted at Mario, frantic. 'God's sake, are we next?'

'Stay calm,' said Mario. 'I think we're okay. He said Serghei knew too much about him to remain alive.'

'Then who murdered the down-and-out and Mariana?' demanded Shani. 'Did he do it?'

Mario calmly put the question to the accomplice whose face they still couldn't see, hidden from view by the tinted visor.

Lowering the gun in his right hand, the man answered Mario.

'He says Serghei did the killing with his uncle. Mariana was too risky to keep alive.'

'Shit!' swore Shani. 'Just wasted a life like that? A good, kind and compassionate life.' She stared down at the body at their feet. 'He lied to my parents, he lied to you, Mario. Lied to me.' Nicolas put his arm around her, which she was more than grateful for. 'I don't think anyone could be more vile than him,' she said.

Mario spoke briefly to the accomplice.

The man responded with a single nod of his head. Then he said something equally abrupt in Romanian.

'What's he saying?' Shani wondered whether he was the same person she'd punched in the face as he sat in his car opposite Skid Row.

'He said his fight's not with us. Serghei promised him thirty thousand dollars to go along with him. We should let him go on his way. To have him around just complicates matters. Agreed?'

'Agreed,' said Nicolas. 'Definitely. But what about this *merde* of an individual's uncle?'

'If he's had a career with the police, he should be easy to track down. I'll report him anonymously to the Chief of Police up in Cluj.'

'Yes, do that,' said Shani. 'You must.'

Mario waved the accomplice away. Tucking the gun into a pocket on his leather jacket, he shuffled back through the corn. Minutes later, they heard the Yamaha start up, its engine then fading into the distance, away from Timişoara.

'What do we do with this snake now?' asked Shani. 'We just leave him here?'

'Why not?' said Mario. 'A stupid man, loaded with greed and selfishness. Let's get the hell out of here.'

They exited the field.

'You two take the BMW,' said Mario. 'I'll take the Suzuki.'

'Looks like rain,' said Shani. 'If we're back in time, I want to show Nicolas the garden. And you can give him a talk on permaculture afterwards.'

'Permaculture?' queried Nicolas. 'What's that got to do with me?'

'It's the future. Before the multinationals poison the earth completely.' Shani glanced at Mario. 'Correct?'

'You could say that.' Mario chuckled at the look of puzzlement on Nicolas's face. 'I'll walk back to the bike. Need to clear my head. See you in twenty minutes or so.'

* * *

'Permaculture?' repeated Nicolas, as they settled themselves in the BMW. 'Sounds like an expensive hair-do.'

'Well it isn't. And I'll be having a crack at it in Séroulé.'

'Here's the deal, then,' said Nicolas, turning the ignition key. 'I'll consider embracing "permaculture", as long as you engage yourself in your thesis. Okay?'

'Depends if Harry Rothwell will allow me to complete it in Séroulé,' said Shani. 'But, yes, it's a deal.' They began to climb the gradient and head back towards Timişoara. 'What do you think of Mario?'

'I like him,' smiled Nicolas. 'Little crazy at times, maybe. But that's just fine. How it should be. Have to say, never heard of anyone using bullets on scales before to weigh herbs.'

Shani found herself laughing. It was a blissful feeling – the feeling of uninhibited wellbeing. 'Eccentric, I agree,' she said. 'It's been a journey for him to put it mildly. Terrific respect for him. He lived for a time in the sewers with other kids in Bucharest. Did you know that?'

'No. He never mentioned it to me.'

'His children are a delight, too. Especially Ana. We appear to have become kindred spirits.'

Nicolas beckoned her to lean into him. 'I love you,' he said.

'Love you, too.' She put her arm across his shoulders. 'Before we go to Cornwall, can we visit Prague so I can show you off to Dusana? You'll be a definite hit with her. No problem.'

'And after Cornwall, the permaculture thing?'

'We'll take everything as it comes.' Shani sat back in the seat as they swept through a series of bends. 'We'll find room for your sunflowers. I know how much you like them.'

'A healthy initiation…sunflower seeds.'

'Are you going to hand over the microfilm to this guy who owns whatever Communications it is in California?'

'Loran Communications,' said Nicolas. 'His name's Joshua Waldo. But only with your blessing. The film belongs to you.'

'Then do it. If he can make something of it, so be it.'

Nicolas glanced across at her. 'Did I say I love you?'

A straight road ahead and Shani leaned back into him. With Nicolas's love, combined with her longing to return to Séroulé, an exquisite opportunity had now presented itself. For sure, there was more to life than sitting behind a desk pushing a cursor around a screen, recalling the past and theorising over whatever.

This was her future. Her here and now. Her beginning, with arms spread wide.

*

Printed in Great
Britain
by Amazon